Dirt

A Frank Kelly Mystery

Vaughn F. Keller

Riverhaven Books

www.RiverhavenBooks.com

Dirt: A Frank Kelly Mystery is a work of fiction. Names, characters, businesses, places, events, locales, and incidents are either the products of the author's imagination or used in a fictitious manner. Any resemblance to actual persons, living or dead, or actual events is purely coincidental. Where data is used, it has been taken from public records.

Copyright© 2020 by Vaughn F. Keller

Published in the United States by Riverhaven Books, Massachusetts.

ISBN: 978-1-951854-11-9

Designed by Stephanie Lynn Blackman

Whitman, MA

For
P.D.

Other works by Vaughn F. Keller:

Behind the Neon: A Frank Kelly Mystery (2010)

Glimpses: Poetry, Short Stories, and Essays (2012)

The Unwilling Pawn: *A Frank Kelly Mystery* (2015)

The Corner of My Eye: Poetry, Short Stories, and Essays (2017)

"If you know the enemy and know yourself, you need not fear the result of a hundred battles. If you know yourself but not the enemy, for every victory gained you will also suffer a defeat. If you know neither the enemy nor yourself, you will succumb in every battle." (Sun Tzu, *The Art of War*)

Chapter 1: Vidal

very year on the first Saturday after New Year's, my next door neighbors, Norman and Nancy Burchill, throw a post-holiday "open house." I always go.

Norm is chair of the Fairfield Republican Town Committee, so the attendees are usually some combination of relatives, friends, neighbors, and local political people. At this year's gathering, Norm's Republican friends were still celebrating Lee Thurman's win to represent Connecticut in the United States Senate. It was the first time Thurman had run for a political office, and he had won at the expense, politically and personally, of a well-known African American who people had thought was a shoe in – at the beginning of the campaign.

Thurman was sworn in on the Thursday before the party. Norm had been the local area lead for the Thurman campaign and was as proud of the Fairfield turnout for Thurman as he was of the fish-house punch he and Nancy served at their party. Thurman had even invited Norm to Washington, D.C. for the swearing in, but Nancy had told him, "No way buddy. This is your party, and you had better be here to help get ready for it."

Norm and Nancy always invite new people who have recently moved into the neighborhood. My neighborhood has changed over the years. Not for the better, in my opinion. It's become dominated by corporate types climbing some kind of ladder, to where, I have no idea. They're commuters who head off to the new high-rise office buildings in Stamford every morning and painfully inch their way home through the Merritt Parkway traffic jam every evening. Most are Republicans.

They're all white and say they've "moved to Fairfield because of the schools."

I've lived here for twenty-five years. That makes me a novelty to them, and they're not quite sure what to do with me. I'm beginning to feel like the stranger. I had asked Eve if she wanted to come with me. She had said, "No way." My fiancée, the former Sister Patricia of the Sisters of Mercy, had worked on the campaign of Thurman's opponent, Gene Douglas. "Thurman's a gob shite and I don't want to hear a bunch of celebratory bullshit. Thurman's campaign reached a new low, and I want nothing to do with the crowd that supported him. You go. I understand. You've got a different relationship with Norm and Nancy."

So, I went. Norm and Nancy had been very kind to me after the death of my wife. Invitations to dinner, inclusion in going out to the movies, watching football games together. Simple stuff, good stuff. Things I appreciated and that were really helpful in keeping me going at the time.

There were several new corporate types at the party who I had not met before and our introductions to one another repeated what's become an old pattern. When I tell them I'm a retired professor of criminology, I see them file me away in their internal social status folder as someone who is "potentially interesting." When I tell them that my students were primarily current or aspiring police officers, and I had taught at a local community college, they move me to a different folder, the one marked "probably boring."

When I tell them I currently work as a private investigator, their interest might or might not get aroused. It depends on the image they conjure up. If the image is that of the sleazy P.I. armed with a camera following the adulterous husband or wife to a motel on the outskirts of some town, I might get a polite, "Oh." This crowd is far too polite to say, "Ugh."

If, on the other hand, the image they manufacture is of the Mickey Spillane or Robert Parker anti-hero drinking coffee spiked with whiskey, whiling away his time in a dingy office waiting for the next

2

case, I might get a curious, "Really?"

You can almost sense the fantasy taking place in their minds. A beautiful damsel knocks on my door. She's on the edge of tears, if not actually crying. She's either very rich or has barely enough money to pay me. She can't go to the police for one reason or another, or has already been – to no avail. Most importantly, I, being the hero of last resort, am her only hope.

The Monday after this year's party was the seventh of January. My workday would have disappointed my new neighbors, at least the way my day began. They would have been surprised, I'm sure, to discover that my office at Nutmeg Security and Investigations is anything but shabby. It is very comfortable, very well appointed, very corporate. And maybe nicer than theirs.

In addition, there are usually a lot of people in the office, although that was not the case on this Monday. Still, I was not alone; Claire, our new receptionist was at her desk in the waiting area. What I was doing, though, would have totally disrupted their fantasies about my professional life.

Rather than having elaborate sexual fantasies, building a house out of playing cards, or making paper clip chains, I was going over Nutmeg's year-end financials, not just for this past year, but for the past three years. With my new status as partner in the firm, my former employer, now one of my partners, Meg DeRosa, wanted to make sure I understood all of the financial ins and outs of "our" organization. Meg had insisted I do "due diligence" before I wrote my check to buy my share of the firm thereby completing our financial transaction. To add to the disruption of the fantasy, I was drinking a very un-spiked cup of Smith Teamaker Meadow Blend No. 67 herbal tea.

Outside, downtown New Haven was overcast and cold. It had snowed all Sunday night but had warmed up during the day on Monday. By two o'clock in the afternoon, most of the snow had become dirty slush. By four, though, the slush had turned into ice and I was not looking forward to the drive home.

3

Thanks to Meg's pushing, I learned that "we," as in Nutmeg Security and Investigations, were doing well. In fact we were doing very well, and I was beginning to enjoy my "due diligence" as I learned how profitable "we" were.

However, my delight at the bottom line was interrupted by the buzzing of my office phone. I punched the intercom button and Claire told me that a Ms. Vidal Banks would like to speak to me.

I assumed she meant on the telephone and said, "My line isn't lit up."

In a hushed voice Claire said, "No, she's here."

I asked Claire, "Did I miss something? Do I have an appointment with her?"

"No. She just walked in and asked if there was any chance you might be available. Should I bring her back?"

"Is the conference room free?"

"Yes."

"Bring her there. My desk is a mess with print outs and notes."

"Will do. Coffee, water?"

"Not yet. Let's see what she wants. Do you think she's a vendor of some kind?"

"A vendor? Not that I know of. I don't think so."

I turned and looked down at the mass of black dog hair that was sound asleep in his bed next to my desk, "Come on, Blackie. Let's go meet this lady." Blackie stirred, yawned, stretched, and got up.

Claire had already delivered the woman to the conference room by the time Blackie and I arrived. Ms. Vidal Banks's back was to me and she was looking out the window. Hearing us come in, she turned and walked towards me holding out her hand. She was stunning, truly beautiful. She was smiling. "Thank you for agreeing to see me, Dr. Kelly." There was something in her tone that let me know that she considered this to be "her meeting." Maybe she was a vendor. I wondered what she was selling.

I guessed she was probably closer to my son Ben's age than to my daughter Molly's. That would have made her somewhere in her early thirties. She was professionally dressed, perhaps a little over the top. She was wearing a tailored navy-blue suit over a bright red silk blouse showing an interesting amount of cleavage. Without her heels she would have been about five-foot-six or seven, but she had on heels, and they were not the sensible kind. She could have been the model for a bank advertising, "Your personal banker."

Vidal Banks was beautiful and was clearly on a mission. So maybe this part of the P.I. fantasy was alive and well. Even if she was selling advertising or something.

I said, "Please sit down," and smiled my best new-partner smile. "I'm sorry, but I don't recall us having met or spoken before."

She chose to sit at the head of the conference table. She said, "Actually, we did meet, but it was very brief. I attended a lecture you gave on identity theft at the Stamford Chamber of Commerce last year. I spoke to you at the reception afterwards. I wanted to thank you for your insights."

I had done several of those lectures around the state. The lectures were Sam's idea of how to get my name out to the business community. Sam DeRosa was Meg's husband, my other partner and a founder of the firm. While Nutmeg was well known for having a robust security business throughout Connecticut, it was not known for having an investigation division. The division consisted of me. Maybe Sam's idea had worked. The "insights" on identity theft Vidal referred to were the result of my spending a few hours on the internet gathering other people's "insights" and putting them into a PowerPoint presentation.

I told her, "I'm sorry, I don't recall." Apparently, I hadn't paid attention to how beautiful she was when she had approached me after the lecture. This time I did. In fact, I couldn't stop looking at her. She had dark eyes, olive complexion, and black hair down to her shoulders. It was her face, though, that was striking. It wasn't perfectly symmetrical, which somehow made it intriguing and compelling, enhancing rather than detracting from her beauty. On the other hand, she was almost too put together, like she was going to a photo shoot.

She said, "I'm not surprised you don't remember me. There were a lot of people there." She was smiling, but it was a textbook smile without much warmth. Maybe she was a vendor, after all.

What was clear was that she knew exactly what she was doing. This lady had had a lot of meetings. I started the way I usually do.

"What brings you in today?" Always "today" as part of the question. Why today, rather than yesterday, last week, tomorrow, or next year? "Today." One word. Sometimes it turned out to be the most important word in the beginning of an interview, and even in an investigation.

"First," she said. "I apologize for just dropping in like this unannounced. I was actually on my way to see a client in the building and saw your firm's name on the office listing downstairs. I recognized the name and made the decision to stop in spur of the moment. I thought I might as well take a chance and see if you were available."

Her professional demeanor had receded a bit, not much, but it was noticeable, replaced with something slightly more straightforward and guileless, with just a hint of embarrassment, and I began to find her engaging.

My brain switched into work mode. She had a "client" in the building, so she was making a professional call and this was her work uniform. I wondered who the client was and thought through the other tenants in the building without coming up with an obvious possibility. She had felt enough urgency, though, to act on the spur of the moment.

I smiled. "I'm glad you did. How can we help you?"

"I'm not sure you can, but I thought it was worth a shot. Let me describe the situation." She hesitated, prepared herself, and began, "My father is, or was – he's dead now – Arnold Nunnely. I don't know if that name rings a bell with you or not. He was killed last October in Boston in what the police are calling a drive-by shooting."

She paused as if wanting that to sink in. "Their explanation for his death is that he was simply in the wrong place at the wrong time, an innocent bystander."

"So, your father was killed in a drive-by shooting," I repeated. "How horrible."

"Yes, in a poor neighborhood. In Boston."

"And...?"

"I think he was murdered."

Her self-protective professional voice had disappeared. Her distress became obvious in her eyes and around her mouth. I sat still. One of the things I've learned in all these years of meditation and martial arts is when to simply breathe, and that's what I did. I breathed into the calm of complete focus.

I sat quietly with Vidal for a minute as I processed her assertion about her father's death. My immediate instinct was to offer the bromide, "I'm sorry for your loss." However, she had said very simply and directly, "I think he was murdered." I didn't yet know what she wanted from me, "from us," but it wasn't sympathy.

I said, "Ms. Banks, would it be okay if I videotaped our discussion so I don't miss anything. Also, I'd like your permission to share the recording and whatever we discuss with one of my partners in the firm, Sam DeRosa. Sam's a former Fairfield police detective and we often work together. No one else would see or have access to the videotape without your permission."

It's usually not good practice to be the only one in the room when you're conducting an interview, especially a first interview in what could be a criminal investigation. It's too easy to miss things: the questions you should have asked but didn't, what the person actually said, or didn't say. Audio recordings are useful; note taking barely so. Sam DeRosa was the only other person at Nutmeg who had investigatory experience but, as president and chief rainmaker, he wasn't always available, so I had recently installed video recording capabilities in both my office and in the conference room.

Claire and I were the only ones in the office that day since Sam and Meg had taken the afternoon off to drive their grandchildren to piano lessons and everyone else was out working on different assignments.

7

Claire was simply too new and too inexperienced to be my second pair of eyes and ears. I wanted a videotape.

Vidal said, "All of this will be confidential, then?"

"Absolutely," I replied. "No one outside of this office will even know you were here without your permission, and that can be withdrawn at any time. In addition, you can ask that I stop taping and that the tape be destroyed if you so wish. The taping is strictly so I don't miss anything and so Sam and I can discuss your situation using the information you provide. If he were here, I would be asking him to join us, but unfortunately he's not."

She had no additional questions and said, "Okay. Go ahead."

I went over to the credenza and opened the drawer where we kept various forms and pulled out the recording permission document. I wrote in my name and Sam's name where called for and gave her the form to sign. "Why don't you take a minute to read this over. It basically says what I've just told you. Would you like some coffee, water? We also have some sodas."

She looked up from where she was reading, "Some water, please." I buzzed Claire on the intercom and forwarded the request.

Water delivered and form signed, I went to the electric panel on the credenza and pushed the record button. The red light went on indicating that the machine was recording. I looked up to make sure that the camera also showed a red light. Sitting down opposite Vidal Banks I asked, "Where would you like to begin?"

Chapter 2: Vidal's Story

I love what I do. The work, Nutmeg, and the DeRosas have all become very important to me. Now I'm doing what I used to teach. I feel alive when I have a case: the tension, the not knowing, the wondering, the exploration. Until I started practicing, rather than teaching, I never fully appreciated how perfectly Arthur Conan Doyle captured Sherlock Holmes' excitement when Holmes would tell the good Dr. Watson, "the game is afoot." I get it now, Sherlock. I really do. When Vidal said, "I think he was murdered," the game was afoot.

She began by asking, "Do you follow politics, Dr. Kelly?"

"Please, call me Frank."

"Thank you. Please call me Vidal."

"I do follow the news, but I've never been personally involved in politics. As you know, I taught for many years, primarily criminology to would-be police officers. It was important that I steer clear of any discussions that were political and outside of my role as a teacher. The last thing they needed, or I wanted, were political arguments in class."

What I didn't say was that living with a theologian who also had a PhD in political science brought politics to the dinner table nightly, especially when my very liberal daughter and her semi-liberal husband were in attendance. On more than one occasion I found myself agreeing with Stan, the two of us facing off against the united front of Molly and Eve.

Vidal continued, "I was raised on politics. As I said, Arnold Nunnely is, excuse me, I still have a hard time saying it, *was* my father. He did oppositional research for a living and was quite successful and well known. He even had a nickname: 'the Assassin.'"

I didn't say anything. She needed to tell the story in her own way. I could go back and ask questions later. Although I was relying on the videotape as my memory device, I also had a legal pad in front of me

9

and jotted down the name, "Arnold, the Assassin, Nunnely."

I did know that Nunnely had been shot in the Roxbury section of Boston about three months ago. Eve had told me about it. Her years teaching at St. Joseph's in Hartford had oriented her more towards Boston than New York. She read *The Boston Globe* online every morning while I read the *New York Times*, delivered to my, our, doorstep in its blue bag. So I had a vague idea who Arnold Nunnely was and how he got the nickname, "The Assassin."

She continued, her voice cool. "He destroyed people for hire. As long as a political candidate would pay, he would dig up dirt on his or her opponent. Usually a 'his' since he worked exclusively for Republican candidates. He would go as deep as the candidate's budget would allow. He didn't only dig up dirt. If a candidate wanted, my father would spread the information – true, half true, or possibly true – through both traditional and social media or merely word of mouth. That way the candidate could maintain deniability about the source of the damaging information. My father would also work through proxies, anything to get the damaging information into people's conversations, tweets, and Facebook streams. He would get one story going viral and when that ebbed, he would start up another one.

"If the candidate wanted, and they usually did, my father would also uncover everything he could that might be damaging to his candidate client so there would be no surprises. Part of my father's job was to alert his client about what might be thrown at him if the opposing candidate had a good oppositional researcher working for him. When it was a primary, and there might be several opponents, it could get very complex. Basically, my father not only knew the absolute underbelly of politics, he helped to create it. He traded in secrets and shame. He was an expert on lies, embarrassment, and cover-ups. Those are his words, not mine. He was not a nice man, and I did not respect what he did, although I admit it fascinated me."

"Do you think he was murdered because of what he did?" I asked.

She leaned forward almost as if telling me something in secret. "He knew things about people. He had hurt people. He could hurt people in the future. Some people hated him. He had destroyed lives; he could destroy more lives. He earned his nickname."

She leaned back and, as if anticipating my question, said, "However, he was my father, and even though we haven't been close for years, I think I still owe him something."

I changed her word to amplify her statement to see how she would react. "You were estranged for a long time?"

"You could call it that. That's a polite word for it. My parents got divorced when I was fifteen. Even before the divorce, I didn't see much of him. He was never home. He worked for candidates all over the country. Big campaigns, small campaigns. He didn't care as long as he was working and making money.

"My mother said his personality changed as he became well known. She said the more he did it, the more demanding and irritable he was at home, whenever he was there. And, according to her, he was also that way when he wasn't at home, when he was on the road."

She paused before continuing and a hard edge came into her voice. "He filled his nights with young women. At first they were political junkies who thought he was so very special and they were stupid enough to think they were special if they had sex with the great Arnold Nunnely. Later, Mom said, he filled the holes in his soul with prostitutes. Finally, my mother had enough and divorced him." Vidal stopped talking.

I waited. I had noticed that Vidal didn't wear a wedding ring. I said, "I'm curious about your name. You go by Banks, not Nunnely."

"I changed it when I turned eighteen. I wanted no connection to him. None. Banks is my mother's maiden name."

Ambivalence is always complicated and often painful. I wondered what the nature of hers was. "You didn't want any connection to him and yet you said you felt you owed him something."

"Owed may be too strong, but yes. Four months ago, he called me and asked me to meet him for dinner after work. I said no, but I did agree to meet him for coffee. We hadn't had a real conversation in years. He had paid for my education and showed up at events, but, beyond that, we were strangers. So, for me, even coffee was a big deal.

"When we met, he was upset. He was gushing with regrets about his life. At first I thought he was pathetic. A man in his late sixties who had messed up his life and now he wanted to make amends, perhaps be forgiven. I'm not sure what he wanted."

She leaned forward to pick up the pen that was on top of the permission form and started twirling it. "After a while I started to believe him, that he really did feel remorse for the way he treated me and my mother and for the lives he had ruined with his work. In retrospect, I'm sorry that even though I believed him, his little speech didn't move me and I was quite cool in my response to him. I assured him he had not ruined my life or my mother's. My mother is happily remarried to a very nice man, and I am doing well professionally. I don't have much of a social life because of the hours I work, but I basically like my life. I didn't want to give him the power to think he had hurt me. I had been better off with him out of my life."

"It sounds like the conversation wasn't pleasant for you."

"It wasn't. He also told me something that was a total surprise. He said he was getting out of the oppositional research business. He said he was working for his last client, Lee Thurman, the new senator. He told me lines had been crossed that scared and sickened even him."

"He worked for Lee Thurman?"

"Yes. Well, primarily for Thurman's campaign manager, Jason McCloud. He also told me that he had saved files for years and years, all on discs, and he wanted me to have them. I told him I wanted nothing to do with them, but he insisted. I told him I'd just get rid of them. He said he understood but asked me to hold onto them for at least a year. He seemed so desperate, I agreed. He didn't come right out and say he was in any kind of danger, but after he was killed, that's all I've been able to think about. He was reaching out, and I wasn't there for him. He wasn't a great father, but he was clearly a troubled man and was

12

asking me for some kind of undefined help or connection. I'm not sure which."

"And then he was killed?"

"Not killed. Murdered." She didn't say anything more.

"You're sure?"

"Yes."

"What leads you to believe that?"

Again, she leaned forward as if punctuating in advance what she was going to say. "Frank, my father kept everything on his laptop and it wasn't in his office or apartment when I cleaned everything out. And there was no cellphone."

"There was no laptop and there was no cellphone in his office," I repeated. Then I asked, "How about at the crime scene?"

"The police say no. He had his wallet with his credit cards and over a hundred dollars. He had his watch. He had his car and house keys, but no laptop and no cellphone. How the hell do you explain that?"

"How do the police explain it?"

"They don't. They just respond by saying he was in the wrong place at the wrong time."

"I can understand why you're frustrated with them."

"That's such an understatement."

I didn't say anything, waiting for her to continue.

When she did, it was a simple request. "I think I do need some coffee, and could I use your restroom?"

When she returned, I brought the conversation back to the relationship, "It must have been stressful becoming responsible for the property and affairs of someone, your father, who you really didn't know that well."

"Yes and no. He had all of his financial affairs in good order and everything had been kept up to date. He'd had the same lawyer for years. They had been law students together, so they were friends as well. His name is Carlos Barlotti. Actually, they worked together at one point. Carlos had copies of all the keys, documents, and contact

13

information I needed. Dad's sister, my aunt Ruth, Mom, and Gary, my stepfather, helped me with everything from the funeral to cleaning out the condominium. Dad's secretary, Leslie Cahill, helped with the office."

"Even with help, it's a lot, especially, I would think, given the circumstances."

"I suppose it was. Surprising, too, in some ways."

"How surprising?"

"It turns out my father was wealthy, and now, to my astonishment, so am I. I'm the sole heir. There was a sizable insurance policy, and I'm the beneficiary. I also inherited the money from his 401K and the sale of his condominium. In addition, he owned the building where his office was. He left me a wealthy woman. I won't have any trouble paying you your fees."

"Vidal," I said, "I'm not worried about you…"

She interrupted, "Well, if you weren't, you should be."

I had no idea why she was becoming testy with me about the fees. Was it the business she was in? I changed subjects. "You've had conversations with the Boston Police Department?"

"I've told all of this to the Boston police, but they still believe it was a simple matter of his being at the wrong place at the wrong time. One other person was killed and two were injured. The police believe it was gang related. The other people were all from Roxbury. But why was my father in a dangerous black neighborhood, and why was he there then?"

"Excellent questions. What are your thoughts?"

"I don't know. The police aren't being very helpful, and every time I ask questions, they treat me with some mix of disinterest and disdain. At times I feel like they are patting me on the head and saying 'there, there, sweetie.' Sometimes I think they're blaming my father for being there in the first place. I've thought of getting a lawyer."

The police blaming Nunnely was entirely possible, I thought to myself. In victimology it is one of the key errors of attribution: the victim brought it on himself. Instead of taking her through a lengthy exposition on the *Just World Phenomenon* and how it corrupted crime investigations, I responded to her statement about a lawyer. "What would you hope a lawyer could do for you?"

"I don't know. That's part of my problem. Perhaps talk to the police. Push them. I don't know. Maybe they would be more forthright with someone other than the victim's daughter. That's why I thought I would talk to you. I don't know what to do, and it's driving me crazy."

I looked out the window. On the far side of the street I could see a mother pushing a stroller. The mother was hunched over, walking into the wind. Cold wind. The hood of the stroller was all the way up and I could see the wind pushing the fabric in from the frame. I couldn't see the child inside.

I turned back to Vidal. "Can we circle back to his laptop? You say he kept all of his information on it but it wasn't in his office, at his home, or recovered at the crime scene. Might he have had it with him and it was stolen?"

"Yes. But the police didn't find it in pawn shops. Nothing else was stolen: wallet, credit cards, not even cash."

"And they didn't recover his cellphone either?"

"No."

"Did he usually carry a briefcase?"

"I don't know."

"You said he gave you copies of everything. I assume that would include electronic files from his computer."

"Possibly. I haven't looked at any of it."

"Would you feel comfortable letting us hold onto the files here. I'd like to review the information in them. We'll keep them locked up and only Sam and I, along with our computer technician, will have access to them."

She said, "I'll be glad to get rid of them."

"Vidal, I want to be honest with you. I'm not sure what I can accomplish, but I'm certainly willing to try. I might be able to get some

15

cooperation from the Boston police, although I don't know. In part it depends on who's working the case. Detectives can be very protective of their turf. I don't know anyone in the Boston Police Department, but I can see what I can do. It may depend on how important they think the case is and whether they're frustrated or not. It also matters how well they're resourced. I know that's not what you want to hear, but it's true. If they have a big case load and they're backed up, they might welcome someone else getting involved. If things are slow, who knows? It's been some time now since the event, so their hope for closing the case and their interest in it may have diminished."

"Are you saying I should let it go?"

"No, not at all, but I don't want to give you any false assurances. We may not be able to do a lot, but we can try."

She didn't say anything and I sat silently as she looked out the window. She turned back towards me, still not saying anything, then she surprised me by looking under the conference table where Blackie was lying at my feet with his eyes closed.

"Your dog or does he belong to the organization? Is he used in your work?"

"My dog. He's not officially used in my work, but actually, he does come to work with me. and he's sometimes referred to around here as Detective Blackie. His full name is Boston Blackie after the old radio detective."

"Is he trained in police work?"

I wondered where she was going with this. "In a way. He's trained in schutzhund, which is technically a competitive sport. The competition includes obedience, protection, and tracking. Some similarities to police work."

"Is he good?"

"Very good. He slips a bit when I get lazy and don't keep up with his training. But that's my problem, not his."

"Does he stay with you all the time?"

"Most of the time. He lives with me and is usually with me." I had absolutely no idea what Vidal Banks was thinking. I realized I wasn't yet used to including Eve as my fiancée and housemate in conversations with strangers. I added quickly, "When I can't take Blackie with me, he stays with my fiancée or one of my children."

"I like dogs. I wish I had one, but with my travel schedule I can't, and my father refused to have one when he lived with us even though he was almost never home. He said they just cost money and why bother. When my mother married, it was still a no-go. Gary said he was allergic."

I didn't say anything. She collected her thoughts. I guessed she was wondering whether or not to say what she eventually did.

"I don't know if I loved my father. That's a terrible thing to say, but it's the truth."

It was hard for her to say it, but she did. I wasn't surprised. She had been building in this direction. A philandering, absent father who wouldn't let her have a dog and, so far, not a positive thing to say about him other than he was beginning to experience remorse and reach out to her. Why would she love him? Still, she said she wanted to find out whether or not he had been murdered.

I couldn't help thinking about the irony. Did Arnold, the Assassin, get assassinated? Why did she care? She had mentioned him paying for her schooling and showing up at events. She wanted this, though, so obviously she was conflicted in some way. I weighed in on the other side of the ambivalence but only with facts and a touch of amplification.

"Earlier you said he paid for your education and showed up for the important events in your life."

"Yes. He did. At first, I thought that was my grandmother's doing, that she told him to do it. I asked her, though, after he was killed and she said he would call like clockwork every month to check in on me and find out how I was doing and what was going on in my life. She said she kept asking him to call me directly, but he said I didn't want to talk to him."

17

"Did you?"

"No. At least not then. I think I was playing out a script that wasn't entirely mine. Well, at least not all of it. Some of it was that I was angry at his having left us, or left me."

"I assume it was your mother who wanted the divorce."

"She did, but he was the one who really left. Years before she actually filed for divorce. Even when I was younger and they were married, I would try to get in touch with him when he was involved in a campaign somewhere, but it might be days before he would get back to me.

"And then not long after the divorce my mother got remarried. Gary's a very nice man. He was a widower and has three kids about my age and, suddenly, I had a new family. My father wasn't part of that. He wasn't part of my life anymore. Even my grandmother, my father's mother, was pushed out of this new family. I think my mother blamed her for my father, which I think is ridiculous.

"My grandmother, Bubbe – I always called her by the Yiddish name for grandma – wasn't about to get pushed out of my life, though. She called all the time. She was the one who gave me my first cellphone so we could stay in touch. Bubbe was not going to let go. You don't push a Jewish grandmother away from her granddaughter and expect to win. She made sure I stayed in touch with my aunt and my cousins on that side of the family.

"My mother and Gary aren't at all religious, even culturally, so every Passover, every Chanukah, Yom Kippur, all of my knowledge of Judaism came from Bubbe and Zaydee, that's Yiddish for grandpa. I even thought about being bat mitzvahed, but my mother was cool to the idea and I didn't care that much. I was really into soccer in middle school, so it never happened. Bubbe was disappointed but said it was my choice. 'Maybe someday, Vidi,' she would say."

I nodded, then asked, "You said you changed your name as soon as you could?" Now I was back on the other side of her ambivalence.

"High school graduation. The older I got, the more distant my father

18

got. Mom and I moved from Fairfield to Greenwich when she married Gary. My life got busier, Zaydee died, Bubbe moved back to Bridgeport to a small apartment and became immersed in the life of the big Conservative Jewish congregation there, and we didn't see as much of one another. I think Bubbe gave up on my father. I heard very little from him, although what I did hear about him from my mother and sometimes in the newspaper was never pleasant.

"Then when he came to my high school graduation, he wanted to take me out for dinner afterwards, but Mom and Gary had already planned a party for me. My father was really angry and made an enormous stink. He had not asked me or them beforehand about dinner. He had this meltdown in front of my friends, and I was horribly embarrassed. I told him to go to hell and to leave me alone. He left and didn't say a word. I started the name-change process, with the blessing of my mother and Gary, the following week."

Time for me to switch again: "You said he paid for your education."

"He did. We communicated through email after high school. I blocked his number on my cellphone. He paid for NYU and for my MBA at Columbia. He would ask me questions about how I was doing, what I was doing, and things like that. I would write him brief newsy replies. Nothing intimate. Nothing real."

"Until coffee."

"Until coffee."

"And he left you his estate."

She shook her head. "I know. Maybe that's part of the reason I want to find out who did this to him."

The number of random and stranger homicides is very small. Usually when they occur the perpetrator is obvious. A robbery goes bad. A disturbed angry person shoots people in a work setting or a school. In homicides, when things are not obvious, you usually begin by learning as much as you can about the victim and then you move out through intimate and work-related circles looking for the big three: motive, opportunity, and means. Since she was already thinking about

19

her father, I said, "Tell me about your father."

"What do you want to know?"

"Whatever you want to tell me. Don't worry about anything being or not being relevant to his death. Help me get to know him. The good, the bad, the things that were important to him, why he did the things he did. Introduce him to me and let me get to know him."

"Haven't I told you enough?"

"You've told me a bit about your relationship with him. I'm also interested in his life, his whole life."

"Like his obituary?"

"Those are usually brief and sanitized."

"You mean more like a Wikipedia entry. He has one, believe it or not. It's short. But he has one."

I laughed. She was definitely an MBA-consultant type, make sure you understand the question and respond to the question with concise, accurate data. I said, "Not quite that formal. Think more along the lines of a biography."

Chapter 3: Vidal and Arnold

efore we begin," I said, "would you excuse me? I need to make a quick phone call. I'll just be a minute."

"Sure."

I called Eve and the call went to voicemail. I left a message: "I may be late tonight. New client. Your bailiwick. Politics. I'm going to ask permission to talk to you about her and her situation."

Earlier, Claire had set a tray in front of where Vidal had been sitting. On the tray was a "Nutmeg" branded coffee urn. Next to it were a creamer, sugar bowl, and Sweet & Low packets along with two "Nutmeg" branded mugs. When I returned, Vidal was pouring herself a cup of coffee. I poured myself one. I felt there was something either I was missing or she was not telling me. "You were going to tell me about your father."

Vidal took a sip of coffee. As she had before, she looked out the window. "There's a great deal I don't know."

"Do the best you can."

I didn't try to explain to her the reasons for doing a detailed victimology. If I understood more about Arnold, I would be in a better position to assess whether or not the Boston detectives had any possible reason to fall into attribution error and think he had it coming to him because he was where he shouldn't have been or if they'd be more inclined to have an attitude of "What else could you expect, stupid?" If they had, their thinking process would constrain them and limit their thinking about his death.

Since I was considering using Vidal's perspective that he was deliberately killed and was an intended victim, I had to get to know him. Was there something in his life story besides, or in addition to, the work he did that would make this murder make sense. Right now, it was still a senseless killing. But it was definitely suspicious.

21

Vidal began cryptically. "I know he was born in Bridgeport." She stopped. Thought. Started again. "Nineteen fifty-one. January third." She stopped, thought, and started again.

"Bubbe told me she was hoping for a New Year's baby. My father was her first born. He has a younger sister, Ruth. His parents didn't have much money."

She was dropping little pebbles of information. There was no narrative.

"Classic Jewish story. Zaydee and his brother Mort owned a dry-cleaning store that their father had started right after the Second World War."

Vidal started to relax and appeared to enjoy the storytelling when her grandparents were the subject. "My grandparents describe Bridgeport as a boomtown during the war. General Electric and Alcoa were big. A very different city than the one that exists today. They said it was very blue collar and vibrant, with big department stores downtown.

"My paternal grandparents are Jewish, Conservative Jewish, and that's how my father was raised. I've been told Bridgeport had a pretty big Jewish population when my father was growing up. Jews had been in Bridgeport since the 1800s, so being Jewish was not a novelty. This was not the case in the suburbs of Bridgeport where there were restricted neighborhoods, restricted country clubs, and all the rest of the antisemitic garbage of the United States."

Vidal's voice changed when she reported this, and I wondered the extent to which she had personally experienced antisemitism. I wondered how important her Jewish heritage was to her. Eve, my in-house expert on all things religious, says that all members of groups that have experienced a diaspora carry with them some anxiety when they are living outside of their homeland and it cascades down through the generations. Whether it is newspaper articles, stories from friends and family members, or personal experiences, the feeling of being different, unwanted, or not quite belonging doesn't go away. All it takes is a newspaper story or a comment to spark anxiety or anger. One generation passes it on to the next.

Vidal paused for a second, took a sip of coffee, then continued. "Dad went to Bridgeport public schools when he was young. In the late fifties things started to change. Companies started closing down their plants. Those who could, fled to the suburbs as real estate prices headed downward. With cheaper housing, blacks and Hispanics started moving in. White flight at its best. As that was happening, the suburbs opened up to Jews, and Bubbe and Zaydee moved to Trumbull.

"This caused a crisis in the family. Zaydee and his brother got into a big fight about whether to open a second store in Trumbull. They split over it, so Zaydee sold his share in the Bridgeport store to Mort and opened his own store in Trumbull. It was a bitter split according to Bubbe. There were accusations of family disloyalty – how could you do this to me – and so on. The brothers never reconciled. Anyway, dad went to high school in Trumbull.

"Financially, things didn't change much from what I understand. Dad told me that he had liked Trumbull. Although the restricted neighborhoods were gone, antisemitism was still prevalent in the schools, but apparently Dad had some good friends and he used to talk fondly of his high school experience. Academically, he did very well in school. He was always one of the smartest kids in the class.

"Frank, is this the kind of information you want to know?"

"Yes, you're doing great." I was beginning to form an image of Arnold Nunnely, but it conflicted with my image of the kind of person who develops a career doing oppositional research. Maybe I knew too little about oppositional research and had made some off-base assumptions. I nodded my head, encouraging her to continue. I was also aware that periodically she shifted from "my father" to "Dad."

"Okay. Well, if you were a Jewish kid growing up in the sixties and had half a brain, you were going to be a doctor or a lawyer or possibly an accountant. Apparently, my father used to love to argue with everyone, so the choice was obvious."

23

I asked, "Was he interested in politics when he was in school?"

"Somewhat. Ran for some offices but never got elected. Bubbe and Zaydee were interested though. They were always talking about it, especially Abe Ribicoff. For Jews in Connecticut, Ribicoff was a big deal. A Jew elected to congress in 1949. Zaydee told me they were thrilled when Ribicoff beat out John Davis Lodge for governor, sometime in the fifties. Bubbe and Zaydee had met Ribicoff when he was campaigning in Bridgeport, and Bubbe still has a signed picture of him hanging in her living room. She's eighty-seven and still talks about it as though it were a few years ago. She'll take my hand and say, 'Three thousand votes, Vidi. He beat one of the most important and richest goys in the state by three thousand votes. The whole state, Vidi, the whole state.' If she had her way, Ribicoff would be alive today and running for president."

"Your dad…"

"I don't know any stories of his running for office after high school, but he certainly heard a lot about politics at home."

"And after high school…"

"He went to NYU, or NY Jew as it was known then. He had a scholarship. This was late sixties, early seventies. New York City. Columbia University had exploded the year before Dad got to NYU. All kinds of anti-war protests. Woodstock. The no-grades movement. The great pudding jump-in at NYU's Loeb Student Union. Dad was in the middle of it all. He loved telling me those stories. Best time in his life he told me more than once. I've seen pictures of him when his hair was down to his shoulders. He got his student deferments but said he might have gone to Canada if he had gotten drafted. According to Mom, he was also doing a lot of drugs. He lost his scholarship and, again according to Mom, barely managed to graduate. He did graduate, a semester late because of make ups, but he did graduate."

"You appear to know quite a bit about your father when he was at NYU."

"Before we had the blow out around my graduation, he took me out to lunch to celebrate my getting into NYU. He was thrilled that I'd decided to go there. I hadn't even told him I had applied. He couldn't stop talking about his time there. He kept saying it was the best time of his life.

"Frank, honestly, I don't understand why all of this biographical data is important. The police never asked for any of it. Shouldn't we be talking about something else, like why on earth he was in Roxbury? I don't know, but I think that's more important."

I understood her puzzlement. "Don't worry, we'll get there. Let me tell you what's on my mind. Here's what we know. The Boston police are working from the hypothesis that your father was accidently killed, not murdered, killed. So that's the lens they are looking at everything through. While there are some big holes in that theory, it also makes some sense.

"You, on the other hand, don't think it was accidental. You believe he was murdered intentionally. Since the Boston police are looking through one pair of lenses, I'm going to look through another. Where they assume it was an accident, I'm assuming it was a deliberate act of murder with your father as the target. They will be investigating with their accidental death glasses on; I'll be investigating from a completely different perspective. To do that thoroughly, I need to begin with your father. If it was intentional, it was done by someone who believed they were better off with your father dead. There may be something in your father's past that brought a person to that belief. I need to get to know your father. Does that make sense to you?"

"Not completely, but I have to assume you know what you're doing. I apologize if I'm being impatient."

"I completely understand. Okay if we get back to your father?"

"Sure."

"You went to NYU for your undergraduate degree."

"Believe me, it had nothing to do with my father. He loved the idea though, and it might be one of the reasons he never questioned paying for my tuition and room and board, but I went for some good reasons

25

and some silly reasons. It's a good school, and at eighteen the idea of going to school and living in Greenwich Village is pretty romantic if you're from a suburb in Connecticut. I'm glad I went."

"Back to your father, what did he do after he graduated?"

"He told me that what helped him decide on law school was the experience of those years at NYU and what was going on in the country. He got serious about law school. According to Bubbe, he had talked about it before. It wasn't new. But now he really wanted it.

"Apparently, he wanted to be a crusading civil rights lawyer. However, with his academic record, no law school would touch him. He had barely graduated. It wasn't that he wasn't smart. He did well on his LSATs, but his grades were abysmal, and he had a hard time getting recommendations from NYU faculty.

"He spent a fortune on application fees. Bubbe and Zaydee were both furious with him for his behavior at NYU and they were very upset about the trouble he was having getting into law school. They blamed him for it, as they should have. They fought with him. Dad moved out and into a cheap apartment with a friend. He got a job at the *Bridgeport Post*, in the circulation department of all places. He drove a truck dropping off papers at newsstands. Mom told me he was also doing drugs like he had been when he was in school.

"It was when he was working at the paper that the University of Bridgeport decided to open up a law school. They got a license from the state, but they weren't accredited at first. It was a wild gamble for any student who applied and got in. They didn't know whether or not they would ever be able to practice law in Connecticut or anywhere else because the school wasn't accredited. Mom told me Dad was of the mind set of 'why not?' The school was accepting anyone who could pay the tuition and fees and breathe. Zaydee agreed to pay for one year if Dad would move home and continue to work at the paper as well as go to school fulltime and get good grades. Bubbe told me it was her idea, and she had to convince Zaydee to go along with it, but he did.

"Dad said yes, delivered papers for the *Post*, and went to school. He

26

did extremely well and my grandparents wound up paying for his second and third years. Dad kept working at the paper and also contributed to his tuition. It was at the *Post* that he got to know the reporters, how the paper operated, and started to get interested in political campaigns and politicians. According to Dad, Bridgeport has always been at least slightly corrupt politically.

"According to my mother, this is the time when he grew up. He stopped doing drugs except for smoking marijuana, and that was not often. Jews typically don't drink a lot, but Dad stopped completely. Later, that changed. According to Mom, he was smarter than anyone else going to school there, so the faculty loved him. They saw Dad as their poster boy for what the school could become. The school did finally get all of their accreditations after a big fight with the state and the Connecticut Bar Association. The school was able to give students credit for the years they attended before the accreditation was granted. Bubbe even wrote to 'my senator Ribicoff' pleading the case for UB and her son Arnie, who had gone to NYU, just like the senator.

"UB Law was really a pretty scraggly school at that point according to Dad, and they had to rely on a lot of adjunct professors. One of them was Stuart Goldman, of Goldman and Bunch in Bridgeport. Goldman and Bunch was, and is, a big and very successful firm and a major player in Connecticut and Connecticut politics. UB convinced Goldman to teach one course – I have no idea what the course was. Goldman saw how hard Dad was working and how smart he was. He took him under his wing, encouraged him to apply for a summer internship at Goldman and Bunch. Dad got it, was very successful from what I understand, and when he graduated, they offered him a position if he passed the bar exam. Dad not only took the Connecticut exam, he took Massachusetts' and New York's as well and passed all three the first time out. I'm told that's very rare. He was on his way."

She took another sip of coffee. I waited for her to go on. She just sat there. She looked at me, or rather through me. I still waited and finally said, "Is something wrong?"

"Everything I'm telling you are things I've heard from other people. I think you should talk to my mother."

"Why is that?"

"She met my father when he was working at Goldman and Bunch. She can tell you what happened there and how it turned his life around, got him into doing oppositional research."

"Do you think she'd be comfortable talking to me?"

"I think so. She knows how frustrated I am with the police. She doesn't know I'm talking to you, but I can ask her and tell her about you. My mother's attitude towards my father has mellowed quite a bit over the years and she feels more sorry for my father than angry at him at this point."

"I'd be glad to talk to her. Vidal, you mentioned the funeral. Would you mind telling me about how you heard about your father's death and what has happened between then and now. You said he was killed on October 19th of last year."

In my head I was trying to put together a timeline. If Nunnely was involved in a campaign at the time of his death, that would have been a few weeks before election day. I added the words "Nunnely killed" after the date on my note pad. I scratched out "killed" and wrote "murdered." *Get in the game, Kelly. You're defining the rules here. Only think murder*. That's the lens I had to use.

Vidal answered my question. "I was getting ready for work when the front desk in my building called and said there was a Stamford detective there to see me. I couldn't imagine what on earth a Stamford detective would want to see me about, so without thinking I just asked, 'What does he want?' Lavanna was on the desk and told me that the detective would prefer to come up to talk to me.

"I was panicking at that point and told her to give me ten minutes and then send the officer up. A few minutes later my doorbell rang and I let the detective in. She was very professional. She told me that my father had been killed in Boston in a drive-by shooting, and gave me all of the Boston police information. After the detective left, I called

Mom right away, told her what had happened, got in the car, and drove to Boston. I called work while I was driving and told them I had a family emergency and didn't know when or if I'd be in. I also called my Aunt Ruth and told her. I asked her to tell my grandmother. I didn't want to be the one to tell Bubbe.

"I had the information from the Stamford detective, so I called one of the Boston names she had given me. By the time I got to Boston, I was fighting morning rush hour, so it took me forever. The Boston detective called me and said he had to leave but that another detective would talk to me when I got there.

"When I finally got to the police station in Boston, I met with a Detective Galvin. He couldn't tell me much except that my father had been killed in a drive-by shooting, and that they didn't know who the perpetrator, or perpetrators, were. Other people had been shot. It was an area known for drug trafficking. There had been gang violence there in the past. He wanted to know if I had any idea why my father would be there. Did my father use narcotics? Why was my father in Boston since he lived in Greenwich, Connecticut? And on and on.

"Then I had to go to the morgue and identify Dad. Frank, I can't tell you what that was like. It was so cold, so clinical. The coroner mouthed, "I'm sorry for your loss," but it was so rote. It was like a movie. He pulled back the sheet. I looked at the body and said that yes, that was Arnold Nunnely, my father. Yes, I was his daughter. There was no Mrs. Nunnely. Yes, I would be responsible for funeral arrangements when the police released the body.

"He wrote down all of my contact information and said he would be in touch. I went back to the police station but Detective Galvin wasn't 'available.' I just sat there in the visitor area for what must have been an hour. No one said a word to me. Finally I left and started driving home. I got as far as the first rest stop on the Mass Pike, pulled over, and just cried and cried. I'm not even sure what I was crying about. I called mom but she was at work. I left a message for her. I thought about calling Bubbe but still couldn't do it. I called Aunt Ruth. She said she would leave work and meet me in Bridgeport and we would talk to Bubbe together. God bless her. I couldn't have gotten through this without Ruth. She and her husband, Manny, have been great.

"Ruth and I took care of all the funeral arrangements. It took several days for the coroner to release the body, which was absurd given their certainty that Dad was an innocent victim in a drive-by shooting and someone else was the target or that a message was being sent to some group. Waiting that long was also against Jewish tradition, and Bubbe was beside herself."

"Tell me about the funeral."

"The funeral? What do you want to know? It was a funeral. My father didn't belong to any church or synagogue so the rabbi at Ruth's congregation agreed to perform the ritual. The rabbi did a very nice job. He had talked to Bubbe, Ruth, and me just beforehand. Ruth spoke. No one else did. I didn't want to. The service was in the funeral home and then at the gravesite. It was a funeral. What can I say?"

"Who came?"

"What difference does that make?"

"If a person has been relatively active up until the time of their death, and has lived in the same community where the funeral takes place, about seventy-five to one hundred people will show up. Usually half are family and friends of family. The other half are friends of the deceased or acquaintances where showing up is expected." The impression I was getting of Nunnely was that he was somewhat isolated. Who showed up might be helpful. Someone might know why he was in Roxbury that night.

"It was small. Bubbe, of course, and some of her friends from her congregation in Bridgeport. Ruth, Manny, and my cousins. Mom and Gary came. My stepsister lives in Colorado and my stepbrother is in Germany in the Army, so they weren't there. My closest friend, Abby, came. Dad's secretary, Leslie Cahill, and Carlos Barlotti were there. There were some people I had never met before."

"Do you have any idea who they were?"

"One of them was the candidate he was working for."

"The Republican, Lee Thurman. Anyone else you didn't know?"

"A couple of college kids who had worked for dad during the summer. Oh, and Stu Goldman. Mom was very surprised that he showed up. She can tell you all about that."

"Anyone else?"

"A woman who didn't introduce herself, to me at least. I think she said something to Ruth. She left right after the funeral and didn't go to the grave site."

I immediately wondered who she might be. I was hoping Ruth would know what the connection was. "Did you have a guest book?"

"Yes."

"Would it be okay if I borrowed it?"

"I don't see why not. Ruth has it."

"Great, and could I get contact information for Ruth as well?"

"Certainly."

"Also, could I have the contact information for the detectives in Boston you have talked to?"

"Sure, I have their cards with me."

"Great, I'll have Claire copy those and give them back to you."

"Do you think you can help?"

"I'm going to try. Vidal, I'll be honest with you, this might take a while."

"I don't care. There's money. Ruth has power of attorney and Dad made her a signatory on his bank accounts. Getting paid won't be a problem."

"I wasn't concerned about that. And would it be okay if I consult one of my resources who has significant information in the political arena?"

"That's fine. Whatever you need. I'll give you names, numbers, whatever, and the files Dad gave me. At the time he had also asked me if I would take all of his legal stuff on. You know, healthcare proxy and that stuff. I had said no. I think it was another way Dad was trying to connect with me, morbid as that seems now. The police found an emergency contact card in his wallet. He had listed me and Ruth. That's how they knew how to find me.

"Frank. Talking about all this. I think he knew. The more I think about it, the more I'm convinced he was deliberately killed."

"You may be right. I'll talk to the detectives in Boston, and to your mother and probably Ruth as well. One last question: why now? Why come to me now rather than a month ago or a month from now?"

She looked down at her hands, picked up the mug of coffee, swirled it around a few times, and then looked up at me. "His birthday. It was a couple of days ago. I always used to send him a card, not call, just a card. I decided I had to do something about this on his birthday. And when I walked into the building and saw your company listed, I knew it was time to act."

Chapter 4: The Partners

Sam, Meg, and I, had been getting together fairly regularly for dinner since Meg first broached the partnership idea several months ago. Most of our meetings had an organizational focus: money, personnel, services, clients. Meg usually called for the meetings and set the agenda. This meeting was different.

After Vidal left, I called Eve and told her about my conversation with this potential client and my plan to ask Meg and Sam to join us for dinner at our house. Eve said she could stay in West Hartford and catch up on some work if I wanted to meet with them alone. I told her, no, I'd like her to join us.

"Why do you want me there?" she asked.

"Because you're devilishly smart, you know more about politics than I do, and this may have something to do with Connecticut politics, specifically the Thurman campaign, and because you live here."

"Are you cooking or are we going to order in?"

"I'm cooking."

I sent Sam and Meg text messages about dinner and the agenda. I included Eve in the message.

Are you cooking? Sam texted.

Yes, I replied.

What time? Meg asked.

I replied to them all, *Poached Salmon with a dill sauce, roasted potatoes, and asparagus at seven with a moderately amusing Sauvignon Blanc and Brigham's Out of the Park ice cream for dessert.*

You got me at Out of the Park, Sam texted back.

Can I bring anything? Meg wrote.

I'll be home by six. Do you want me to pick up anything on the way? Eve asked.

I'm all set, was my group reply.

After dinner the four of us made light work of getting the table cleared, dishes rinsed and into the dishwasher. We were on to ice cream and coffee in the living room. Sam, ever the detective, did an objective recap of the report I had provided at dinner. After he finished, Meg asked the real question of the meeting. "So, you've told this Vidal Banks you would be willing to try to help her and you want our blessing to go forward."

"Basically, yes, and to give me your thoughts."

"Of course we'll take her on," Sam said. I could feel his competitive juices flowing. He missed detective work. Most of his time was spent dealing with security issues. Protecting walled-in condominium swimming pools from the neighborhood kids was not his idea of excitement. The possibility of a murder investigation, though, that was something else.

"I get where the Boston P.D. might be seeing this as a dead-end case," he said.

Meg was playing with her cellphone. "In Boston whether it's dead end or not might depend upon who you are."

She looked up at us to make sure she had our attention. "Are you ready? Since 2007 Boston Police arrested somebody in ninety per cent of the cases where a white person was murdered, and forty-two percent of the time when a black person was killed. They have two hundred and fifty-four unsolved black deaths and only six unsolved white murders. Boston has the biggest clearance rate gaps, by race, of any major city in the United states."

"You're kidding," I said.

"Not according to what I'm reading."

"I'm not surprised by the gap," Sam said.

"I agree. But this big?" I added.

"Why the gap?" Eve asked.

Sam looked at me to indicate that he expected me to answer. I did. "Black on black crime, or even suspected black on black crime, often gets pushed to the back burner. Police priorities are political like

34

anything else. White privilege is alive and well in every police department, even when its murder."

Eve said, "This may be pushing the statistics and may make no sense, in fact it's very cynical, but say someone wanted to kill a white person and minimize the police department's attention. According to those numbers, would it make sense to make it look like a black person was the target?"

"You're right. That's cynical," Sam said, seeming to get a little hot under the proverbial collar. "You're assuming there's systemic racism in the department and someone is using it to cover up a murder. I think that's a stretch. I don't buy it. Nah."

Meg immediately responded. I felt I was watching a long-standing disagreement play out. "Sam, cool your jets. Boston has had racial trouble for years and you know it. Keep an open mind. Don't move into your knee jerk 'defend the police' mode. We don't know enough and Eve may be on to something. Don't dismiss it."

I stepped in. "Drive-by shooting on top of it. Any information about their clearance rate with drive-bys?"

Meg was still googling away. "Not yet. Wait a minute. These aren't drive-bys, but listen to this. One thousand unsolved murders in three black neighborhoods since 1970: Mattapan, Dorchester, and Roxbury. Where was Nunnely killed?"

"Roxbury," I replied. The professional criminologist in me started to get pedantic. "Look, we know that the United States, and especially our cities, have abysmal clearance rates for murder. There's a dramatic gap between clearance rates for whites and clearance rates for minorities, not just in Boston, everywhere. It sounds, though, like Boston is worse than most cities.

"It's been a couple of years since I've looked at the data, but Boston may be an outlier on statistics that are already horrific to begin with. I don't think we should dismiss Eve's conjecture. I agree, the idea that someone would set Nunnely up this way may be a stretch. It's wild to think that someone could use a drive-by shooting in a minority neighborhood in a city with a dismal record of clearing black murders as a screen to obscure who the real target was. If that's what happened, it's both brilliant and about as dispassionate as you can get."

"You're saying it was a professional hit." Sam offered it as a statement not a question.

"Possibly." I answered. "From Vidal's story, I haven't heard about any family squabbles that would lead me to think about any kind of intra-family passionate motive for killing Nunnely. I still want to check that out. So far, we just have the one story from Vidal. I need to talk to some others. That leaves friends and work as the next most likely circles to look at. Given what he did for a living…"

Sam jumped in. "You're thinking work."

"If he was the intended target. Given the damaging information he had about people, it makes sense."

"You don't think there might be a chance that Boston is right and that it was simply a drive-by?" Sam asked.

"Simply a drive-by murder?" Meg said.

"Come on. You know what I mean," Sam said.

Meg was still googling. "When was Nunnely killed?"

"Last October," I said.

"This is unbelievable. Listen," Meg Said. "Eight homicides last October: Mattapan, Dorchester, and…"

"Roxbury," I guessed.

"When in October?" Meg asked.

"Nineteenth."

"Right at the end, the very end of this rash of murders in October."

"All drive-bys I'll bet," Sam said.

"Not all," Meg answered.

I came back to the question that was central in my mind. "Why was he there? Why was he there then? If we can answer those questions, we can probably figure out whether there are dots to connect or not."

"Frank?" Eve said.

"I know. I'm thinking the same thing. Seeing the murders piling up in October, did the killer set this up so the police would lump it in together with the others?"

"Oh, come on," Sam said.

"I know. It's a stretch, but…"

"Hell of a coincidence," Meg said looking up from her googling.

I didn't fully understand Sam's reluctance to consider the possibility that we were dealing with something that would require a sophisticated plan and impeccable execution. But if he found it hard to entertain the possibility from a distance, I could imagine how difficult it might be for the Boston police who were in the midst of a series of murders.

I brought the conversation back to where I knew we would all be comfortable. "Can we talk about next steps? I'd like to commandeer the small conference room to set up a white board, and I'd also like to store the information Nunnely gave Vidal there."

Meg answered for both of them, "Of course."

"I'll change the pass code on the door so only the three of us have access," Sam said.

"Make that four," I said. "I may need Jackie to help out with the files when we get them."

"Who's Jackie?" Eve asked.

"She's our computer guru," Meg said. "Part time now. Hopefully full time when she graduates in May."

"Okay. In fact, I'll ask Jackie to change the codes," Sam said.

"Thanks. I want to begin with family and friends and see if I can eliminate any motives there. Conflicts, grudges, any negative feelings. We already know Vidal was very conflicted about her father."

"And she is now a very wealthy woman," Meg said.

"But she came to you asking for help," Eve said.

"It's far too early to eliminate anyone," Sam said.

"Alibi?" Sam asked.

"If this was a professional hit and she was responsible, she would have one. Sam, would you look at the videotape of my interview with Vidal tomorrow and tell me what you think?"

37

"Sure," Sam said.

"Also, do you know anyone in the Boston P.D. I could talk to? Vidal gave me cards for the people she's spoken with, but it would be better if I had a personal introduction."

"No one comes to mind, but let me think about it."

For the next hour we talked about who I should talk to: Vidal's mother, aka Nunnely's ex-wife, his sister, secretary, his lawyer. We decided it made the most sense to begin with the ex-wife. Sam agreed to make some calls to see if his network could make any connections into the Boston Police Department for me. Meg said she would send a contract with a request for a retainer to Vidal. Sam and Meg left a little after nine o'clock.

As we were getting ready for bed, Eve asked me if something was going on with Sam and Meg.

"I have no clue. You picked up on it, too?"

She gave me a *how could you miss it unless you were a complete idiot* look.

My response was not exactly insightful or profound. "They seemed rather tense with one another."

"You think?"

"I'll ask Sam tomorrow."

"Don't you dare. If he or Meg wants to say something to you, they will. You don't say anything."

"You're right."

"Thank you, darling, but sit. There's something I want to talk to you about."

I did what I was told and sat on the edge of the bed.

"I'll say this as plainly as I can. I love you and I do not want you to get hurt, let alone killed. If this was a professional murder and you go after this person, you're going to be in danger. I'd like you to be alive for the wedding I'm planning in June. You have a starring role, and I want you in one piece, preferably without any holes."

"I'll be fine," I said lightly. "I'll have Blackie with me." Blackie

38

looked up from his bed at the foot of our bed when he heard his name.

"Frank, be serious. You were shot at and almost killed last year."

"Aren't you glad I wasn't?"

"Frank!"

"Are you saying you don't want me to do this?"

"Yes. I don't want you to do this. If I had my way you'd go back to teaching or come to love security work. I'd probably put a cocoon around you, but I know I can't do that. I *can* however ask you to be super careful though, and please do not do anything alone like you did last time. Please promise me that."

"I promise," I said. I didn't know if I'd be able to keep the promise, but my intentions were good.

I couldn't sleep. I got up and went online and dug out the Boston newspaper articles from October. The focus was on the gang leader, Tom-Tom Garcia. Tom-Tom. I wondered how he got that name. His was the lead name in every article, a leader in one of the gangs that had been terrorizing Roxbury. The articles talked about the gangs and the neighborhoods. I wasn't familiar with any of it. I realized Boston might as well be a foreign country as far as I was concerned.

Arnold Nunnely got only one line in the *Herald* story where he was referred to as a political operative from Connecticut. The articles focused on the other victims even though they had only been wounded. They identified an Yvonne Wilson as Garcia's girlfriend and Charles Braxton was referred to as an associate of Garcia, and their names came before Nunnely's in every article. A couple of the articles referred to Nunnely as an "innocent bystander." One article went on to list other innocent bystanders who had been killed or wounded in recent Roxbury or Mattapan shootings.

I thought more about the promise I had just made to Eve. During my four years in the Navy, it was a time of relative peace in the world. Getting shot at was something I had not even contemplated. In all the years teaching police at the college or the Academy, the number of times a criminal shot at one of my students was negligible. Last year when it happened to me, I wasn't prepared for it, psychologically. I had been prepared with the weapons I needed, but I was still too much of a novice, even at my age, to have prepared my mind.

Eve knew this. She didn't want me to get hurt, let alone killed. I didn't want that either, especially now. I was happy, probably happier than I had ever been in my life. I thought more about my promise to her before I turned my computer off and went back to bed.

Chapter 5: Eve

O n the drive down to Greenwich the next day to meet Vidal's mother and stepfather, I turned on the radio. Tom Odell's song "Grow Old With Me" came on, and I sang along:

And our hands they might age
And our bodies will change
But we'll still be the same
As we are

I am getting older, but I still have a lot of piss and vinegar left in me, to use one of my father's favorite expressions. I had better. I don't know why, but the song from *Bye Bye Birdie* popped into my head: "I've got a lot of living to do." I smiled and said out loud, "God bless you, Eve Karam."

It had been a little over a year since Eve had come into my life. Professor Eve Karam, formerly Sister Patricia of the Sisters of Mercy. Now we lived together, in sin, she would remind me. Her decision, I would remind her.

Our relationship had changed so much in that year. It had started when Eve had been an enormous help with a case I was working on. With her two, not one, mind you, but two, doctorates – one in theology and one in political science – she had led me to understand what was happening in the country of Turkey and helped me to gain an appreciation of the Islamic religion.

I had fallen in love with her. Totally, completely, crazy teenager in love. When I became sane again, I found I loved her even more. So, being the good ex-Catholic Catholic, I of course asked her to marry me. After alternating sleeping arrangements between our two homes for six months, it seemed like the right thing to do.

However, compassionate and brilliant and loving as she is, she also has the capacity to be an incredible wise ass. In her most wise-assed

41

way, her response to my proposal had been, "I was married to Christ. You think you can do better?" How on Earth was I supposed to answer that? Fortunately, she saw my puppy dog rejected look and quickly pulled my ego out of the mud.

She had said, "I'm sorry. I was teasing. Frank, were you being serious? I thought you were just playing. You're really serious? At our age? You want to get married? Are you sure?"

"Yes," I had said. "I'm sure."

"Wow." Was her first reply. "I need to think about that," was her second. "Can you give me a couple of days?" was her third.

Two days later she had said, "No, Frank, at least not yet. I've never thought about getting married. Maybe I'm being greedy, but I've just been loving, absolutely loving spending time with you, getting to know you, your family, friends. I love waking up with you in the morning. You've given me an appreciation for what a mature, wonderful relationship can be, which I never expected at my age. But this is, wow, marriage, this is something else."

I don't know what I expected. Well, I guess I expected her to feel the same way I did. Silly me. Ego back in the mud.

My god damned mud. Would it ever go away? Had my marriage to Patricia just been a charade for a lot of years that produced two children, now both adults? I know I was legally married, and I would like to think *really* married for at least some of those years. But then came the discovery: Patricia had been having an affair, a longtime affair, eight years longtime it turned out, with a property developer she worked with. Patricia was his real estate agent. He was her client. I was clueless. People always say, "He must have known." Bullshit. I didn't know. An automobile accident took them both. My wife died with her lover.

So my ego takes a mud bath fairly easily when it comes to relationships. Oh, and my first wife's name was Patricia, the same as Eve's religious name. How's that for some irony?

Eve had seen my reaction to her less than excited response about my marriage proposal and pulled me out of my muck, at least partially, to where I could at least breathe. She had said, "Frank, I love you. There's absolutely no question in my mind about that. You're a wonderful human being; I'm happy when I'm with you; I've come to feel an incompleteness if we're not together for two or three days. How about we live together for a year and see how we do? You've been married, lived with someone, and raised a family. All of this is very new to me."

Not trusting what she had just said so sweetly and honestly, I acted like an adolescent idiot and had said, "Do you want to date or something so you can be sure?"

That really pissed her off. She let me have it. "Frank Kelly, sometimes I would like to kill your wife if she weren't already dead. I am not her. Let me repeat that: I am not her. No, I am not saying I want to date around as a way of being sure. Been there, did that when I left the religious life, remember? I'm saying I just never imagined being married, and I need to get used to the idea as a possibility."

A month later we stopped bouncing from one bed to another. She rented her condominium to a new faculty member at the college of Albertus Magnus in New Haven and moved into my house in Fairfield where we now reside in sinful bliss.

Three months ago, the Wednesday before Thanksgiving, she blew my mind. She proposed. I had put the idea aside. Well, sort of. She hadn't been able to sleep. It was five o'clock in the morning. She rubbed my back until I turned over. Then she rubbed other parts of me and made love to me. Then we held each other. Eventually I had fallen back asleep. She got up. An hour later she came back into the bedroom carrying two mugs of coffee. I was already somewhat awake when she handed me my mug and asked, "Are you awake enough to talk?"

"Getting there," I said. *Uh oh. What's up? This can't be good*, screamed through my brain.

"Francis Xavier Kelly, will you marry me?"

Part of me wanted to give her a wise ass remark and say something like, "Can I think about it?" Fortunately my non-stupid side prevailed.

43

Thank the goddess! I said, "Yes." One word. Then I did have to pay her back. I just had to, "Eve Karam, you do realize, of course, that I have not ascended into heaven and I do not sit at the right hand of God. Do you really want to marry someone beneath your former station in life?"

With that she had yanked the pillow from under my head and hit me with it, almost spilling my coffee all over the bed. My now fiancée of less than a minute was very quick and she said, "My former station. Do you really want to go there? You are so lucky I am part Buddhist, abhor violence, and right now am trying very hard to practice loving kindness."

Then she hit me again, only lighter and said, "Actually, I like practicing loving kindness on you and would like to do so until I get it right and, as you can see, that may take a while." Then she hit me again, lighter still, and bent down, kissed me on the top of my cowering head and added, "Think you can tolerate my learning curve with this marriage thing?"

My more mature self was waking up and I had said, "If you can tolerate mine." I looked at her. "It really is new for me, too, you know. I love you."

"I love you, too."

No way in hell did I ever imagine hearing what she said next. She said, "Are you up for springing this getting hitched thing on everyone tomorrow at Thanksgiving dinner?"

Tomorrow? Thanksgiving? I was able to squeak, "I think it's a wonderful idea."

She had then started predicting responses, beginning with my children. "I know Molly will be delighted. She's asked me at least three times if we were ever going to get married. I'm not sure it matters as much to Ben."

"Yes, it does," I contradicted. "He's asked me when we were going to get married. In some ways I think it may be more important to him than to Molly. He wants to make sure you'll always be here."

That had caught her by surprise. "I will. Oh, God, Frank. I want to always be here." With that, tears formed in her eyes. She took my mug from me and put the two mugs down on the nightstand and lay down beside me.

Now it was my turn. Eve's family was coming from various parts of New York and New England to be with us for Thanksgiving, the first extended family gathering with us hosting as a couple. I was not going to try to predict, so I asked, "What about your family? Do you want to just spring this on them at dinner? You sure you don't want to talk to them first?"

She had answered with absolute certainty. "Are you kidding? Immigrant Catholics with a daughter who left the religious life and is living with a man without the benefit of marriage? My mother will be over the top and my sibs, who, don't forget, always thought I was nuts for going into the religious life, will want to party. It also helps that everyone really likes you, Molly, and Ben. You too, Blackie."

Blackie had joined us on the bed. Eve started petting him. After a minute Eve turned my world on its axis starting, of course, with getting me back. "Of course, you have to understand that it does help that you have a dog and Jesus didn't." And then came the turning. It came with a change in her voice that moved us both into a land of intimacy that Eve had just created for us to explore.

She stopped petting Blackie and leaned towards me. "Frank, I think, no, I know, I've learned more about love from being with you than I ever knew existed. So, again, yes, Francis Xavier Kelly, I want to marry you and spend the rest of my life with you if you will have me."

I couldn't get any words out this time and just nodded. We held each other in silence.

Blackie, of course, interrupted this moment of perfection with a sharp bark to remind me I had a chore to attend to. "I'll make this quick," I said.

"You'd better. I'll get breakfast together while you take him out and then we have some plans to make."

Eve's predictions had been right. Molly was thrilled and

immediately started telling us what we needed to do to have the perfect wedding. Having married "Stan the man" a year before, she was now an expert on all things having to do with weddings. Ben had been a little more subdued but immediately asked if he could be my best man. I hadn't even thought about having a best man. It turned out he'd been thinking about it since Eve came into our lives. Unlike me and Eve, my offspring already knew we would get married and were just wondering when. Her family, as she had predicted, was delighted. *Ecstatic* was the word her mother used.

When I told Sam and Meg DeRosa the Monday after the Thanksgiving weekend, Meg's response was, "It's about time." Sam said something to the effect of, "It was never in doubt."

Odell's song ended as I turned onto the Greenwich exit.

Grow old with me
Let us share what we see
And oh the best it could be
Just you and I

Chapter 6: The Ex-Wife

Money *Magazine* ranks Greenwich, Connecticut, as the twelfth best place in the United States to live. An easy commute to New York City's Grand Central Station via Metro-North Railroad, it's home base for several hedge fund companies and people who have lots and lots of money. The median house sells for around two million dollars, and one year over a hundred houses went for more than five million. And this was where Vidal's mother and her stepfather Gary lived and where Vidal had lived after her mother married Gary. And it was where the late Arnold Nunnely lived. The old tune went through my head, "Nice work if you can get it…"

Driving through Greenwich and the walls guarding the mansions on either side of the road, I couldn't help but think about comparative real estate values. I told myself our – maybe if we were lucky – five hundred-thousand-dollar house in Fairfield was just fine. I tried to turn my envy into a judgmental critique of conspicuous consumption and the accelerating disparity of wealth in the United States. Driving through Greenwich, it was not hard to do, and I enjoyed my self-righteousness.

When I had called Estelle Liscom, the ex-Mrs. Arnold Nunnely, she was very polite. Reserved but polite. She said she would be glad to talk to me about her former husband. She suggested an evening meeting so her husband could join us. Or, protect her from me, I thought. I had no difficulty with that and packed my audio recording equipment in my L.L.Bean canvas briefcase, hoping that she and Gary would allow me to record our conversation.

I dressed my six foot frame, consistently one-hundred-and-eighty pounds of fifty-five-year old damned good physical shape into my uniform of L.L.Bean chinos, L.L.Bean button down blue shirt, sans tie, and covered my non-L.L.Bean Glock with my L.L.Bean blue blazer. It was cold, so I also wore my L.L.Bean long winter coat. Such is my no thought dress code that I adopted when I first started teaching.

Years ago, on our way to pick up a sailboat Patricia and I had chartered for a week, we stopped at the L.L.Bean store in Freeport, Maine. For me, it was love at first wander. I pledged my loyalty to the world of Bean, even if it meant a sporadic tirade of abuse from my daughter. She so disapproves of my sartorial conservatism she once gave me several Christmas presents perfectly boxed in L.L.Bean boxes she had squirreled away, but they all contained merchandise from other, far inferior I would add, haberdashers and were more appropriate for a Manhattan twenty-year old. I laughed as I was supposed to and those items still reside in a far back corner of my closet. Even my son, Ben, thought they were a bit much and didn't want them.

The Liscom home was actually modest by Greenwich standards, meaning slightly under two million. It was a Georgian brick colonial with a couple of white pillars holding up a small portico so you wouldn't get wet while waiting for the door to be opened by the genteel Greenwich occupants. Tailored shrubs on either side were protected against the cold by materials of unknown origin. I was right on time, and the door opened within seconds of being rung.

I don't know what I expected, but Estelle Liscom wasn't it. After all, she was "Greenwich," had a very put together daughter, and I expected a type. Estelle was the opposite. She was a bit dumpy, no make-up, maybe five-foot -two, short gray-going-white hair, wearing loose fitting jeans and a sweater.

Gary didn't look the way he'd imagined him either. Taller than Estelle, he was also heavier than Estelle by a great deal, with a large stomach that came down over where his belt probably was. What was left of his hair was white. Glasses hung on a chord around his neck and dangled over his buttoned-to-the-top cardigan sweater.

They invited me into their living room which was comfortable and filled with pictures of children at various ages from birth into adulthood. I saw several of Vidal.

"Would you like some coffee, water, soda?" Estelle asked.

I declined. I asked permission to record our conversation after telling them about my meeting with Vidal. Of course, they knew about that already. They granted permission, not reluctantly, but warily. I concluded they were seeing me for Vidal and for no other reason.

After polite chitchat about weather and traffic, which went on far too long, I launched the question that I knew would get things going, "Vidal thinks that her father was deliberately murdered. Do you?"

Gary's answer surprised me. "I can believe it. I don't know, but it wouldn't shock me. Given what he did, he must have known a lot of things that people would not want to have made public, and I'm sure he had a lot of enemies. You spend your life digging around in other people's garbage and you're going to develop a stench, and Arnie stank in more ways than one."

Wow, did that question generate some heat!

Estelle cooled it right down. She said, "I have no idea. When Vidal told me Arnie had been killed in a drive-by shooting and she didn't think it was an accidental death, I thought, at first, she was imagining things. The more she told me about her conversations with the detectives in Boston, the less I thought it was possible, you know, that he was killed on purpose. However, when she told me that she had been to see you and that you thought it was likely that it was intentional, and Gary said he was sure it was, that's when I started to consider it."

Oh, Vidal, how did you misrepresent what I said? I didn't want to contradict what Vidal had told them, but I didn't want them to think that I was sure he had been murdered. So, I said, "Let me clarify my thinking at this point. I can understand how Vidal, given our conversation and the conversations she has had with the detectives in Boston, might have concluded that I was agreeing with her. My thoughts are a bit more nuanced. What I want to do, for the purposes of my investigation, is to assume it was an intentional murder. In part, I want to do this because the police are assuming it was not. This way you have people looking at what happened from two diametrically opposing viewpoints, a kind of dialectic. We may discover different information that way and, hopefully, it will get us closer to what actually happened."

"You must have an opinion though. What do you think?" Estelle asked.

"I understand that this may sound fuzzy, but I'm assuming he was intentionally murdered in order to guide my investigation, but do I know? Not yet."

"He's hypothesis testing," Gary added.

"Exactly," I said.

"What do you need from us?" Estelle asked.

"First, I need to know who Arnie was and how he got to be the man he was." They had referred to him as "Arnie," so I followed them. He was "Arnie," not Arnold.

"Then I'd like to know about any people Arnie had conflicts with and anybody you know of who might have a grudge or might want to see him harmed. Who might benefit from his death?"

"I don't think you need me for this," Gary said. "I'm not exactly objective. The man was a horrible husband and a lousy father." With that Gary started heading for the stairs that led to the second floor. "I'll be watching TV in the bedroom if you need me."

Estelle didn't say anything to him as he left. She waited for Gary to walk up the stairs and disappear. We heard a door close. It wasn't a slam, but it wasn't gentle either.

She said, "I'm sorry. He hates Arnie. To some extent he's right. Arnie was not a good husband and he was far from a good father, but Gary didn't know the old Arnie, the one I married."

"Tell me about the Arnie you knew. How did you meet?"

"Well, I met Arnie when he first started working at Goldman and Bunch. I was working as a sales representative for an office supply house, and Goldman and Bunch was one of my accounts. Arnie was a first-year associate and full of energy and, because he was the lowest of the low men on the totem pole, he got to handle some of the mundane issues like office supplies. I was incredibly attracted to him. I had only been to college for two years, a community college in upstate Connecticut, and all I knew of the political things that were taking place were from reading. And here was this rebel, former rebel, he would say, who had been in the middle of it. Also, he was Jewish, real Jewish, not like my family. As an example, at my family Passover my father would say, 'We can pass over this and pass over that' when we would read from the Haggadah. In Arnie's family, you read every word. I loved that. I loved his parents and his sister Ruth.

"In a little less than a year, we were married. Arnie was still living with his folks believe it or not. We found this wonderful first-floor flat in the Black Rock section of Bridgeport, and it was magical. We'd take walks down to St. Mary's-by-the-Sea. With our two incomes, we could afford to eat out at good, but inexpensive, restaurants. We developed some friendships with other young couples in the Black Rock area. Life was pretty much everything I could have asked for.

"Like any associate in a fairly large law firm, Arnie worked fifty to sixty hours a week. My hours were nothing like that, so while he worked, I nested. We both wanted children, two of course. I became pregnant in our second year of marriage, right on my schedule." Estelle laughed. "Arnie had wanted to wait another year or two until it was clear he was on track to become a partner, but I couldn't wait to be a mother.

"He was getting a great deal of positive feedback at the firm and we never doubted whether or not he would become a partner. He had the billable hours he needed, actually more. Clients liked him. He did a lot of work for Stu Goldman, who was his champion at the firm. You need a champion at a law firm."

"I've heard that from my son. He's an attorney at a firm in New Haven. He's an associate. He works those kind of hours."

"It's not easy. Vidal was born in March, the twentieth. Goldman's wife was diagnosed with Alzheimer's the following September. He left

Dirt: A Frank Kelly Mystery

the practice in December to take care of her. He was close to retiring anyway, but his wife's illness changed his plans. Then everything went sideways for Arnie."

"In what way?"

"A year after Goldman retired, the managing partner, one of the only partners in the firm that Arnie had not done much work for, a specialist in corporate law, brought Arnie into his office and told him that he was welcome to stay with the firm as an associate as long as he would like, but it was unlikely that he would ever be considered for partner. Do you know why?"

"University of Bridgeport," I guessed.

"You got it. It didn't matter that Arnie had graduated Summa Cum Laude or that he had sweat blood for the firm and had high reviews from clients and the other partners. He didn't have the damned pedigree of a top-tier law school for the firm to brag about."

"That must have hurt," I said.

"Hurt? Arnie was devastated. He called Goldman and told him. Goldman already knew but said he wasn't in a position to get involved. That added to the hurt. I was stunned when Goldman showed up at Arnie's funeral. Maybe he felt guilty. Who knows? I had nothing to say to him. He was fragile, stooped over, using a walker. A nurse or somebody was accompanying him. I know this sounds cruel, but even after all these years, I didn't want to talk to him."

"You hold him responsible."

"I do. To this day, I think if he had simply made a call it would have changed the course of a lot of lives."

"What did Arnie do after he got the news?"

"Vidal was an infant. I wasn't working. Arnie stayed. He wanted to walk out the next day, but he didn't. He felt betrayed, though, and hated every minute of it. As an associate he wasn't making a lot of money. After a couple of months, a friend of his who had also graduated from UB called him about an opening at the state prosecutor's office in Bridgeport. Not much more money, but some. It offered more job

52

security and Arnie loved litigation. He also knew that it was more likely he'd get picked up by another law firm if he had the state prosecutor's office on his resume. And, if he ever wanted to go into private practice doing defense work, the prosecutor's office was a good place to start. So, he applied, and got the job."

"Did that work out for him?"

"At first. He loved it. The hours were not as long. He enjoyed the negotiations, the arguments, and the plea bargaining. He loved being in court. He loved working with the police, formulating cases that would lead to convictions. He used to kid about how the former rebel who fought against the system was now 'the man.'

"He got involved in some major cases and started becoming fairly well known in some political as well as criminal networks. He was the lead prosecutor on a big political corruption case."

"So, things were going well," I said.

"Yes, for a while. Arnie wanted to put off having a second child. After the political corruption case he thought he would get a promotion and it might mean moving to another district in Connecticut. It didn't happen. The reason?"

"Not again."

"Yes. Again. An unwritten law seemed to exist. If you graduated from the University of Bridgeport School of Law you were fine as a worker bee, but that was as far as you were going to go in the state of Connecticut, which is a small state to begin with. Then, to add on, the legal community is small. Of course it didn't help that the University of Bridgeport was failing economically and the law school had separated from the University and had become part of Quinnipiac University. And then, to save the University the Bridgeport, the board of directors accepted a bail out from the Unification Church."

"The followers of Sun Myung Moon. The Moonies," I added. "I remember when that happened."

"The Moonies now controlled the board of directors. Bottom line, Arnie's degree was from the University of Bridgeport Law School, or

Moon U as it became known. If Arnie had gone to school a few years later, his law degree would have been from Quinnipiac and everything would have been fine."

"How did he react?"

"You can imagine. How would you react? He started to drink. He was furious at first, then he became sullen and moody. He stopped working as hard as he had been. 'Why bother,' became his favorite saying. We heard about a house in Trumbull and, since it didn't appear we would be leaving the area anytime soon, we bought it. Now I became the one who didn't want to have another child, not until he got his act together and made his way back to the old Arnie. I went back to work, and we became distant from one another. Our marriage wasn't horrible, but it wasn't what it had been."

"What happened next?"

"The following year, after he got passed over, he decided to go into private practice. My going back to work meant we would have some income while he got started. Also, he had been approached about doing some work for the city of Bridgeport if and when he ever did go into private practice. He was a good lawyer, worked hard, and people liked him."

"What kind of work?"

"Really, it was stuff the city attorney didn't want to deal with so he farmed it out to other lawyers. Sometimes it was defending the city in a nuisance lawsuit. Sometimes it was dealing with a real estate issue or taxes. Arnie was good. He was thorough and he worked fast. He was well trained in the world of billable hours, only now he was minimizing hours rather than maximizing them. Larry, Larry Brundred, was the city attorney then, and he gave him a lot of work. What it also meant was that Arnie was getting a name for himself, an independent name. He had an office, hired a legal secretary, and things were looking up again. He knew everyone in the district prosecutor's office and kept those contacts. Basically, he made problems go away for Larry, for the city.

"Others started coming to him, too. They weren't big cases, some weren't really cases at all. You know, write a threatening letter about cleaning up your tree which fell on to my property. Talk a prosecutor into letting little Johnny go back to college and have his license suspended while he was away at school after he had been arrested for a DUI. It was back to the long hours, but they were his hours and he got paid for every one of them. He was taking on everything that came his way and no one gave a damn where he had gone to law school. He was admitted to the bar in three states and got results. That's all that mattered."

"And how were things between the two of you?"

"Good again, when he was home. He was driven, though. His need to make his mark after what had happened to him was enormous. He was rarely home for dinner. He wasn't drinking as much as he had been, but he was still drinking. He would say he was having dinner meetings. He probably was, but I'm not so sure they were all necessary.

"Then, since we were living in Trumbull, he approached the city attorney there about doing the same kind of work he'd been doing for the city of Bridgeport. It didn't develop into anything, but he was approached about running for office in Trumbull. By Republicans. Trumbull was always somewhat of a purple town, and Arnie, by this time, was fed up with just about every institution, including political parties. He had a few meetings with the local party leaders, but turned it down. As I said, Connecticut is a small state. Shortly after turning it down, he got a call from a Republican candidate for attorney general, a guy by the name of Joe Thew. He wanted to know if Arnie would be interested in doing some research for him on his opponent. Guess who the opponent was?"

"I have no idea."

"His former boss, the one who didn't promote him, Dominic Christanso, the Deputy Chief State's Attorney who was running for public office for the first time. Arnie salivated at the opportunity to stick it to him. Thew won thanks to Arnie, who had dug up cases where Christanso had played favorites on plea bargains or squelched cases, like burying a DUI for the governor's brother-in-law, and Arnie dug it up. And, for the cherry on top of the dirt sundae, he discovered Christanso had a quid-pro-quo sexual liaison with one his staff members who he promoted after she threatened him when he tried to break it off.

"Arnie destroyed Christanso and loved every single juicy minute of it."

"And that's how Arnie got involved in doing oppositional research?"

"Yes. That's when he tasted political blood for the first time. That was the birth of Arnold, the Assassin, Nunnely. It was also the beginning of the end of my marriage to Arnie Nunnely, the struggling young lawyer who kept getting beaten down and kept getting up again."

"I take it Arnie changed?"

"Money, power, grandiosity, travel, affairs, cynicism. I could go on, but I think you get the picture. You don't need all the gory details."

It was clear that she didn't want to tell me about the end of their marriage, and I really didn't need to know the details. I was getting a picture of how Arnie became Arnold the Assassin. I did need to know more about his oppositional research practice, but they had been divorced for a long time and I needed to know about his current life and circumstances. I asked her anyway, "Do you know anything about his current practice?"

"No. Nothing. His secretary, Leslie Cahill, still works for him, believe it or not. I talked with her briefly at the funeral. She'd know."

"One last thing. Did Arnie have any conflicts or problems with family members or friends that you know about?"

"No. But then I know almost nothing about his recent life. We've had very little contact with him for years. Gary and I would see him at family events once in a while, but that's it. His sister Ruth tried to include us. If it involved Vidal, we would include Ruth and her family and, of course, Bubbe – I call her that, too. Arnie would come sometimes. Sometimes he didn't."

I thanked her for her time, and offered to keep her posted on what I

56

found, but she said she would find out from Vidal and that it wasn't necessary. I interpreted that as, "Gary doesn't want me involved."

As I drove home, I thought about Arnie, Estelle, and Vidal. I thought about Estelle and Arnie, full of dreams and taking walks along the water at Saint Mary's-by-the-Sea. I thought about breaks, good and bad, and timing. If Arnie was murdered, I wanted to find the person who was responsible. Some lines from *Death of a Salesman* found their way into my consciousness: "He's not the finest character that ever lived" but "attention must be paid," and "He's not to be allowed to fall into his grave like an old dog."

I thought to myself, *I'm going to pay attention, Arnie. I'm going to pay attention.*

Chapter 7: Off to Boston

When I got home from my meeting with Estelle and Gary, I thought I'd better learn something about the Boston Police Department before I paid them a visit. As usual, I became fascinated. The academic juices started to flow and what I thought was going to take five minutes became a couple of hours.

I learned that the Boston Police Department is the oldest police department in the United States, the largest in New England, and the twentieth largest in the country. It was modeled after the London Police Department. Its beginnings can be traced back to a "night watch" and a "day watch," all the way back to the 1600s.

Inclusion has not always been its strength. When the first Irishman was appointed to the department, one Barney McGinniskin, Boston blue bloods, the so-called Boston Brahmins, were outraged and some even claimed it was the end of America as they had known it. Poor Barney didn't last long. He was fired after a couple of years for being both Irish and Catholic. I could relate to Barney. Those were the same reasons Patricia's parents didn't want her to marry me. Barney, in eighteen fifty-two, me in the nineteen eighties, same shit, one difference. The Irish took over the Boston Police Department while I lost Patricia to a WASP, a wealthy WASP. The department still had inclusion problems, only now it was black and brown skin that was underrepresented in a city that is fifty percent minority.

I wasn't surprised to find out how large the department is, employing two thousand cops and about a thousand civilians, covering three zones and eleven neighborhood districts, and all of it organized into bureaus, one of which was the Bureau of Investigative Services – my kind of people. I expected homicide, drugs, and forensics to be housed there. I was surprised, though, that it also included a Family Justice Center. Family Justice Center? I dug deeper: sexual and physical abuse, domestic violence, children and elder abuse. Calling it a Family Justice Center sounded so pristine compared with what they actually dealt with. Was the title a euphemism or an aspiration?

Arnie was killed in Roxbury, District B-2. B-2 included the neighborhoods of Roxbury and Mission Hill. So the police in B-2 had the job of serving and protecting about eighty-thousand souls. But what different souls they were.

Mission Hill was full of college kids, medical people, and a wide range of assorted others, and then there was Roxbury which sought to be known as the home of "Black Culture in Boston." It made sense being ninety-two percent African American and Hispanic. Roxbury and Mission Hill – I wondered who got the bulk of the attention from the Blue in District B-2. I told myself to go easy and damp down on my cynicism.

However Wiki also told me that the crime rate in Roxbury was around forty percent higher than the national average. That translated into one out of every twenty-five people in Roxbury being a victim at some point. Roxbury's unemployment was double the national average. Wiki didn't give me underemployment. I can't imagine what that could be. Forty-two percent of the population was under twenty-five. Academic test scores were forty percent lower than the national average. That translated to a lot of young black and brown kids un- or underemployed with a mediocre to lousy education.

Roxbury would be a breeding ground for gangs. Poverty and hopelessness were the potting soil and fertilizer of gangs whether in Boston in the U.S. or Tegucigalpa in Honduras. Gangs were all about the power to provide safety, belonging, and economics to the chosen ones and their allies. Turf, "owning" a geographic area of any kind regardless of how small, was the metaphor for strength, whether it was a block, a neighborhood, or, in some cases, a building. Drugs, prostitution, theft, and extortion would be the job opportunities for gang members.

Although the word ghetto is no longer politically correct, it seemed

59

to me that if there weren't physical walls around Roxbury, there were a hell of a lot of socially constructed ones of race, class, education, health, employment, and on and on. Many of the walls were invisible, unless you lived there. The suburbs did everything they could to make sure those walls stayed strong.

I thought about Westport, the next town over from where I lived in Fairfield. Westport had just fired their outside law firm. The reason: the firm had dared to represent a developer who sought to build affordable housing – in another town. Not even in Westport.

Some people would get desperate enough, and courageous enough, to leave, just pack up and leave, but they were rare. I wondered whether the residents of Roxbury would be granted asylum someplace in the United States. Clearly not in Westport, Connecticut.

Well, at least the Boston Police Department put its new district headquarters in Roxbury, and the police supported a Roxbury women's basketball team.

The next morning I huddled with Sam. It was another New England gray January day after another night of mixed snow and rain. I was getting tired of them. Sam was in a gray mood as well.

He came in complaining, "I hate having to leave my car out in the driveway. The fucking snow and rain froze last night and I must have had an inch of ice on every damned window. I'm going to get one of those automatic starters so I can look out my kitchen window, press a button, start the car, and wait to go out until the defrosters have done their work."

"Assuming you've remembered to leave them on," I said. Not exactly a helpful response on my part.

"You taking lessons from Meg? That's exactly what she said."

I thought it wise to change the topic. "Claire brought in an assortment from Dunkin. Want something?" I know, police get maligned and stereotyped for eating donuts. Sam actually does love donuts, although Meg tries in vain in restrict his consumption. "So they don't become conspicuous in front of you," she would say referring to

Sam's slight pot belly. Sam, however, often snuck one if someone else in the office brought them in.

Donuts, though, were not top of his mind this morning. It was his car and ice. "I want my son to get his damned stuff out of my garage so I can have my garage back." Sam and Meg's son Tony had recently moved and, in the process, had "borrowed" some garage space to store things that he and his wife weren't sure would fit in with their new home decor. I didn't respond to the garage issue and waited for Sam to change the subject.

Getting no solace from me, he moved on and said, "Watched the video yesterday. Vidal. Strange name."

"Means *life* in Portuguese," I told him.

"Thought the family was Jewish."

"They are. Apparently Arnie and Vidal's mother, Estelle, went to a lecture by a woman whose name was Vidal and they both liked the name. Vidal's middle name is Esther after her great grandmother."

Sam picked up on my use of Arnie. "So, its Arnie not Arnold?"

"Yeah. That's what Estelle and her husband, Gary, called him. What do you think now that you've seen the video?" I asked.

"We'll do what we can for her," Sam answered. "What the hell was her father doing in Roxbury? Why that night? We figure this out, and we'll have a pretty good idea of whether this was premeditated homicide or the unintended killing of a bystander."

I agreed then filled Sam in on my meeting with Estelle. He asked some questions as I gave him my report. He asked about Gary and his anger at Arnie. "Why is Gary so pissed at Arnie this many years later? He won the girl. Sounds like he's got a good relationship with his stepdaughter. What's he so angry about?"

"I don't know. He left us and went upstairs after a couple of minutes. I never really talked to him, and Estelle didn't say why he was as intense as he was. You aren't thinking Gary might have something to do with this, are you?"

"I don't know. You're the professor. Family. Anger. Could be something we don't know about. You know the data," Sam said.

"Have to consider it," I said. "Spouses, friends, and acquaintances are responsible for more than eighty percent of all homicides." I wondered if I had missed connecting some dots. It was clear that Gary had no use for Arnie. "I can circle back and find out what that was all about," I said. "Vidal may know."

"Who knows?" Sam said. He took a long swallow of his coffee. "About the Boston P.D. Sorry, but I turned up nothing yesterday. I called all the people I know who I thought might have contacts in the department. Nothing. Afraid you'll have to go in cold turkey. When are you thinking of contacting them?"

"Today. If the case team is willing to, I'd like to meet with them face to face. I think I'll get more that way than if I talk with them on the phone."

"Absolutely. Want me to come with you?" Sam asked.

"Not at this point. If it gets squirrely, it may make some sense later. Let's see how it goes. At this point we don't even know if they'll see me."

"Tell them that you're going to be in Boston anyway, on another matter. That way they can't say you don't have to bother making a special trip," Sam said.

"Good idea. We have all of the paperwork we need from Vidal?"

"Yep. I went over it with Meg yesterday afternoon while you were out looking at wedding venues with Eve. How'd that go?"

I chuckled. "We only saw two that we have any interest in. Molly, of course, had told us exactly where we should hold the wedding and the reception. I've had to remind my darling daughter that this is our wedding and, when I want her advice, I'll ask for it. I reminded her that I stayed out of her plans when she and Stan got married. Eve, of course, said it was not a big deal and that Molly's excitement and suggestions were sincerely an offer of help and coming from a place of love."

"To which you said?"

"I know. You're right."

"Eve is right, you know," Sam said. "Your kids worship you."

"I doubt that, but I do know they're happy about us getting married. I guess I could show Mol a bit more loving kindness."

"Loving kindness?" Sam asked.

"It's a Buddhist thing. I learned about it from…"

"Eve," Sam finished my sentence.

Three hours later I was on the road. On a good day it takes about two-and-a-half hours to drive from New Haven to Boston, interstate routes 91 to 84 to 90. On a bad day, meaning rush hour going around Hartford and then rush hour getting into Boston, it can be an hour longer.

Vidal had given me three Boston Police Department business cards – a sergeant detective, Colm Ganim, and two detectives: Joseph "Brud" Dolan, and Alice Malone. This was the homicide squad assigned to the "Nunnely case."

When I called, I had gotten Joseph Dolan who said, "Please call me Brud." He had been polite and professional. He had referred to Arnie's death as the Garcia case. Okay, a case by any other name is still a case and all that, but labels matter, and I both understood and accepted his perspective. Arnie didn't rate having his name on the case. Arnold Nunnely's death, from what they'd decided, was an accident.

Charles Braxton and Yvonne Wilson, the other two who were shot, were still alive and had recovered from their wounds. Dolan and Malone were focused on catching whoever had killed Tom-Tom Garcia. It seemed that Arnie was about as important as roadkill as far as they were concerned.

Dolan said "no" to my bringing Blackie. Fortunately, it wasn't going to be too cold to leave Blackie in the car when I was with Dolan and Malone. Eve was disappointed that I was taking Blackie with me. Sometimes Blackie went off to college with her. She had convinced the administration that the kids relaxed more when she was counseling them about their spiritual journeys if Blackie was available to be petted or just lying there.

But today he would be with me, traveling to the setting of the radio and then TV detective from the fifties: "Enemy to those who make him an enemy, friend to those who have no friend."

My gun was another matter. Massachusetts has the toughest firearm laws in the nation, including restrictions on Glocks. Glocks are okay for various law enforcement groups but not for civilians. Even though I am legally a Connecticut State Marshal, it would be a silly pissing contest to get into when I was asking for their help, so I would not be wearing my Glock 23 concealed under my jacket.

When I was teaching, I never paid much attention to guns other than as an academic series of problems. Forensics, proliferation, weapon of choice, and things like that. That changed when I joined Nutmeg and started carrying a concealed weapon every day. My attention to weapons changed infinitely more when I was shot at and forced to kill the two people who had been trying to kill me.

Since that happened, I've practiced more with my Glock 23. I also wanted a weapon that was more powerful and more accurate than the 23 that I could leave in the car, a "just-in-case" gun. Upon the recommendation of Pat Brady at Nutmeg, a guy who was a walking weapons encyclopedia, I bought and spent hours with a Glock 20.

Pat insisted, "Reliability, Frank. I don't care how powerful a gun is. If it isn't reliable, it doesn't matter. Stick with Glocks. You can count on them. Get the 20."

I did what he told me to do. The magazine held fifteen 10mm rounds. With a barrel approaching five inches, it was barely small enough to carry concealed, so it lived in its holster in the locked glove compartment of my car along with a box of ammunition and two magazines loaded and ready to go. Massachusetts or not, I was leaving it there. I doubted that anyone from the Boston P.D. was going to ask me to open a locked glove compartment or would hassle me if it was there.

I made sure I had all the paperwork they might want: P.I. license, marshal's badge, and a representation letter from Vidal Banks. With

Blackie in the "way back," I drove to Boston to meet Brud Dolan and his partner Alice Malone.

I had just gotten on to the Massachusetts Turnpike when I got a call from Vidal.

"Frank?"

"Hi, Vidal." Her name had come up on my Outback's information screen. "What's up?"

"A couple of things. I got a call from Detective Dolan. He said you were meeting with them and he wanted to make sure it was okay with me for them to talk to you. I assured them that it was. When are you seeing them?"

"In about an hour."

"He didn't sound pleased that I hired you."

"I'm not surprised. We'll see how it goes."

She changed topics. "How'd your meeting with Mom and Gary go?"

"I think fine. Did your Mom or Gary give you any feedback?"

"Mom liked you. Gary thinks I should just leave this alone and let the police handle it. Also, Mom wanted me to tell you that she forgot to mention Carlos Barlotti. I told her I already told you about Carlos. Mom thinks he might have been still working with Dad when Dad was shot. Carlos was at the funeral."

"Great. Would you text me any contact information you have? I'll get in touch with him."

"Okay. And please let me know how it goes with Detective Dolan. Are you meeting with his partner, Alice Malone, as well?"

"Yes. He said I would meet with both of them."

"Good. I liked her."

"I'll call you on the way back from Boston and let you know how it went."

"Thank you."

When we sat down around a conference table at the office of the Bureau of Investigative Services, I showed Brud Dolan and Alice Malone my marshal's badge and my brand-new license as a

Connecticut private investigator. I didn't tell him what a job it was to get that. With Sam's retirement on the horizon, we couldn't wait for the mandatory five-year apprenticeship that it takes to get a private investigator license in Connecticut. Sam and I pushed and cajoled and leveraged and finally got the Connecticut bureaucrats to accept the four years I had spent in the Naval Investigative Service as well as consider my career teaching criminology. Eventually they relented, and I am now probably the only licensed P.I. in Connecticut with a PhD. It impresses some people. I don't think it impressed Dolan.

More importantly, I showed them the letter from Vidal Banks authorizing Nutmeg Protection and Investigation to investigate the death of Arnold Nunnely. Between Dolan's telephone call with Vidal, her letter, my badge, and my license, they'd have to work pretty hard to not at least be polite to me.

Chapter 8: Brud and Alice

J oseph "call me Brud" Dolan was a neither person. He was neither tall nor short. He wasn't fat, nor was he slim. He wasn't young, nor was he old. He was bland. Even his skin and hair color were bland. Business casual allows for multiple layers of sartorial sins. Brud believed the ads for wash and wear and was wearing un-pressed gray slacks and a rust colored shirt that had faded.

Alice Malone was dark skinned with kinky short hair, young enough to be Brud's daughter, and wore pressed black slacks and a heather green sweater over a yellow blouse.

They were polite. It was trained politeness, enforced politeness. Brud and Alice offered me water, coffee, and "How can we help you?" The delivery was professional, rehearsed, agreed upon. Everything led me to conclude that they had one goal: I was to be handled, disposed of, and sent on my way.

I understood why Vidal felt she had been patronized when she had talked to them. Brud had no interest in engaging me. Alice had apparently been willing to express some degree of humanity to Vidal, but then Vidal had just lost her father. I hadn't lost anything and was a distraction from their busy schedules.

Must all police stations use the exact same conference tables? Must every wall be beige, puke green, or gray? At least the chairs were relatively comfortable and the bottle of water that I accepted was no better or worse than any other bottle of water that promised it came from some crystal clear, undefiled, and undisclosed spring someplace.

After we got through the sharing of my credentials, Vidal's letter of authorization, the polite chit chat about the traffic, the weather, and my drive to Boston, I decided to be empathic to their situation but threw in a bit of experience and expertise just for good measure.

"Folks, I've been training police and working with different departments for thirty years. My hunch is you see me as a waste of your time. I'll try to take as little of it as possible. However, my client has lost her father and his death doesn't make any sense to her. Basically, that's why I'm here. I know she's talked to you, and I may be going over things you've already discussed with her, but like you, this is what I do. I may have a different take on what did or did not happen to her dad. I don't know."

Alice seemed to respond to my attempt to join with them and said, "I know she's upset. How can we help you and her?"

"Well, to start, I'd like a copy of the reports: coroner's, forensics, crime scene investigation, the 'murder book' if that's what you folks call it here. The newspapers said one other person was killed, a Tom-Tom Garcia, and two other people were wounded but not critically, Charles Braxton and Yvonne Wilson. I'd like to know about them. Mostly, I'm just interested in your thoughts about what happened and why."

"We can get you copies. It may take a while," Brud said.

Alice added, "I know Vidal thinks her father was not an innocent by-stander, but there's absolutely nothing to indicate he was anything but that."

"I understand," I replied. "Would you take me through what happened. What's the narrative you're working with?"

"It will be in the reports," Brud said.

"I'm sure, but perhaps you can add some flesh to it."

Alice was more accommodating but still working from the "handle this guy script." Her voice was a monotone, "Short version. The shooting took place on Friday, October 19, a little before seven in the evening. Tom-Tom Garcia, his girlfriend, Yvonne Wilson, and his lieutenant, Charles Braxton, were walking in the 'H Block' when a car drove by, stopped, and someone shot them using an AK-47, according to the ballistics. We know that Garcia and Braxton were members of the Hell's Kings gang. The Kings have been trying, without much success, to move in on the Steel Guerillas. The Guerillas may have had enough. There is another possibility that our gang people have come up with. They think that it may have been a coup."

"Interesting. An internal coup," I said to buy some good grace.

"Perhaps Tom-Tom was coasting," Alice continued. "Our people think someone or ones believed they could do a better job."

Brud Dolan continued the narrative. His tone was patronizing. "Apparently Nunnely was waiting for someone, or he was lost, or he may have been waiting for the bus that stops at the corner of Humboldt and Homestead. We have no idea why he was there. His daughter didn't know, and his secretary didn't know. We think he might have been trying to buy drugs. Everyone we talked to said he didn't use, but people don't always know, and a lot of suburban types come into this neighborhood to score because they can be anonymous. Why Nunnely was there at that spot at that time, we have no idea. Nada."

Alice jumped back in. She was more polite. "Garcia, Braxton, and Wilson are a different story. It's their neighborhood. Wilson said they had been out surveying their turf. Making their presence known. It was a nice evening. Maybe it was just an evening walk. It was getting dark, but there was still some light."

"Witnesses?"

Brud jumped in. "In Roxbury? You kidding? One older man. From across the street. Sitting on his stoop. He said he was wondering what a white guy was doing just standing there in that neighborhood. Our witness saw a dark sedan stop. Then he heard what he thought was gunshots. When the sedan pulled away, he saw people on the ground. He ran inside and had someone call 911. That's it. One old man."

"Video?"

Brud Dolan's cynicism was getting to me. He answered my question with, "A wonderful picture of a stolen car with a stolen plate. And we suspect the car is the same one found on fire six hours later in Providence, but we can't be sure."

"Burned out car. No fingerprints. No DNA. No fabric. Sounds very professional," I said.

"You think?" Brud patronized. "These gangs are not exactly novices at killing one another and getting away with it."

"You sure it was the car?" I asked, maintaining my calm.

"Same make and year. VIN number gave us the color which corresponds to the witness and video. Highly unlikely coincidence given the timing," Alice said.

I shook my head in agreement and said, "Vidal told me you were convinced it was a gang killing."

Alice said, "There is no evidence to indicate otherwise given what we know about the Kings and the Guerillas. For that neighborhood, nothing else makes any sense. I have some questions about the internal coup theory, but I can imagine something like that."

I nodded, considering the scenario.

"Also, there's one other thing," Alice added.

"What's that?"

"Nunnely was also shot with 22 longs."

"22 longs. Seems strange. So Nunnely was shot with two different guns?" I said.

Brud took the lead on the explanation. "First shot didn't kill him, so a second shooter made sure there were no witnesses. As I said, these guys know what they're doing."

Alice tried to be sympathetic. "Look, I'm sorry that her father is dead. But he's not the first innocent person to be caught in this kind of shooting. We've lost young kids. We lost an older woman last week who worked at one of the hospitals. In that shooting there was no one else around. It's like she was target practice or an initiation."

"How the hell do you apply your investigative theories to that, Dr. Kelly?" Brud said.

I smiled and stared him in the eyes. They had obviously looked me up and seen that I had written articles on crime investigation for journals. I could have argued, but it would have been pointless, and I wanted to get whatever cooperation I could so I said, "You don't."

"You're damned right you don't," Brud added. "You hope for a break, usually from another case. You leverage someone and hope they'll cough up a lead. Most of the time, you just add to your list of cold cases, and we have lots of those."

Brud Dolan was as hard as concrete. Criminals were hardened. Police were hardened. Everyone was hardened to accept the unacceptable. I wondered what that would do to Brud and Alice as human beings after too many years of being hardened.

I said, "I plan to go down and take a look at the crime scene. Any objections?"

"It's a free country," Dolan said. "Daytime, you shouldn't have any trouble."

"If I have questions after I read the reports, okay if I get back to you?"

Brud Dolan had gotten up and was walking towards the door. Alice kept the polite police façade going. "Of course. After you read them, you might want to reset Ms. Banks assumptions about what happened. I think that might be easier for her. Senseless killings are just that, senseless, and that's what this was."

I said, "One last thing. Since I'm going to the neighborhood, would you give me the contact information for the witness. If it's okay with the two of you, I'd like to talk to him."

"I don't see any problem with that," Alice said. "However, if he says he doesn't want to talk to you, don't bother him. I don't want him calling here telling us you were harassing him."

Alice pulled out her mobile phone, looked up some information, and jotted it down on the back of her business card and gave it to me.

"Thank you," I said and handed them each one of my cards in exchange for the one Alice gave me.

I had one more question, "Sorry, just had a thought. Vidal told me that her father always had his laptop and cellphone with him. I would think that would be especially true in the middle of the political campaign he was involved in. My understanding is that neither were found at the crime scene."

Brud said, "And your question is…"

"Were there any remnants of either in the burned-out car, the one you think was used by the assailants?"

Alice looked at Brud. He answered, "No. They would have been destroyed beyond recognition in the heat anyway."

I wasn't going to argue with him. I was confident they never looked. I thanked them for their time. I hadn't insulted them or argued with them. I patted myself on the back for not bolstering their resistance. Actually, I was sympathetic. It's hard to work day in and day out with only rare moments of success. Alice must have picked up on my *I'm on your side and I get it*, approach because as I was leaving she had added, "It will take me a few hours to dig out the reports that you want and make copies, but if you can stop by later this afternoon, I can have them for you."

Brud looked at her as though she had deserted him but didn't say anything.

I said, "Thanks, I really appreciate that."

Chapter 9: H Block

When I got back to my car, I glanced at my watch and realized the meeting had taken just over thirty minutes. I had been handled, but I had avoided a confrontation, gotten some information, and, more importantly, I was invited to come back in a few hours to pick up critical documents.

Blackie greeted me warmly. He needed a walk and I knew just where we were going to go: the H Block, where Arnie had been shot. "Enough," I said to the tongue lapping at my ear. "We'll go in a minute."

I reached into my briefcase and took out a file of newspaper clippings that Claire had put together for me. She had put a post-it note on each of the top two articles and had scribbled yellow highlighter over the titles. On the first sticky note she had written, "Can this be true?" On the second she had written, "OMG. How can people live there?"

The first was from an independent community newspaper called *The Universal Hub*. A new kind of journalism, it collected all sorts of pieces of information from blogs to emails and then formed them into a local narrative.

H Block: Where children are shot in a gang war that goes back decades

By adamg on *Sat, 01/12/2013 - 3:43pm*

The Globe reports today that Gabriel Clarke, the 13-year-old choirboy shot at Humboldt Avenue and Homestead Street while walking to church last night, is in critical but stable condition.

His shooting is just the latest in an endless string of gun violence in an area just north of Franklin Park known as H Block because most of the street names start with H -

> Humboldt, Homestead, Harold, Harrishof, Holworthy - and in
> the area around the Bromley-Heath housing project in
> Jamaica Plain.
>
> The H Block Gang and the rival Heath Street Gang have
> been shooting at each other — and at completely innocent
> bystanders — since the 1980s. Children and teens who have
> nothing at all to do with the battling often wind up as victims
> as gang members just drive onto their rival's turf and start
> firing.

I wondered just how many gangs were in that area. The article went on to name all the children who had been shot in and around the H Block. The article was from 2013, seven years ago, but as I read other clippings, things didn't seem to have changed dramatically. The H Block and Heath Street gangs weren't the only gangs in Roxbury. The Orchard Park Trailblazers and the Columbia Point Dawgs fought, diminished in influence, then regained it. And then there were Hell's Kings and the Steel Guerillas. Innocent people died in the process.

Claire had marked another piece, one from 2015, and underlined sentences that clearly disturbed her. It was from *The Boston Herald*.

> By CHRIS VILLANI and O'RYAN JOHNSON |
> PUBLISHED: September 11, 2015 at 12:00 am |
> UPDATED: November 18, 2018 at 12:00 am
> A predawn shooting death that traumatized shellshocked
> residents on Roxbury's crime-plagued Holworthy Street
> yesterday is believed to be a targeted killing, police said.
>
> Police Commissioner William B. Evans told the Herald that
> police responded to reports of multiple shots about 4:45 a.m.
> Evidence markers showed at least 12 shell casings. The victim
> died in a small alley between two apartment buildings. The
> back window of a small SUV that was parked up the street had
> a bullet hole in it.
>
> "We are canvassing the neighborhood, looking at the video
> cameras and talking to neighbors to try to find out who was

74

responsible," Evans said.

Police Lt. Michael McCarthy said police believe the victim was targeted.

- Related: <u>Violence terrifies mom, daughter</u>

"He was known to police. We don't believe this was random," McCarthy told the Herald.

A woman who a neighbor described as the mother of the dead man's child staggered with grief as she walked down Holworthy Street toward the scene yesterday morning, crying out "No, no," through tears.

"<u>I live in a cemetery and I'm sick of it,</u>" one resident said. "The worst thing is hearing the mournful cry like I did this morning. Let's see how many more have to die. I have been in the middle of the crossfire with my 3-year-old daughter."

Referring to the 2013 Boston Marathon bombing manhunt, she added bitterly, "<u>We can shut down the entire city, the entire state, to catch two bombers but we can't catch anyone around here.</u>"

Neighbors insisted yesterday the victim was not involved with gangs.

"He was always there for somebody," a friend of the victim said, declining to give her name. "He would never say no to anybody ... He was there for you, he was always there for you ... He ain't gang-related or nothing."

City Councilor Tito Jackson, at the scene around the corner from the award-winning Trotter Elementary School, said, "I am here to support the family who lost their father, son, and their loved one. ... We are right next to the Trotter School. No young people should have to walk past a crime scene on their way to school."

Holworthy Street is part of Roxbury's notorious H-Block, which has been plagued by gang shootings for years.

A woman who lives across the street said, "My son woke up at 4:40 to gunfire, that's a sin. <u>They call this street H-Block for</u>

a reason. It's like being in prison. My kids have heard more gunshots in real life than they have in the movies."

There were about fifteen articles in the file. Adults, young adults of various ages, and children had been killed. One could not help but conclude that the police were helpless to stop the violence. Claire had attached a note to the last one: *I can get more if you want, but there are hundreds.* She had also texted me the same question and I had responded: *Not now. This is plenty. THX.* I needed to digest these before asking her to spend any more time pulling together what was in print or online.

The more I read, the more sympathetic I became to the Dolan and Malone hypothesis. The community and political pressure on the police to stop the violence in the H Block must have been intense. The detectives' perceptions and assumptions had to be shaped by both the pattern of violence in the H Block as well as by pressure from elected officials. But even if Arnold Nunnely was an innocent bystander, as Dolan and Malone believed, I felt we still had to answer the nagging question, "What was Arnold Nunnely doing standing at a bus stop in the H Block of Roxbury on a Friday evening in October?" He had an election coming in a couple of weeks. Still, I was finding it harder to hold on to the perceptual glasses I was trying to wear – Arnold Nunnely was intentionally murdered.

GPS navigation systems are wonderful. I love the one in my car. I also use one when I'm sailing. GPS does not, however, tell you whether or not an area is infested with pirates, poverty, or potential danger. GPS will get you where you want to go, but once you are there, you're on your own. Mine did get me to the H Block and to the bus stop on the corner of Humboldt and Homestead.

I parked on Humboldt behind a maroon van with "The Lord Is My Shepherd" printed in big white letters across the back window. Across the street was a Jehovah's Witness Kingdom Hall.

I parked in front of a group of light brown, two-story rowhouses that looked like they were fairly new. There was a stoop in front of each unit. I thought there was a good chance one of these stoops was where the witness was sitting when he saw the car go by and heard shots.

Leaving Blackie in the car, I walked back and forth in front of the houses. I looked over at the bus stop from each stoop and imagined a car going by. If one of these was where the witness had been sitting, he would not have been able to see the shooter, driver, or passengers because the car would have been by him before he heard the shots, but I wanted to check out the other corners to make sure this is where the witness had been sitting.

I did have the name and telephone number for the witness written on the back of the card Alice Malone had given me, but I didn't want to call yet. I didn't have an address, so I didn't know if the witness was in front of his own house or someone else's home.

I walked back to the car, opened the back, put Blackie on lead, and had him jump out. I took a few minutes to simply look around. I saw nothing that would have screamed *be careful*. On the opposite corner, next to the Kingdom Hall, was a brick building that looked like it was a power station. The bus stop was directly in front of it. Across the street, on Homestead were a couple of triple-decker apartment buildings. They were gray and brown with the exception of one that was painted an orange pink. It stood out, not in a good way. There were patches of yards here and there.

I knew from my GPS that I was only a few blocks from Franklin Park. I had heard about its zoo and knew the park was enormous. As close as this neighborhood was to the park, gentrification was nowhere in sight. Was the violence suppressing real estate values?

I gave Blackie the command to heel, "Fuss." He came around to my left side, his right shoulder precisely aligned with my left knee, and we began walking. When we crossed over Homestead, I saw a fenced-in area with some yard space on the corner and thought that might be sufficient to his needs. We walked over to it and paused so he could relieve himself. I noted that no one was out on the streets or waiting on either side of Homestead for a bus to come. No one. I wondered if this was normal. It was the middle of the day on a weekday. It was winter.

The weather, though, was clear and unseasonably warm. I wondered if there were any stores in the area.

I walked across the street to where the victims would have been walking or standing. I was dealing with a cold case, a several months old cold case, so there was no tape marking off where the victims had been shot. There were no markers showing where shell casings might have been picked up. Given the backdrop of the power station and the fence which protected it from intruders, I wondered if that was also part of the perpetrator's planning. Knowing the history of random victims in all of the gang shootings I had been reading about though, I doubted that the gang members would have considered the backdrop. A professional, however, might have, if he or she wanted to minimize collateral damage.

I decided to walk a couple of blocks in all directions. I wasn't looking for anything in particular. I was just trying to get some feel, some sense of the neighborhood. I walked down Humboldt to Hutchings, took a right on Hutchings and walked another block paralleling Seaver Street and Franklin Park. I took another right when I reached Harold Street. I went up Harold to Homestead and took a right to complete one quarter of my circumnavigation of the crime scene.

I did the same thing with the other three quarters. Nothing. Absolutely nothing stood out that would have indicated danger of any kind. If I didn't see or feel it, and I was looking for it, Arnie might have felt some discomfort because it was a strange setting, but I doubted whether anything would have put him on alert. I also wondered if this was a strange setting to him. Had he been here before?

I did find some small neighborhood grocery stores and a pharmacy a couple of blocks up Humboldt. Still, only a couple of people were out on the streets. I received quick glances but no stares. That surprised me. Blackie is a big, pure black German Shepherd. People always stare at Blackie. I doubted that people were being polite. Were they assuming I was police?

Questions and more questions were going through my mind. No one, neither Vidal nor the police, had mentioned how Arnie had gotten there.

Had he walked from Franklin Park? If so, why was this man from Greenwich, Connecticut, in Boston's Franklin Park? Did the bus stop have nothing to do with why he was in that spot? Had he driven to the area and was waiting for someone to get off the bus rather than his waiting to get on? If so, what had happened to his car? Had he visited someone who lived close by and not used his car because of the reputation of the neighborhood? Was he planning on taking the bus someplace else? That didn't make any sense to me. Arnold Nunnely would have used Uber or Lyft or taken a cab, or maybe even a limousine.

I had no answers. The other thing that bugged me was the disconnect between all of the articles I had read, the description of the H Block from Dolan and Malone, and my visual impression of the neighborhood. I, a middle-aged white man, had walked through this reportedly very dangerous neighborhood and felt safe as could be. So much for the validity of first impressions.

I knew the reputation of H Block. I knew better than to trust my preliminary observations. What would Arnie have known, if anything?

Chapter 10: Joseph Lewis

I called Joseph Lewis. When I introduced myself, he said, "A private investigator, a real P.I.? About the shooting across the street. Sure, why not?"

He didn't live in one of the rowhouses where my car was parked. He lived in one of the triple-deckers on the opposite corner. I told him I had Blackie with me, but I could leave him in the car if he would prefer.

"I'm a dog person, too. My 'Lady' gets along with everybody, so if your dog won't eat mine, bring him along. It's fine."

"I assure you he won't. Gentle as can be."

"It's the third floor. That okay? I can come down if you want. My daughter's on the first floor. My wife's there with the kids. Be a bit noisy, though."

"Third floor's not a problem. I'm across the street. Be there in a minute if that's not an inconvenience."

"Sure. I'm just watching re-runs."

Three floors later I knocked on his door. He answered, looked at Blackie and said, "Jees. That dog is big."

"He is that. Blackie, say hello." Blackie sat and held out one paw.

"I'll be damned. I can't even get Lady to sit. She's too old to start trying now. Like me." He leaned down and shook Blackie's paw. Standing up he held out his hand and we shook. "Joe Lewis," he said. "Named after the boxer. Different spelling, though." I introduced myself and I shook hands with the Joe Lewis named after Joe Louis. "Come on in," he said. "Lady, you see that?" he said in the direction of a worn couch occupied by a small, furry combination of breeds. Lady got down from the couch and walked over to Blackie.

"In ordnung," I said in German, Blackie's command language, to release Blackie from work mode. I dropped his lead. The two dogs circled each other assessing permission before they proceeded to sniff one another's rear end to find out each other's mood, how healthy they were, as well as age, sex, and a lot of other information which we don't fully understand, but they do. Joseph Lewis and I stood there watching the ritual for a minute.

"Never understood that. But they all do it, sniffing one another's butt," he said.

"Incredible sense of smell. They can be trained to sniff out everything from narcotics to infection, and even when a diabetic is in trouble and going into hypoglycemia."

"We should have one of them around here with all the diabetes we got in this neighborhood. Here, sit down." He pointed to a wing chair facing the television set. He sat in an old leather recliner next to the chair he had indicated for me.

Both comfortably seated, I made some mental notes. Joe Lewis was probably in his mid- to late-seventies. He was a few pounds shy of being what a physician would classify as severely obese. His skin was very dark and the contrast with his full head of short white hair was striking. When he smiled, it was exuberant.

"So what on earth does a P.I. want to talk to me about? I'm sorry, but I'm getting a real kick out of this. You ever watch the *Rockford Files*? I love the old *Rockford Files*."

"Sure," I said. "James Garner. I loved where he lived, a trailer right on the ocean."

"Yeah. And his father. What a character."

Technically, it's called *joining* in interviewing. You find some common denominator that lets the other person know that there is something that brings you together. At most, I may have seen two or three reruns of the *Rockford Files*, but that was enough.

"I have to admit, when I watched them, I never thought I'd ever be working as a private investigator some day, but here I am." That did the trick and got us on to the purpose of the visit.

"You're here about the shooting at the bus stop. If they didn't kill innocent people, I'd be for letting them go at it and kill each other off.

81

Maybe we should send them off to some field someplace and let them have at it, you know, like the Civil War," Joe concluded. He paused for a moment and then continued. "It didn't use to be that way when I grew up here. It was a nice neighborhood. We had the park down the street. It was a good place. If I could, I'd get the hell out of here but my daughter and her kids live downstairs, and my wife takes care of the kids while my daughter's at work, so we're stuck. I just hope the kids don't get involved with none of this gang stuff. They're girls and they're still young, so it's okay for now. They're too young for the gangs to be interested in them, you know, recruiting them. They recruit girls, too. A couple more years and I don't know what we'll do. This is our home."

"Hard choices. I don't envy you," I said simply.

We both sat in silence. The past and the future were both in the room, memories and dread.

I brought us back to the present, "So you think it was gangs?"

"Of course. What else? Garcia. Everyone around here knows him. No loss him gone. Scum. Deserved it. The others with him? They were with him, they deserve it too. Shame about the other guy. I don't know who he was, but he had nothing to do with it. Just standing there. Happens all the time. Sometimes it's little kids."

He got more agitated as he talked. He was describing a third-world country in the middle of Boston. I was tempted to learn more but brought the conversation back to why I was there and tried to do it in a way that would not contradict what he had told me.

"I know the police agree with you that it was a gang shooting. Actually, my involvement in the case is because of the bystander. His name was Arnold Nunnely, and his daughter hired me. What we're trying to figure out is why he was there in the first place. His daughter, her name is Vidal Banks, is trying to make some sense out of all of this. I know you've told all of this to the police, but would you mind going back over it again for me?"

"Sure. The guy had a daughter?"

82

"Yeah, in her thirties."

"I didn't know that. Her name's Vidal?"

"Yes. It means *life* in Portuguese."

He shook his head slowly and looked down. His mood had softened at the mention of a daughter, and his voice was low as he started recalling what had happened. "Well, me and my wife were across the street visiting with some old friends, the Wells. They live in one of the duplexes on Humboldt. We had ordered Chinese in and had just finished dinner, and I wanted a smoke. Margaret doesn't allow smoking in her house, so I had been banished to outside.

"I was just sitting there on their stoop minding my own business, smoking, looking around. It was a nice evening. Just starting to get dark. I saw a car drive up to the bus stop and the white guy got out. You said his name was… I'm sorry, what was it again?"

"Nunnely, Arnold Nunnely."

"Yeah. Sorry. Anyway, this Nunnely gets out and is just standing there at the bus stop. I see Garcia and a couple of others walking his way and I think to myself, I hope they don't hassle him, start anything. A couple of minutes later this other car goes by and it blocks my view so I can't see the bus stop or the people. It slows down, stops, and I hear gunshots. I've heard enough of them to know they were gunshots. I'm pretty sure they're coming from the car, so I take another look at the car, you know, a close look. Then it speeds up and I can see what had happened. Garcia and this Nunnely are both lying there, on the ground. The girl's still standing up, but I can see she's been hurt. The other guy. He's holding onto the mailbox.

"I go inside and tell Margaret and my wife to call 911, and I start to go back out and my wife screams at me to stay inside, so I did. I looked out the window, though, and saw another car had stopped. My wife pulled me away from the window and I didn't think to see what kind of car that one was. I did know what the first car was that I seen that had slowed down, the one where the shots came from. I told the cops. I gave them make, model, and color. I couldn't see a license plate, but I knew that car. My cousin has one. I told the cops they find that car, they find the shooter. I'm sure of it.

"So, we stayed in the house looking out the window. Five, ten minutes later we hear sirens and a whole bunch of cop cars show up. That's when I went out and went over and told them what I saw. It was a mess. Blood everywhere. About fifteen minutes later a bunch of ambulances and fire trucks show up.

"Cops told me to go over and sit on the stoop where I'd been sitting when I saw it happen, and that's what I did. One of them had already written down my name and address. About a half hour, maybe an hour, later a detective comes over and talks to me and I tell him everything I had already told the other cop. And then the next day, Saturday, two different detectives come to my apartment and I tell them the exact same thing all over again."

"Do you remember if their names were Dolan and Malone?"

"Yeah, they were. They gave me their cards. I think I still have them someplace."

"Mr. Lewis…"

"Joe. No one has called me mister in years."

"Joe, you say a car drove Nunnely to the bus stop. He didn't walk there? He was dropped off?"

"Yeah. I figure someone dropped him so he could get the bus. I don't know."

I didn't say anything for a minute. I was just trying to process what Joe had told me.

Joe added, "Maybe someone didn't want him to walk there if he was visiting someone. Could be. Or maybe they weren't going where he wanted to go. Car was coming from the direction of the park."

"Hard to know," I said. "Joe, anything else you remember, say from the time you went out to smoke until when the first detective interviewed you."

"Like what?"

"This is where it's tough because I really don't know. Did you notice anything out of the ordinary?"

"Other than a well-dressed white guy standing at a bus stop on the corner of Humboldt and Homestead at seven o'clock on a Friday night?"

"That's not usual?"

"You're kidding, right?"

"The white guy or the well-dressed part?"

"Both." Joe was smiling, playing with me.

"You said he was well dressed. In what way?"

"I don't know. Hard to describe. Clothes looked expensive."

"Was he dressed formally or informally? Tie? Suit?"

"I don't remember any of that. He had a jacket on. Might have been leather. You know, the nice kind. Expensive."

I asked, "Had you ever seen Nunnely before? Around here, anyplace else?"

"No, never."

"I'm curious about the second car, the one that stopped after the shooting. Can you tell me anything about that car?"

"Not really. Sedan of some kind. I was sort of out of it at that point and there was a lot of excitement in the house about what had just happened. I figured they had just stopped when they saw people on the ground, saw blood, didn't want to get involved, and got the hell out of there. That's what happens here. People don't want to get involved."

"Did either car stop long enough for somebody to get out, grab something, and get back in the car?"

Joe thought for a minute before answering. "Possibly the car where the shots came from. I can't be sure though. Frank, when I heard the shots, I may have turned away. I didn't want any trouble."

"But you're certain about your description of the car."

"Absolutely. Something clicked in my head. I even thought for a minute that it was my cousin's car."

"Your cousin's car?"

"Yeah, but it wasn't his."

"You sound certain."

"He's been in trouble before. When he was younger. Some gang stuff. I was worried. I called him later, after the police left. I told him what had happened, including the car. He got angry as hell at me, but he told me he was in Quincy all afternoon with his wife and kids and they were still there."

We stayed at it for another twenty minutes or so. I tried every trick I could think of to try to jog his memory, open up new channels. I tried them all: sounds, smells, what he was doing, what he was thinking about. We didn't get anywhere, but not for lack of effort. He wanted to help. At one point I said, "I'm not doing very well, Joe. What do you think Jim Rockford would be asking you?"

He laughed. "I think you're doing just great, Frank. I think you're just not working with someone who has a good memory."

I did the standard, "Here's my card. Please call me if anything comes to mind no matter how small." I hadn't taken any notes. I knew about the car that the shots came from, but there were two new pieces of information. Arnie had been dropped off and he was better dressed than Joe was used to seeing at the bus stop. I also had another piece of information. Another car had stopped and then driven away. One other thing was clear – everyone but Vidal was sure this was a gang shooting and nothing more.

Blackie and I said our goodbyes to Joe and Lady, went back to the car and drove back to the Investigation Bureau offices. As promised, there was a packet of files waiting for me at the reception area. I was grateful they were ready and we were going to get out of Boston before rush hour began in earnest. We had just gotten onto the Massachusetts Turnpike heading West when my mobile phone rang. It was Eve.

"What time do you think you'll be leaving Boston?"

"How about right now?"

"Perfect. How would you like to have dinner in Hartford? We can leave Blackie in my office at school. I have food here for him, so your pride and joy will not go hungry."

"Darling, I'd love to have dinner with you but, unless I am mistaken, this is not a date-night dinner. What's up?"

"Expanding your knowledge base. Dinner with Dr. Henry Gore."

"And what pray tell is a Henry Gore?"

"A professor of political science at one of my multiple alma maters. Henry's an expert on the two-party system, electoral politics in the United States, and just for you, an expert on the history of political campaigns in the United States."

"And, of course, oppositional research," I said.

"But of course. He lives in West Hartford and is free this evening. Since you have to come through here anyway, I thought I would give Henry a call and invite him to dinner so he could meet you. When I mentioned what you were doing and Nunnely's name, his first response was 'that piece of shit,' and then he said he would love to meet you and talk about his favorite topic, 'the destruction of any resemblance of fair fighting in our fucked up democracy.' I am quoting him."

"Of course."

"It's a Monday night, so we shouldn't have any trouble getting into Salute. You're paying, of course."

"Of course."

"What time do you think you'll get to Hartford?"

"In about two hours if I don't hit any traffic."

"Okay. It will be an early dinner. Come to the school and we'll drop Blackie off, then we'll fetch Henry and go to dinner."

"Salute is expensive I assume."

"Not for a partner in a successful security and investigations firm. I do believe you were bragging about the bottom line recently."

"Salute it is."

Chapter 11: Henry Gore

First things first. When we reached the campus, I took Blackie to do his business. Once back in Eve's office he ate, drank, and retired to the bed she kept there for him. Eve was already packed up and ready to go, the thoughtful student not wanting to keep her professor waiting. "Henry's going to meet us there. He's always on time."

The two of us drove to downtown Hartford and the restaurant. On the way, I told her about my visit with Dolan and Malone, the articles I had read, my visit to the H Block, and Joe Lewis.

When I was done Eve said, "You're wrong: it's not like a third-world country; it is a third-world country. We have people seeking asylum to get into the United States who are fleeing the same thing you're describing in the H Block."

"The words asylum and refugees crossed my mind."

"Here, it's the same thing in North Hartford. Smaller scale, but the same kind of violence. It's a drug-based economy and no one seems to care. The competition is fierce and the way to get competitive advantage is to increase your human resource base through recruitment and build market share by killing off your competitors. Drug capitalism in the streets. Doesn't matter what country you're talking about. Same dynamic. Maybe we should set up an asylum process for our own citizens."

I thought back on my visit with Joe. He was a good man. A caring man. I wanted to offer Joe Lewis and his family asylum. I caught myself thinking, "Stop the white savior shit, Kelly," and took a deep breath.

"What's that about," Eve asked.

"Nothing."

We arrived at Salute and parked in the lot next door. Once inside, the maître d' escorted us to the table where Henry Gore was waiting. Seeing us, he stood up, came around the table, ignored me, held out his arms, and Eve went right into them for a big hug. He was tall, thin, in his mid-forties with wild uncombed hair and a scraggly, just-worth-bothering-about, goatee.

"Too long, Eve. Too, too long. How is my favorite nun?"

"Not a nun. A sister. And you know damned well I left the religious life."

"Oh, bull. You'll always be a nun."

"You're impossible."

"Of course I am. It's how I maintain my reputation as an enfant terrible. Without it, I would be one more lowly associate professor of who-gives-a-damn."

Eve unwrapped herself from Henry's arms, took one of them, stretched it out towards me and said, "Henry, meet my fiancé, Frank Kelly."

Henry shook my hand. "I know all about you from my search on Google. I approve."

"I'm glad," I said.

"Let's sit and drink. I understand you're paying."

"I am."

"Wonderful. We read the menu from right to left then, and we drink from the top shelf. We members of the professoriate don't usually eat in this den of political corruption."

Salute was across the street from Bushnell Park. On the other side of the park was the Connecticut State Capital building. Salute was a watering hole for Connecticut politicians and those who wanted to influence them. We were early, though, and there were only a few people at the bar and fewer diners.

The restaurant was like those in political capitals throughout the United States with its leather, wood, excellent food, and bar tenders who remembered names and favorite libations but were deaf to conversations.

Henry ordered a Belvedere Vodka martini. "See, I'm not going to break the bank. Belvedere is better than Grey Goose and costs less. Only pretentious capitalists committed to conspicuous consumption drink Grey Goose. They would never dare to do a blind taste test. They're blind to everything, especially us lesser folks anyway."

I ordered a seltzer with a splash of bitters. Eve ordered an iced tea. We still had to drive back to Fairfield. Henry had Ubered to Salute and would Uber home. He obviously planned to have more than one martini.

We weather chatted, and Henry and Eve catch-up chatted until our drinks arrived. Henry's impersonation of an enfant terrible diminished as he and Eve talked and I began to see why she liked and respected him.

"There's something about the first sip of a perfect martini that almost, but not quite, could make a deist out of me," Henry said and immediately went for a second sip that was longer than the first.

"Okay, Kelly, what do you want to know about the farce we have made of our elections? Let me start by saying this is always the case at the national, and sometimes at the state, level. I understand you're looking into the death of the Assassin. You do understand that he was the worst of the worse, a practitioner of destruction, a master of corruption, a man worthy of being a Marvel Comics villain."

"I take it you didn't like him."

"I loathed him, him and his ilk." He paused for another sip. "Actually, I had a grudging respect for the Assassin. Brilliant at his chosen profession. He changed the game, and you have to respect game changers even when you loathe them."

"How did he change the game?"

"When the Assassin..."

"Could we have a little respect for the man and use his name?" Eve interjected. "He is dead, and he has a daughter who cared enough about him to hire Frank. Besides, from what Frank has told me, he had some really bad breaks that got him into the business."

"Always the nun. Excuse me, sister. I know, nuns are cloistered. You weren't cloistered. Okay, Nunnely it is. Or would you prefer Arnold?"

"His family called him Arnie," I said.

"Arnie! Oh, no. That is so human. This hurts, but okay, Arnie. Okay, when Arnie entered the oppositional research business it was all about votes, quotes, anecdotes, and photos. It still is, but Arnie took it a step further."

"Votes, quotes, anecdotes, and photos?" I said.

"Okay. Example time. The oppo scours public documents and pulls together every vote the opposing candidate ever made, every time they opened their mouth that contradicted their current position, or said anything that was contrary to polling. Photo files are gone through. They also find every story that ever circulated that could be used to indicate the person is a schmuck. Think of Mitt Romney tying his damned dog to the top of his car.

"You can actually tie a juicy quote directly to a drop in the polls. For example, after Romney made the comment in a fundraising meeting with fat cats that he didn't give a damn about the forty-seven percent who weren't going to vote for him anyway, his polling numbers dropped the next day. And then there was Clinton – Hillary, not Bill – and her referring to some of Trump's supporters as 'Deplorable.' One of the dumbest moves ever. She saw what happened to Romney when he dumped on Obama supporters with that forty-per-cent comment and four years later she does the same thing. Basic law, you can dump on your opponent all you want but not on your opponent's supporters. Not only did her poll numbers drop, blue collar bars all over the country had signs saying, 'Deplorables welcome here.' Idiocy, pure and simple. And then of course she had to apologize." His agitation called for another sip of martini.

"Photos?" I asked.

"Dukakis riding in a God-damned tank. A twenty-eight-year-old Dukakis campaign kid organized the photo op supposedly to make it look like Dukakis was commander-in-chief material. Instead, he looked like an idiot and the reporters were rolling around on the ground they were laughing so hard. Or how about the picture of the man of the people, John Kerry, our Naval war hero, out wind surfing. Like every red-blooded American male wind surfs off of Nantucket. The Bushies loved it and used it: 'John Kerry, whichever way the wind blows.' The picture that was supposed to make Kerry look vital and masculine made a great ad for Bush, and Kerry provided the picture. The one I love the most is the least qualified candidate of all time, Sarah Palin, in front of turkeys being stuffed into a decapitating machine while she's talking about using her power as governor to pardon a Thanksgiving turkey.

"Almost all oppo work is headed in one direction – make the opponent look like a phony, a hypocrite, or a fraud. Sometimes just digging around finds the ammunition. It was a kid working for the Obama campaign and digging through campaign finance records that came across John Edwards four-hundred-dollar haircut. Edwards was touting his concern about their being two Americas, one rich and one poor. It was his whole damned campaign for Christ sake, and the guy got a four-hundred-dollar haircut. What a putz."

"How did Nunnely change any of that? Sounds like it's been going on for a long time."

"Campaign shit has been around from the beginning. Even since colonial times. Alexander Hamilton wrote a piece that was published by a Philadelphia paper in which he accused Jefferson of having a love affair with one of his slaves. Hamilton wrote it using a pseudonym, Phocion. The affair was true, of course, but most people didn't know it at the time.

"You think Trump calling Rubio 'little Marco' or Hillary 'crooked Hillary' was new? Name calling isn't new. Jefferson's people referred to Adams as His Rotundity."

"And Arnie's contribution?" I asked.

"Ah, Arnie. Arnie created narratives. Arnie delved into the psychology of voting. He wanted to know why people voted the way they did and went after that. He understood that people told themselves a story about the candidate they supported that was positive, heroic in the best of cases, but they also told themselves a negative story about the opponent, especially at the national level. Your Arnie wanted to create a narrative of negativity that led a voter to think, 'I could never vote for that person.' A narrative is not a one and done. It is a story.

"I don't know whether he was involved in the W-campaign against Gore, but it's a damned good case example of creating a negative narrative. That was the other thing about Arnie. He often stayed in the shadows, a puppeteer who worked through the identified campaign communications director. There might be an oppo researcher of record. That person would be doing the typical votes, quotes, photos, and anecdotes work. Meanwhile, and behind the scenes, Arnie would be creating the narrative. He would decide what came out, when, and through what medium. He would feed the press and the internet more scabrous flesh to add to the narrative he was developing. Arnie was a prosecuting attorney. He laid out the case why you, the voter, must convict the opposing client of being a horrible human being who must be sentenced to never achieving the political position he or she was running for. Arnie designed stories to persuade you that this candidate was dangerous or they were a fraud. Above all, they were guilty. You, the voter, were a member of the jury and Arnie was leading you to say to yourself, 'I will never vote for this person no matter what…I am never going to let this person get into office.'

"His client candidate couldn't do it blatantly, so Arnie became the master at feeding the press and the internet monsters. He used the press as you would use witnesses in a trial. He would feed them stories and do so in a way that they would publish and create the narrative for him. They rarely had an idea where the story was originating, but even if the story wasn't true, it would always be plausible."

"You mentioned the Gore-Bush campaign," Eve said.

"Perfect example. I don't know if that was Arnie, but it sure looked like his work. Here's the message, 'Al Gore is a liar and you can't trust a thing he says.' Good old Gore supplied all of the raw material, but somebody, maybe Arnie, said to themselves, this is the narrative that

93

will work. We want voters to convict Al Gore of being a liar! Gore invented the internet. Really!"

Henry stopped talking and glanced around. Our waiter saw him looking and came in our direction. Henry held up his glass and pointed at it. The waiter came over and asked if we wanted another round. Eve and I were not yet halfway through our drinks. "Two olives this time," Henry said to the waiter.

After the server had retreated, Henry said, "Counting olives helps me keep track." Eve and I just glanced at one another. Henry saw us. "Don't worry. Last one. I only pretend to be a drunk. But then there will be wine at dinner, won't there?"

"For you." Eve said. "We still have to drive back to the school, get Blackie, and then we both have to drive home."

"Blackie?"

"My dog," I said.

"Oh, so you do understand what an unthinking ass Romney was tying his dog to the top of his car."

"I do. You were talking about Al Gore and how Arnie might have worked for Bush." I didn't know how far past the second martini we might have Henry's attention, so I wanted to stay on track.

"Poor Albert Gore, no relative of mine by the way, thank God. Gore not only was dragging the chains of Bill Clinton's blowjob in the oval behind him, he also never got the distinction between compulsive self-aggrandizement and legitimate pride of accomplishment. Fine line there. So, whether it was Arnie or someone else working for Bush, the liar narrative was a masterful job. Whoever it was, they fed the press every semi-truth, misstatement, and outright falsehood that Gore had ever uttered or, and this is important, might have uttered. The Bushies and their PACs provided all of these morsels to the press on a diamond studded platter. Whoever was pulling the strings, they kept it going over and over and over again. Finally, the press believed it and were actually attributing statements to Gore that the poor fellow never said, but he might have said. That's when you know you've won."

"What about Trump? His lies don't seem to matter," Eve said.

"They don't matter to his base. Clinton getting a blowjob in the oval didn't matter to his base. The oppo and the negative narrative you create on your opponent will always fire up your base, but the oppo your opposing candidate flings at you will roll off your base's back. You're fighting for that wonderful one standard deviation from the mean, that sixty-eight percent of the electorate that leans but doesn't fall head over heels one way or the other. That's the jury. That's the group you want to vote to convict your opponent of being a fraud or a phony, or in Al Gore's case a liar. If you can convict them of being a danger to the Republic, so much the better."

"One standard deviation, sixty-eight percent. I thought it was only about ten or twenty per cent of the electorate that was in the swing area," I said.

The second martini arrived with two olives. Henry took a small sip and sighed. "It's never as good as the first."

Henry put his drink down, looked at me, and in a tone worthy of a professor talking to a non-studious student said, "Frank, where were you in nineteen seventy-two? Not old enough to vote. Nixon against McGovern. Nixon won forty-nine of fifty states and, here it comes, drum roll please…"

Eve, of course, knew the answer, "Sixty-three percent of the popular vote. Biggest popular vote difference in American history."

"You were paying attention," Henry said to Eve.

Eve tilted her chin down and looked at Henry over her glasses. I recognized that *don't be an idiot* look she was giving Henry.

"I didn't know that," I said.

Over enunciating each word for effect Henry said, "Democrats do not like to be reminded of George McGovern. Sixty-three percent." Henry took another sip of his martini.

"What about Obama?" I asked. "I don't remember any votes, quotes, photos, anecdotes, or any big narrative against him."

"Oh, yes. Obama the cool, Obama the clean. Republicans had a hard time with him, so they used guilt by association. They went after his pastor. Remember Jerimiah Wright? They had plenty of fodder with that fellow. Obama wrote a great speech in response, but then Wright couldn't keep his big mouth shut once he had a big audience and Obama had to run away from him as fast as he could. And then McCain and Palin tried desperately to hang Bill Ayers around Obama's neck, a great big heavy albatross, but Ayers turned out to be a little sparrow. There was nothing there, or at least not enough to make any difference.

"McCain had a hard time with Obama. Not enough out-of-the-mainstream votes in the Senate to hang on him. Obama is incredibly sharp on the stump. No 'I misspoke' moments from the cool one, or very few.

"The Obama family. Great pictures and no stories. Romney had it easier than McCain because Romney had four years of Obama policies. He had an entire administration record to go after. Still, what story could Romney tell? Romney-Obama was a much cleaner lefty versus righty battle. But then Romney's poor mutt was riding on top of the car, and his master didn't give a shit about forty-seven percent of us.

"People do dumb things, Frank. People who go into politics are no brighter than anyone else. Case in point, wasn't Arnie working for Lee Thurman?"

"Yes," I said.

"What a piece of work. Thurman, our new senator from Connecticut, had no political experience. But he had lots of money. Lots and lots of his own money. And he had lots of money behind him. My beloved state of Connecticut just elected an oligarch who was funded by oligarchs. And a decent man was defeated at the last minute because your boy Arnie did his job. Sorry, Eve, but dead or alive, Arnold Nunnely was an assassin working for an amoral oligarch who would do anything to get elected."

"What are you implying?" Eve said.

"Nothing specific. But when someone like Thurman emerges out of the blue the way he did, and outspends his opponent to the extent he did, and then there is a dramatic negative that was revealed that close to the election, certain to sink the other candidate the way that it did, I believe somebody wanted something, and they wanted it very badly, and it wasn't just to win."

Henry finished off his second martini just as our food arrived. He ordered two glasses of wine, one each of the most expensive wines on the menu that you could order by the glass, a Justin Vineyards Cabernet Sauvignon and a Sonoma Cutrer Chardonnay.

"Two glasses of wine at the same time?" Eve asked.

"Surf and turf my dear. The cab is for the filet and the chard is for the scallops. A piece of fillet, a sip of cab. A piece of scallop, and some chard. Have you never done this?"

"No. I can't say that I have," Eve answered.

I did everything I could to stop from laughing my head off. I asked a question instead. "What are you *not* saying about Thurman's election?" I asked.

"I don't trust Thurman's win. Something about it doesn't pass the sniff test."

I didn't say anything. Eve bowed her head slightly. I knew she was saying a private grace. The three of us ate silently for a minute. Henry stopped eating and looked at me. He swirled the cabernet in his glass. When he stopped, he said, "You must have read or seen *All the President's Men*, Frank. I'm not your deep throat here, although I wish I was. If your Arnie was assassinated the way his daughter believes, then I have one piece of advice: follow the money, Frank. Follow the goddamned money."

Chapter 12: Files

"Three hits, center mass, 22 longs," Sam said after he finished reading the autopsy report.

"Isn't that an assassin's kind of gun?" I asked.

"It is. This was no accident. He was no bystander. He was also hit in the shoulder with something bigger. Might have been the same weapon used on the others."

"That's the AK-47. Dolan and Malone told me two shooters, two weapons."

"Looks that way. How the hell did those dolts in Boston explain away three perfectly grouped shots as unintended?"

I looked up from the file I was reading. "All the forensics indicate it was intended. This was no accident that he was there at the wrong time and place. Simply, Dolan and Malone wanted me gone. Politely gone, but gone. I wanted the files, not a pissing contest, so I played nice."

"Did they give you the autopsies for the other victims?"

"No, and I didn't think to ask. Maybe there's something in the crime scene reports about where they were hit."

We had the various reports spread out on the small conference table in the room we had commandeered for the investigation. We were mapping people, timelines, and actions on the white board. We were drawing relationships where we knew they existed. Sam opened up another file folder and started working through all of the technical data, photographs, weather information, setting, blood spatter, and on and on. There were no photographs of Charles Braxton and Yvonne Wilson. Because of their wounds, they had been taken to Tufts Medical Center before the crime scene team had arrived. Sam pulled out the pictures of Tom-Tom Garcia taken from multiple angles. "Stomach wounds. Two shots. Lower abdomen. Below the stomach. Colon. He might have survived it. Best guess, bullets rattled around, tore the lower aorta and, from the amount of blood, he bled out, quickly."

He showed me the pictures of Arnie and Garcia side by side. "So, Arnie gets hit with three shots grouped tightly together in the middle of the chest, Garcia gets hit with two shots in the lower abdomen, Braxton and Wilson survive, and we have no idea where they got hit, and yet Dolan and Malone contend that Arnie was an innocent bystander who was killed so there wouldn't be any witnesses. And yet two witnesses *were* left. Why didn't the shooter with the AK-47 kill Nunnely? That would make more sense, especially since he shot him once. I cannot, for the life of me, understand the logic they used to come to the innocent bystander conclusion. Let's call them and ask. They stonewall us, we talk to their boss. What's his name?"

I picked up my phone and turned to my notes app. "Galvin, Colm Galvin. Let's wait on calling anyone until we get through all of these files. I want to know if they were able to tell from the blood spatter who was shot first, second, third, and fourth. If the car was moving, even slowly, they might have been able to figure that out. If Arnie was shot first, the only reason to shoot the others was either to prevent identification or as cover for killing Arnie, make it look like a gang killing."

"Or..."

"We know there were two shooters and two guns. Maybe there were two targets and two completely different sets of motives," I said.

"If it was gangbangers, they wouldn't give a shit about identification or cover unless..."

"Unless what?" I asked.

"What if it was a paid hit? What if someone hired a gangbanger to kill Arnie, make it look like a gang hit, and they lucked out and were able to take out a rival gang leader in the bargain because he just happened to be there?"

"Wow. Hiring gang members to assassinate Arnie. That seems like a stretch to me. And Arnie was there at that precise time because?"

"Who knows? I'm just speculating," Sam said.

99

We spent the rest of the morning going through the documents. We read the reports of the investigating detectives. Galvin had interviewed Wilson and Braxton in the hospital. He'd also interviewed Wilson at home. Both times she said little beyond, "We were just walking, minding our own business. I got shot. I didn't see who did it, but I know it was the Guerillas."

Galvin also did a second interview with Charles Braxton. Braxton said the same thing Wilson had: "We were just walking, minding our own business. I didn't even see this Nunnely guy before we were shot. I told you, I never seen him before."

Dolan and Malone had done the interviews in the immediate area. There was an interview with Joe Lewis. There were interviews with Joe's wife and his friends, the Wells. And there were interviews with other people in the neighborhood.

I looked up from reading the interview reports. "Sam, there is no mention here of a second car. According to their notes, neither Wilson nor Braxton mentioned a second car stopping. Why not? Apparently, neither did Joe Lewis. It makes no sense. You're Wilson or Braxton. You've just been shot. You're hurt. Your buddy is lying in front of you bleeding out. A car stops. Aren't you going to ask for help?"

"You would think so. You're sure going to remember a car stopped," Sam said.

"And no mention of a second car in Dolan's interview with Joe Lewis. Joe told me about a second car stopping. Why didn't he tell the police? Or, if he did, why isn't it in the interview report?"

"More stuff we need to ask them. I'm starting a list."

I spent at least thirty minutes with the blood spatter pictures and report. It was thorough for Nunnely and Garcia. Since Braxton and Wilson were alive, the technician had not bothered to photograph or make any notes about them. I had attended seminars on blood spatter analysis but was no expert. Actually, I was more of a skeptic. So much depended on the expertise of the technician. I couldn't see anything that would indicate who had been shot first, Nunnely or Garcia. I was working from the assumption that if Nunnely was the target, he would have been shot first. It was an assumption, though, and I could have been projecting my own *what I would have done* thinking on to the mind of the shooter.

We kept at it until lunch time. The white board had names on it, but that was all. There were almost no action words on the board or any connecting lines. Not a one beyond the links between Garcia, Braxton, and Wilson. What Sam and I agreed on were three things. First, Arnold Nunnely had been the target. Second, the Boston detectives must have horse blinders on to see only one possibility, that this was a gang hit and Arnie was collateral damage. Third, no one had told the police about a second car that had stopped, not Joe Lewis, not Yvonne Wilson, not Charles Braxton. Or they had all told the detectives about the second car and the detectives had deemed that the information was irrelevant so it was not anyplace in the reports.

There was also something very strange in the autopsy report about the inventory of Arnie's personal effects. It included his wallet and watch. It included credit cards and cash, but there was no phone and no computer. There was no way that, given what he did for a living, he did not have a mobile phone with him at all times, maybe even two. Computer maybe, but he'd never be without a phone.

Also, in the on-going investigative reports, there was no mention of Vidal and her belief that her father was deliberately killed. She had spoken with one, or both, of the Boston detectives multiple times. She told me she mentioned the missing computer and phone to them. Nothing. It was like they'd never talked to her. Based on the absence of Vidal and her suspicions in their reports, I wondered who else might have talked to them but was left out.

Sam and I called Boston's PD after lunch and got Galvin. Dolan and Malone were working on another case and were not in the office. Galvin was not thrilled about talking to us. This was one cold case among many cold cases. As far as he was concerned, this was a case of turf disputes between two rival gangs. The bystander was not a child or a mother or from the neighborhood. He was white. He wasn't even from Boston. Arnold Nunnely had no relevant constituency producing pressure. And now this P.I. was getting involved, asking questions, taking up time, and generally being a pain in the ass. Of course, he didn't say any of this.

Sam listened on the speaker phone. I said, "I can't thank you folks enough for your cooperation with the Garcia-Nunnely case. I know it's an old case, and I'm just now getting up to speed. I know that you've tried to be helpful to the daughter, Vidal Banks, and I appreciate that.

"My partner, Sam DeRosa, and I have spent some time with the files that Detective Malone was kind enough to pull together for me and we have a couple of questions if you don't mind."

"What do you want to know?" he said.

"We noticed that Garcia was shot twice in the lower abdomen and, given the picture of the entrance wounds and the amount of blood, we assume that he bled out. Nunnely, however, was shot three times in the chest and must have died instantly. His shoulder wound from the larger caliber bullet would not have killed him. We were wondering what you folks thought about this difference and also if you were able to conclude who was shot first. Basically, we're curious about what your scenario is for the event."

Galvin paused before answering. "After you left Monday, I met with Detectives Dolan and Malone to discuss the case. Now remember, this case is a few months old and we have no named suspects, let alone arrests. There is no activity on the case at this point because there are no leads to follow up on. The interviews were all inconclusive and the crime scene investigation was also not helpful in identifying any leads, let alone suspects.

"Regarding the scenario, we assume that the perpetrators were stalking Garcia and his companions. Their decision to take a walk that evening was prompted by the weather according to Wilson, but she said this was not unusual for them, that they had done a similar thing the previous couple of days. We believe that this presented an opportunity for the perpetrators. They followed the three of them and waited until they would pass by an area that would not present a backdrop of a play area or a residence. When they approached the bus stop, the perpetrators drove up to them, slowed down, stopped, and shot them. Mr. Nunnely was standing at the bus stop and could see the perpetrators and might be able to identify them, so he was shot. Because he was standing still, he made an easier target. Wilson and Braxton believe that the two of them and Garcia were shot first and then Nunnely.

"The car then sped away. It was identified by a Mr. Joseph Lewis. We inspected footage from one of the city's video surveillance cameras and found a car matching Mr. Lewis's description that was consistent with the time period for the shooting. We were able to identify a license plate for the car. We later learned that the license plate had been stolen from a vehicle in Worcester the previous day. A car matching the description was found in Providence, Rhode Island, where it had been set on fire. The vin number of the vehicle indicated that it was stolen in Bellingham, Massachusetts, the morning of the incident. Because of the fire, there were no fingerprints, DNA, or fiber to provide any useful forensic information."

Sam looked at me and I nodded to him. Sam said, "Hi, this Sam DeRosa. I work with Dr. Kelly. Were you able to get any information about the second car?"

"What second car?"

I answered, "When I interviewed Mr. Lewis, he said a different car stopped a few minutes later and then it sped off. He said he couldn't identify it other than to say it was a sedan of some kind and it was light colored."

"I have no record of his ever mentioning a second car."

Sam asked, "Wilson or Braxton ever mention a second car? A car that stopped?"

"Not to my knowledge."

Sam continued the questioning. "Did they mention anyone getting out of either car and taking something?"

103

"No. Like what?"

Sam said, "Mr. Nunnely's computer and cellphone, or a briefcase."

"No."

Sam nodded to me and I said, "I want to make sure I understand what happened. Sorry if I'm sounding a bit dense. Neither Wilson nor Braxton mentioned a second car, one that stopped, although Joe Lewis saw one. And no one saw anyone get out of either car."

"Not that I know about. It's been a few months now. I went back over the report after you met with Dolan and Malone, so I'm looking at the same information you are. I'll ask Dolan and Malone when they get back."

For the first time, I felt like Galvin was paying attention rather than reciting. I said, "One other thing we noticed. In the listing of his effects, there was no mention of a mobile telephone or his laptop computer. We find it especially strange that there was no phone given his current involvement in a political campaign and yet he did have his wallet, with cash and credit cards, and an expensive wristwatch that were listed as on him at the time of the event."

Now he asked me a question. "You think someone wanted his cellphone and got out of the second car when it stopped and grabbed it?"

"And possibly his laptop computer as well. Just wondering. Seems strange to us that he didn't at least have a cellphone."

"You said political campaign. Exactly what did he do?" Galvin asked. "I don't remember."

"He was a political consultant who conducted oppositional research. He collected dirt on people, and he was killed just weeks before an election he was involved in. The timing adds to our suspicion"

"Now I remember. His daughter did tell us that. You're thinking she might be right."

"We're looking into it."

"I'm going to talk to Detectives Dolan and Malone when they return. I'll ask about a second car stopping and about his not having a mobile

104

phone or computer on his person when he was examined and processed."

"Thank you."

"I'll have them call you. And would you please call us if you discover anything that you think might be useful?"

"Of course." I then added, "Before we hang up, something else has been bothering me. The shooter with the AK-47. If Nunnely was a witness who had to be eliminated, why didn't he shoot Nunnely more than once. Why did a second shooter, with a far less powerful weapon, shoot him three times center mass? If they didn't want to leave any witnesses, we're wondering why they left two."

Galvin didn't say anything for a minute. I could hear papers being moved. Finally, he said, "I don't know. I'm going to talk to Dolan and Malone."

After I hung up Sam said, "I think you've made a friend. Not sure I would want to be Dolan or Malone when he talks to them."

Chapter 13: Vidal at Home

I wanted to get back in touch with Vidal and tell her what we had done so far, as well as what we had learned or not learned. I called her on her cellphone and asked if she was free for dinner. I was concerned that she hadn't sent us the materials that Arnie had given her. After Henry Gore's suspicions about Thurman's win in the last election, I wanted to get whatever she had into our office where we could go through it and where I knew it would be safe.

Vidal didn't answer so I left her a voice message. And then I waited. After an hour without a response, I decided to google her to kill time until she returned my call. She popped up first on her company website.

Her firm, Strategic Alliances, was based in Stamford, Connecticut. Their website said they did strategic consulting. They worked with all kinds of organizations – from start-ups and non-profits to Fortune Five Hundred companies. They didn't list any clients. Privacy, I assumed. You didn't always want people to know you needed help with your strategic dilemmas. They did give some examples of projects they had worked on.

Vidal was listed as a "Senior Associate," a project lead, "Responsible for working with senior executives to solve their most vexing problems." I was impressed. The website biography included her academic accomplishments as well. She graduated magna cum laude from NYU. Being in the top five per cent of her MBA class at Columbia earned her the Dean's Graduation Honors with Distinction. She may not have had a close relationship with her father, but she sure inherited his academic abilities.

I looked at other Google references. She was on LinkedIn but not on Facebook or any of the other social media sites. After I finished searching for information about Vidal, I spent time reading more of the clippings that Claire had pulled out for me about gangs and Boston. The more I read, the more difficult it became to reject the hypothesis that Dolan and Malone were using. Three hours went by and still no response. I sent her a text message.

I reopened the police reports. Braxton and Wilson had been asked if they knew who had shot them. They had both answered no other than blaming the rival gang. They had been asked if they had seen who shot them. They both answered no. They had been asked if they knew who had been shot first, second, and so on. Braxton answered no. Wilson said she thought that the three of them were shot before Nunnely, but she couldn't be sure. They had been asked if they recognized the car. Again the answer was no.

Another hour went by. I googled more stories about oppositional research. George W. Bush won the 2000 South Carolina primary because his campaign manager, Carl Rove, conducted a state-wide survey with the question: "Would you be more or less likely to vote for John McCain…if you knew he had fathered an illegitimate black child?" Rove then followed up with a well-orchestrated whispering campaign. At the time McCain had been out campaigning with his dark-skinned daughter who he and his wife had adopted from one of Mother Teresa's orphanages in Bangladesh.

I didn't know much about the Pizzagate story until I read the Vox article. I wondered who came up with the idea and started it rolling. Would Arnie do something like this? Given what Carl Rove and Bush did to John McCain, I was coming to believe there were no limits to how low candidates would go.

An astonishing number of people believe Pizzagate, the Facebook-fueled Clinton sex ring conspiracy story, could be true: **Especially if they're Trump voters.**
By Peter Kafka Dec 9, 2016, 11:27am EST
Here's a question I never thought I'd ask: Do you think Hillary Clinton is connected to a child sex ring being run out of a pizzeria in Washington, D.C.?

If you voted for Donald Trump, there's a decent chance

you think it's true. Or, at least, you're not sure, one way or another.

Nearly 50 percent of Trump voters think the Pizzagate theory is either true or could be true, according to a new poll released today from Public Policy Polling.

It's yet another reminder that "fake news" — an admittedly lousy term used to describe a wide range of untrue things on the internet — has a depressingly receptive audience.

In this case, the non-story is a made-up tale about Clinton, her associates and an underage prostitute network. It started up this fall in dark corners of the internet, but quickly bubbled up through Facebook, which weaponized the meme with its sharing tools.

And it's the same tale that prompted Edgar Welch, a 28-year-old North Carolina man, to drive to a Washington, D.C., pizza place on Sunday, armed with a semi-automatic assault rifle, so he could "shine some light" on the claims. He was arrested after firing the gun inside the restaurant.

Finally, when I heard from Vidal, she was in her professional mode. "Frank, I'm sorry it has taken me so long to get back to you. I've been in an all-day meeting. I'm in New York and won't get home to Stamford until around seven, seven-thirty. Is that too late for you? You're coming from New Haven?"

"No, I'll be home by then. I live in Fairfield, so I won't have to fight traffic at that hour. Seven or so is fine. Is that going to be too late for you? For dinner?"

"No, I rarely eat before eight, when I do eat. Lately it's been a frozen dinner or a peanut butter and jelly sandwich on nights like tonight."

"I've got an idea. If this would work for you, why don't I pick up some takeout. I know a great Thai take out restaurant."

Her professional voice modulated into a different key. "You have no idea how wonderful that sounds."

I called Eve and told her the plan. "Actually, that works out well," she said. "Molly has wanted to get together for dinner. Wedding stuff. I'll see if she's free."

Blackie and I headed home where I got him settled. Then, a little less than half an hour before I was supposed to be at Vidal's, I picked up takeout from Whoopi Thai in Fairfield. The food was always good regardless of the name of the restaurant. Bringing Vidal dinner was a wonderful excuse for me to order their mango curry with duck. Vidal wanted sautéed vegetables and brown rice. Healthy, but boring. I picked up a bottle of chilled Riesling from the liquor store across the street from the restaurant and drove the thirty-five minutes to Stamford. An hour earlier and it would have taken me at least twice as long on the Connecticut Turnpike. I was happy she would be getting home after seven.

Vidal's contact information was in my cellphone and I relied on GPS to wind my way through Stamford to the waterfront area known as Shippan Point. She lived in the Harbor House complex, and her building overlooked a canal coming in from the east branch of Stamford Harbor. There were docks in front of her building. I could imagine Eve and me living there with our sailboat, the one we didn't own, nestled into a slip that we could look down on from our balcony every morning while we had coffee.

Vidal showed me around her unit. It was a quietly elegant two-bedroom, two-bath penthouse unit which succeeded in rounding out my fantasy. "Beautiful spot," I said, looking out the sliders onto the deck and down onto *my* slip just waiting for *my* boat.

"Thank you. It is lovely. I've been here for three years, and I do enjoy it when I'm here, which isn't often enough. It's also super convenient. Much of my work is in New York and some weeks I'm close to being a commuter. I can be at the railroad station and on a train in a few minutes. I can also get to the New York airports without too much difficulty, and I can be at my office in ten minutes. It's nice that Mom and Gary are close, one town away, in Greenwich. This location really works for me.

"Someday I'd love to have a boat sitting at the dock, but I'm afraid that's years away from now, and who knows what life will be like six months from now, let alone a couple of years?

"Shall we eat? And thank you so much for doing this. The thought of going out to eat was…"

"Painful," I offered.

"Very. I hope you're not offended."

"Not at all."

Over dinner I told her about my trip to Boston, the meeting with Dolan and Malone, my trip to the H Block, and my interview with Joe Lewis. I told her about the time that Sam and I had spent going through each file, then I asked her, "Do you want me to take you through what we learned from the files? Some of it is not pleasant. Or I can give you a summary. It's up to you."

She said she wanted all of the details. I took her step by step through the police reports, forensics, and finally the medical examiner's autopsy report and pictures. I started to shuffle the pictures back into the envelope but she stopped me.

"No, I want to see them."

"Are you sure?"

"Yes. When I identified him at the morgue, all they showed me was his face. I want to see the pictures."

I complied and handed her the photographs of her father. In some, from the crime scene, he was clothed. In the ones from the medical examiner he was nude. She studied each one and handed them back to me without saying a word.

I waited. I returned the pictures to their folder and put them back into the oversized envelope. She still didn't say anything and I had no idea what was going through her mind. I decided to be blunt. "Sam and I believe your suspicion was accurate. We believe your father was murdered."

Still, she didn't say anything. She played with her chop sticks and pushed her vegetables around. When she looked up, she said, "I know he was." She returned to her chopsticks. This time when she looked up she said, "Someone wanted to murder him. Why? Why would somebody do that?"

I didn't answer. She continued to look directly at me and answered her own question. "Secrets. Or revenge. Or both. He hurt people. They wanted to hurt him back. Maybe it was revenge. Payback.

"It may have been that damned computer program of his – all the things that people were afraid would be made public. There are a lot of people, Frank. Probably several for every campaign he worked on. This time, though, he knew something was different. He was scared. It wasn't my imagination."

"No, it wasn't your imagination. And I think that the squad commander in Boston, Colm Galvin, is entertaining the possibility that your father was the primary target, or that there were two targets. I don't know if that will change what they do or don't do, but I think it will change the level of cooperation we get from them."

"Why now, Frank? He had done this work for years. Why on earth now, when he was getting ready to retire? Once in a while I find myself saying, 'Dad, what did you do?'"

"And we don't know. Clearly something was different. Your father seeking you out and wanting to talk to you is telling. Wanting to give you information he had saved up for years. You said his mood was different, he was scared. You also used the word 'remorse' when we met in New Haven. By the way, do you know if anyone else knew he was retiring? Any possibility of a 'tell all' book that people might have been concerned about?"

"I don't think many people knew, and he would have told them not to share anything. His secretary, Leslie Cahill, would have known, I'm sure. Carlos Barlotti would have known. Others? I doubt it."

"I want to understand what was happening that led to the changes you saw and we also have to move away from talking about generic people who might have wanted to hurt your father. There might be

111

hundreds of people who at some point or another were furious with him. We have to narrow the field down to specific individuals who wanted to hurt him in October and who might have actually done it."

"How will you do that? Do you mean something like that means, motive, opportunity formula you see on T.V.? Does that really work?"

"It's crude, but as a thought framework it has value. It's usually more complex than that, but it helps. You said you didn't know much about his business dealings, past or present. Who should we talk to? Who knows the most about what he was doing, and perhaps thinking, before he was shot?"

"Two people immediately come to mind: Leslie Cahill and Carlos Barlotti. Even if Carlos wasn't involved with Dad's business right now, he had been for years. When Dad and I met, I asked him how Carlos was. He said fine and that they still got together for lunch or dinner once in a while."

"We'll start with them. How about your mother or stepfather?"

"Dad would never tell them anything, and they would never ask."

"His sister? Mother?"

Vidal laughed. "They hated what he did and who he did it for. Other than my father, the Nunnely's are died-in-the-wool Democrats. Politics, and especially my father's work for Republican candidates, became a taboo subject at family dinners. Manny, Ruth's husband, would start something every once in a while, and Bubbe would shut him down. No, politics was a forbidden topic when Dad was there."

"Would he talk to them about retirement?"

"Maybe, but I doubt it."

"Anybody else you can think of who would know what he was doing at the time he was shot?"

"He always had trackers working for him when he was involved in an active campaign."

"Trackers?"

"A tracker is someone who follows an opposing candidate wherever they go. They use tape recorders, video cams, conversations with the opponent's staff. They'll try to join the opponent's campaign staff if they can manage it. A tracker will try to record everything that is said, whether it's for public consumption or not. They want to get something that's indisputable.

"I read recently about a tracker who was caught waiting outside a senator's office in the Senate Office Building in Washington. The tracker was trying to secretly record the senator's hallway conversations. That was supposed to be a no-no in the building, an informal agreement between Republican and Democratic staffs. Apparently, nothing is off limits anymore.

"I'm sure Dad hired trackers for the Thurman campaign. Oh, you should probably talk to people in the Thurman campaign as well."

I pulled out a pen and made a note on the file.

"Frank, don't forget his clients in all this, the candidates who hired him. One of his jobs was to find material that could be used against his client, say Thurman, so the client could be prepared to respond or get the story buried. Burying a story can be critical. Trump is a good example. Stormy Daniels. *The National Enquirer* bought her story, and not just hers. *The Enquirer* bought several and buried them. Trump isn't the only one who practices buy and burn."

"Did your father ever do something like that?"

"I don't know for sure, but I have no trouble believing that he did. I think my father did anything and everything."

"Vidal, I'm surprised you know so much about his world given how little you knew of your father's business and how little you saw of him."

"I know. My mother doesn't get it either." She paused and then continued. I felt like she was being careful now in how she expressed herself. "I don't know specifically what Dad did, his campaigns, but I was curious about his work, so I was always reading political news stories. I'm not quite a political junkie, but close. I was also fascinated by the similarities to the strategic work that I do. CEOs, politicians. I think they have all read Sun Tzu's *The Art of War*."

"Interesting. Makes sense." I wanted to add, *Like father, like daughter*, but I didn't. I stayed on task.

"I will talk with all of the people you mentioned and the Thurman campaign people, if they'll talk to me. One other thing I'd like to talk to you about is the missing cellphone, his computer, and the materials he gave you."

"He didn't give the files to me, he sent them to me. By FedEx. I had to sign for them."

"He sent them to you through FedEx?"

"Signature required. Yes. I can only imagine he thought that was safer than someone seeing my estranged father showing up at my doorstep with a box of who knows what. Remember, he was scared. He may have thought he was protecting me in some kind of cloak and dagger, bizarre way."

"He may have been right. I'd like to take the box with me when I go if that's okay with you."

"Certainly. I have no reason to have the files here, and no time to even look at them if I wanted to."

"You mean you haven't opened the box."

"No. I offered it to the police, but they weren't interested."

"And you weren't?"

"Yes and no. Time, Frank. It's all about time. I don't have any."

We ate silently for a few minutes. My curried duck fulfilled its promise, as always. I thought about Vidal's assessment of her father's state of mind and how soon after their meeting he had been murdered. He had been prescient. He had been in danger.

As we ate, I began to wonder what had been happening in the killer's world between then and now. Did he or she get what they wanted, whatever that was? What were they doing right now, while we ate our dinner?

I broke our silence. "I know this may feel like overkill to you, but let me suggest that you and I communicate by phone and email from now on. Let me take it from here with the Boston P.D. I'd like the killer, whoever it is, to think you're living your life just like before any of this happened and that you have nothing to do with me or with Nutmeg. I'm also going to do the same thing with your family. Any contact will be electronic or by telephone."

"You sound concerned. Is it something specific?"

"Well, yes and no. Your father's laptop is missing. There was no cellphone among his effects although his wallet, credit cards, a sizable amount of cash, and an expensive watch were not touched."

"I still can't believe he wouldn't have had a cellphone."

"Neither do I. I think it's possible that it was taken somehow when he was shot. Laptop and cellphone missing. Given what he did, I've got to go on the assumption that information was in some way behind the motive for what happened to him. In addition, since nothing unusual has happened since his death, I'm assuming that whoever is responsible thinks that the information they were concerned about is no longer a threat to them. I would like them to continue thinking that way.

"However, my digging around may spike their anxiety. I think it's best they think I'm working for someone in the political world who might be concerned about the information your father had rather than working for you."

We spent some time talking about her life as a consultant. "We aren't as big as Bain or the Boston Consulting Group, but we're growing. Primarily, I crunch data and make digital presentations for corporate executives. My job is to convince them that I am the smartest person in the room and know more about their business than they do, which is sometimes the case. Basically, it's our data versus their egos, and whoever wins gets to be a hero and make a lot of money. We make a lot of money."

After we'd cleaned up from dinner, I packed up my research and then placed it on top of the box Vidal had from her father. I don't know what I expected, but the box Vidal gave me was not very big. It was one of FedEx's heavy materials boxes. It was marked 18x13x11-3/4. Someone had handwritten *fragile* on it, and it had a FedEx "Please Handle With Care FRAGILE Thank You" sticker on each side. It weighed maybe ten or fifteen pounds. Given the size and the weight, I had a hard time believing it contained years and years of files on the campaigns Arnie had been involved in.

When I got home and took Blackie for his pre-bedtime walk, Eve decided to come with me. The January night was cold, but it was a dry, clear cold, and the night sky was filled with stars. A cold front had arrived and done its job reminding us how beautiful New England could be on a winter night.

I described Vidal's condominium to Eve and my fantasy about living on the water with a dock and boat in front of our house.

"Sounds lovely. Why not? We can do that. You know, Emily wants us to sell this house and move to Milford. Milford's on the water." Emily was Eve's best friend, the one who brought us together, and a partner in the law firm where my son worked. It was all very neat and tidy and a tad nepotistic.

"She would, would she? Would you like to move?"

Eve stopped walking. My *uh-oh* alarm went off. I stopped.

"Honestly?" she said.

"Yes."

"I like where we live, Frank, but it's your house. It's where you and Patricia raised your children. I want us to have our home, one that we choose, one that we build our life in. It could be a tent or a cabin in the woods someplace, or a condominium on the water with a dock and a sailboat tied up there. As long as it's ours, I don't care where it is or what it is."

"I didn't know you felt that way."

"I'm sorry, but I have been. Just recently, really. I think the wedding planning..."

"Don't be sorry. I've thought about selling the house on and off ever since Pat was killed. I think its inertia that's kept me there."

"So, you're open to the idea?"

"Yeah. I'm more than open to it. I love the idea."

"Whew. Okay, if I call Em tomorrow? I'm sure she knows a broker in Milford. Milford okay? Or we could look in Branford or Stratford? They're all closer to New Haven, so the commute wouldn't be as long for either one of us. I would like to have some separate office space. I could use space in another room, like our bedroom, but I'd rather have my own office."

By the time we got to bed, criteria had been established for our new home on the water down to the east-west orientation so we could have both sunrises and sunsets.

Chapter 14: Carlos Barlotti

When I called Carlos Barlotti late the next morning, he was eager to talk to me. He said, "Anytime. Name the place and the time."

"Would right now work? Where do you live, Carlos?"

"Norwalk. I'll come your way. Where are you?"

"I'm in Fairfield right now. I live here. My office is in New Haven, but Fairfield is closer for you."

"You know the Circle Diner?" he asked.

"Sure."

"Perfect. I'll be going against traffic. Be there in thirty. I'll be the old guy wearing a New York Jets hat."

There are diner people and non-diner people. I'm a diner person. Carlos was a diner person. He was older than I expected, about seventy-five, I guessed. Overweight, he sort of waddled in from the parking lot. He was wearing his New York Jets watch cap and a big parka. I was waiting for him at the cashier's station. The hostess handed us our menus. "Booth or table?"

Carlos answered for both of us. "Booth."

When we sat down, he didn't even wait for the waitress to arrive. "Arnie was killed, you know. I don't know who pulled the trigger, or who hired whoever pulled the trigger, but he was murdered."

So much for any small talk or *good to meet you* niceties. I asked, "How can you be so sure?"

"Because he was scared shitless. I've known that man forever, worked with him, been his friend, been his lawyer, and it's the first time I've ever seen him scared, really scared."

"When did you last see him?"

"Two weeks before he was shot. We had dinner at my place. My bet, given what he told me, it has something to do with the last campaign."

"What did he tell you?"

He nodded in the direction of the waitress coming over to get our order. He clearly didn't want to say anything in front of her.

She asked, "What can I get you, gentlemen? Are you ready to order?"

"Coffee for me. Haven't looked at the menu yet," Carlos said.

"Coffee?" she asked me.

"No, thanks. How about some sparkling water?"

"Be right back with your drinks." She left.

"Vidal hired you, right? Makes sense. She knows this wasn't an accident. She was worried about him. I'm surprised she waited until now. Boston cops aren't doing shit."

"So, you knew Vidal was worried about her father, before he was shot?"

"Yeah. She called me and told me. Then at Arnie's funeral she said she tried to talk him into quitting the campaign and he said he'd like to, but he couldn't."

"I'm a bit confused. I was under the impression they didn't see much of each other and she didn't know too much about what he was doing."

"That was true up until about a year ago. Then she started talking to him on a regular basis, first on the phone, then a meal once in a while. Surprised him. They talked quite a bit on the phone from what he told me. He was so happy he didn't know which way was up. For years she wanted nothing to do with him. That girl's nose is so stuck up she'd drown in a rainstorm. And now, all of a sudden, she's interested in Daddy. Bullshit."

"What do you think changed?"

"My hunch: Lee Thurman. I think she wanted to get in with Thurman's crowd. I think she wanted clients. I think she wanted introductions."

People lie. I know people lie. Usually I can pick it up. I didn't expect this. Had I misread Vidal this badly? The waitress came back with our drinks and took our lunch orders. After she left, I said, "I'm surprised that they had been talking and getting together for a year or more."

119

"I don't think she wanted her mother and her stepfather Gary to know. Arnie was not a great husband and only slightly better as a father, and that's when he was around. It was not a 'we'll always be friends' kind of divorce, and Vidal sided with her mother. Can't blame her.

"Don't get me wrong. I loved Arnie. He was a good friend. But family was never his top priority. Arnie loved power and he loved being a kingmaker. He also loved being around money. When I was working with him, we charged top dollar and we delivered. Boy, did we deliver.

"Arnie loved the big reveal, that's what he called it, the big reveal. Early in a campaign we'd be like moles. You see, every political candidate's trying to create this golf course. It's all green and beautiful and makes you feel like you want to play with him or her on their perfect golf course.

"Now, our client hires us to burrow into the dirt of the opponent's life and create mole hills all over their opponent's pristine golf course. The poor opposing candidate starts to see mole hills but they wouldn't know what we had found or who we would feed it to: press, social media, rumors. Our job was to make sure no one would want to play on his or her golf course with all those mole hills: rumors, connecting dots that hint at things. Shit like that. We'd get the opponent too busy playing whack-a-mole to go on the offensive.

"And then we would wait for the big reveal. Whammo, two or three weeks before the election, we'd set off the dynamite on the eighteenth hole. The poor schmuck wouldn't have enough time to do any decent backtracking or damage control. The beautiful golf course that the opponent's campaign had spent months designing and building was now a piece of shit. Baboom!"

"I understand Arnie only worked for Republicans."

"It was personal and professional. On the professional end, it was money, morals, and methods. They have the money, lack morals, and have the mechanisms to get the job done. Behind that, though, he had been screwed by Democratic elites, first at Goldman and Bunch and then in the prosecutor's office. He thought they were all a bunch of phonies. Clinton was the only one he had any respect for. Slick Willy knew power and how to use it. Left the White House in debt and a couple of years later, he's a multi-millionaire. Despite his scandal, he got more Dems elected to Congress in the mid-terms. It had never been done before. And they said Reagan was the Teflon President? Bullshit. Clinton was the real Teflon guy."

Carlos was a talker. He talked fast and he was enjoying himself. However I wasn't learning anything, so I asked him, "Do you know who killed Arnie?'

"No. No clue. Long list though."

"Who's at the top of your list? You said you thought it might have something to do with this last campaign."

"Maybe Gene Douglas, Thurman's opponent. Arnie destroyed him. Didn't just wipe him out in the election, he did him in totally. Guy's never going to run for office again, ever. He's got to get out of politics. I can't see Douglas doing it himself. I don't know. Maybe. But he sure would know how to get someone to do it for him."

"Why do you say that?"

"Douglas is from Waterbury. He also spent a lot of time working in Hartford. Either city, you got enough money, you can hire somebody to do whatever you want. He was also big in Bridgeport. If he wanted to hire somebody, no problem. He'd know who to talk to to get it done. Given what Arnie did to him, the guy had to have wanted payback."

"Anyone else?"

"You mean currently angry enough or feeling threatened? Cause in the past... "

"Let's stay with current involvements."

"Something was going on with Thurman's campaign. Arnie didn't tell me a lot, but there was too much money somehow, and there were two different PACs that were spending money like they had a private mint. It seemed like they didn't want to simply beat Douglas, they wanted to push his head under water and drown him so he'd never run for anything else ever again. Or they wanted Thurman to get this enormous win and set him up for something big, really big."

"The Presidency?"

"Maybe eventually, or maybe right away. Obama only served three years of his first term in the senate. Talk about fast tracking. Thurman looks great on paper. No voting history to weigh him down. Great family. He wins big in a purple state, and it would get people's attention.

"He had already creamed his opponents in the primary. Thurman beat out two possibles, and they didn't have a chance they were so badly outspent. Not just media. Ground game. They tried calling it a grassroots campaign. You can call it whatever you want, but it costs a lot of money when you're paying your organizers and canvassers top dollar to go door to door.

"Think about it. Thurman had raised money for the party, a lot of money, but this guy has never run for anything, not even dogcatcher. And now, suddenly, he's running for the Senate. He winds up dipping into his own piggybank. Okay, I get that, but in all, he spends roughly sixty mil to Douglas's ten. Not all of it was Thurman's money, but a major chunk was. And that's the money that was reported. And then you had these two PACs. I have no idea how much the PACs actually spent. Thurman destroyed Douglas. Big, big numbers, but it was a very pricey win."

"Something about it bothered Arnie?"

"If there was shit going down in the campaign, and Arnie indicated there was, heavy duty shit, Arnie knew about it and wasn't cool with it. Whoever wanted Thurman to win might have wanted to make sure Arnie had nothing to say to anyone. I heard that the federal prosecutor might have been taking a look at the campaign financing. Someone might have gotten worried, Arnie might have picked up on it, and that would have scared Arnie."

"If there was a financing problem, would Arnie have known?"

"Probably. He was very good at his job, and his job was to know everything on both sides of the fence."

The waitress came with our meals. We stopped talking until she had walked away. "I understand his laptop is missing and that's where Arnie kept everything."

"Not everything. Just current stuff. Older stuff, he had everything backed up going back years. You think J. Edgar Hoover had files on everybody? Arnie was one of the first people to go digital. Everyone does it today, but Arnie was way ahead of his time. The man fully understood the power of information."

"What do you mean?"

"Relational databases. Years ago, when I was still with him, Arnie read some articles and decided to become a master of a relational database and, to top it off, he's going to learn how to design his own. So he gets hooked on this Larry Ellison guy and his company, Oracle. He studies, goes to trainings. He doesn't want to hire somebody else to do it because of the information he plans on putting into this thing. Then it becomes a damned hobby with him. You work for Arnie, you learn how to put data into *Secrets*."

"*Secrets*?"

"That's what he called his program."

"Did you use *Secrets*?" I asked.

"Oh, no. Only Arnie knew how to use the program. I could put information into *Secrets*, but only Arnie could get data out."

"What kind of stuff did you input?"

"It could be anything from notes to video or audio files. Let's say one of our trackers is at a campaign event for an opponent. The tracker is going to use their cellphone to record whatever the opponent said. Then they would send that video to Arnie. Or, if the tracker couldn't be obvious and could only do an audio recording, they'd try to get physically close to the opponent, turn on record, eavesdrop, and send the audio file to Arnie. Articles? Download them. Send them to Arnie."

"So a tracker couldn't input information?"

"No way. They were usually part-timers or consultants. I could. His secretary Leslie could. But that was it."

123

"I'm impressed," I said.

"Don't be. Today both parties have their own organizations and that's all they do. Picture scavengers or enormous vacuum cleaners sucking up dirt and storing it. The Dems have American Bridge. The Republicans have America Rising. They're both set up as super PACs which gives them a lot of freedom of movement and less financial accountability. America Rising not only collects data on Democrats, today they also collect data on any federal employee who says anything negative about Trump or any of his people."

"Did Arnie work with America Rising?"

"When it suited his purpose. They wanted *Secrets*, but no way in hell was he giving it to them. They begged him for it and even offered him a fortune.

"Frank, Arnie was ahead of all of them. This Jewish kid from Bridgeport wrote the damned book. Politics has never been a game for wimps, but Arnie? Arnie was something else. He was a warrior."

"He sounds more like a mercenary to me."

"Yeah, he wanted the big bucks, but he loved the war, and he only worked for the good guys."

"So, in his world, that means Republicans."

"Yep."

"Did he have any competition?"

Barlotti sat back as though deep in thought. I had no idea what was going through his mind, but from the way he was acting, I thought he was deciding whether or not to tell me something. Finally, he said, "There is one group that also works for Republicans that is getting a lot of business. It's called Project Veritas. It's connected at the highest levels of the Republican party. They use ex-spies, Brits and U.S., and they infiltrate. They treat the Dems and their supporters as enemies of the U.S. who must be destroyed. They have their spies copy documents, record conversations, anything, and then feed it back to Republican campaigns. They also do disruptive stuff. What is different about them is they go beyond the candidates: they try to damage the organizations

124

that usually support the Dems."

"For example?"

"Frank, this group has a lot of juice. Arnie tried to steer clear of them."

"Come on, Carlos, can you give me an example?"

"Okay. This one got some play in the press. They infiltrated the AFT headquarters…

"American Federation of Teachers."

"Yeah, but they got caught and there was a law case. Arnie would go after candidates; these people go after anybody who they think stand in their way."

"*They* being?"

"The conservative Republican movement."

"Would they…"

"Nah. Arnie would be a fly to them, and one who was on their side, at least they would think so."

"Was he?"

"He was changing. He had questions."

I was not going to tell Barlotti that I had at least some of Arnie's information sitting in a box in the trunk of my car. It was beginning to feel more like a box of explosives.

I was, however, going to have a conversation with Vidal Banks. It was not one she expected. Why the hell would she lie to me? And what was all this shit about how she became a political junkie because she was "interested" in what her father did?

I thanked Carlos for his time, paid for lunch, and left a voicemail for Vidal Banks. "Her nose is so high in the air she'd drown in a rainstorm." I had a hard time getting that image out of my head as I drove home. Eve had sent me a text message: *I'm home. We need to talk.*

Chapter 15: Leaving the Homestead

Eve's Prius was in the driveway when I got home, but she didn't respond when I called out to her. I went upstairs, but still no Eve. I came back down and went into the kitchen and glanced out onto the deck as I was opening the refrigerator.

Eve was sitting in one of the teak chairs I left out all winter in anticipation of an occasional day of warmth. She had the hood of her parka pulled up and her arms were wrapped around herself against the cold.

I opened the slider and went out onto the deck. "You okay? It's freezing out here."

"I think I blew it with Molly. She's really mad at me. Hate would not be too strong. I am now officially the wicked stepmother, or stepmother-to-be maybe."

"What the hell happened? Come on in. It's too damned cold out here. What on earth are you talking about?"

We went into the kitchen, and I could see she'd been crying. I helped her out of her parka. "You want some coffee or something?"

"I'm going to go wash my face. I want the last hour back. That's what I want."

"Come on, can't be that bad."

"Oh, yes it can," she said as she headed for the hall bathroom.

I turned the kettle on and got out a couple of mugs. I pulled out the basket with its assortment of teas and placed it on the counter. I selected a peppermint tea for myself and waited for the water to boil.

I sat at the kitchen counter waiting for Eve to come back from the bathroom. When she did, she didn't say anything. She went about selecting a tea for herself and pouring the hot water into both of our mugs. Her eyes were swollen but the traces of tears had been washed away. I sensed they could return at any second, so decided it was best to say nothing.

She began, "When Molly and I had dinner last night, we had what I thought was a very relaxed and nice time. I think she did, too. We talked about wedding stuff and she offered to give me the binder she had made up of wedding ideas that she had collected for her wedding. I didn't want to offend her, so I said I'd love to see it."

Eve stopped talking and took a sip of her tea. "Well, she came by while you were having lunch with what's-his-name."

"Carlos Barlotti."

"She came by to drop it off. That's where the trouble started. The timing could not have been worse."

"How?"

"I had just gotten off the phone with the real estate broker that Em had recommended. She had told me about several condominiums that are on the market right now. One in Stratford, two in Milford, and a couple in New Haven. All of them are on the water. The ones in Stratford and Milford have docks that come with them, and I was getting really excited. Then Molly walked in with her damned binders. I'm just getting off the phone. I'm excited about the condominiums and rather than keeping my big mouth shut, I start to tell her about them. Frank, I'm sorry. I should have said nothing."

"So…"

"Frank, I should have waited for us to talk about how we were going to tell the kids."

"What did she say?"

"Why would we want to move? This is where we live. This is our home."

"Wait a minute. She doesn't live here anymore?"

"Oh, yes she does. This is where her family lives."

"What else did she say?"

"Isn't this house good enough for me? Where would we have Christmas Eve and Christmas? A condominium wouldn't be big enough for everybody? Dad doesn't want to move, does he?"

"Jesus. What did you tell her? I hope you told her I wanted to do this."

"I didn't say anything. I was floored. I knew what a big mistake I had made. She slammed her notebooks down on the counter and left. I can't tell you how sorry I am. I feel like a complete idiot."

"Come on. Okay, maybe we should have talked about it, but you were excited, and she was surprised. She was also being a twenty-four-year-old brat. She's married and lives with her husband. Ben has his own apartment, but I'm supposed to maintain the homestead for her? You can move in, but only as long as she still has her bedroom here? This is bullshit."

"Frank, this is deeper than that. This is about losing her mother, and me taking you away, and now the house. Christmas Eve and Christmas. Come on. And she didn't have any control of any of it. Let's face it: I blew it."

I didn't know what to say. I was pissed at Molly, felt sorry for Eve, and felt really stupid for not having thought about Molly and Ben in all of this. Eve and I had done a good job of preparing them and telling them about our getting married. I just never thought the house and moving would matter that much.

"You didn't blow it, hon. I did. I should have predicted something like this. This family is not exactly the perfect T.V. family. She really talked about Christmas Eve and Christmas?"

"And room enough and where the decorations would go."

"Okay. I get it. Shit. Christmas was always our one Ozzie and Harriet moment. No wonder she went there.

"Some of this you know. Some of it will be new to you. Pat's family is from Indianapolis originally. She came to the East Coast to go to school and stayed because of a guy she met. Three or four guys later, we met. Her brother went to Austin. Then her parents retired to Florida. Basically, Ben and Molly knew they existed, but there were some years they didn't see any of them. When they did, it was usually at a wedding or a funeral."

"No cousins?"

"Three, but they don't know them. They're older. I don't even have addresses for them."

"And you're an only child."

When Eve said that, I was unprepared for the feeling of aloneness that struck me. I tried to talk my way out of it. "Yeah. My mother died when I was in the service. Her family was from Toronto, and after Mom died, we gradually lost touch with them.

"And then there was me and my father. He was anything but an easy man to get along with. He had a younger brother he was estranged from over some business deal that went south. He did not approve of my school or occupational choices. I was supposed to be a lawyer, preferably a tax lawyer like he was. He didn't think Pat should work, and if I had been a lawyer, she wouldn't have had to. My father was a devout, sanctimonious in my opinion, Catholic who thought the sun rose and set on the Jesuits."

Eve said, "He was Francis Ignatius Kelly and you are Francis Xavier Kelly. You were supposed to go to Fordham and went to UConn instead. How did you wind up with an ex-religious? You nuts?"

"Brains, beauty, and sex. In addition, you are kind, and generous, and Blackie and my children like you."

"Liked, as in past tense with your children."

"This will pass. I guarantee it."

"Maybe. So, tell me about Christmas."

"After Mom died, Dad moved back into New York where his tax practice was. After Pat and I got married, Dad would come up every Christmas Eve and spend the evening and Christmas Day with us. We've always had a guest room, even when we just had a small apartment. After we bought this house and the kids were born, Dad was always with us and we always made a big deal out of Christmas. When the kids were young, we would go to an early Mass and come back and have dinner. Christmas morning we'd open presents, usually go to a movie Christmas afternoon, and then Dad would head back to the city around eight o'clock.

"When the kids got older, we graduated to midnight Mass. When they started having significant others, they were included. There was never any question about where everyone was going to be from noon on Christmas Eve to Christmas night. Christmas Eve night the kids always slept in the bedrooms they had had since they were children. Dad always had the guest room up until he died five years ago."

"Stan?"

"Stan, too. He had no choice. Marry Molly, marry Molly's Christmas."

"What about other holidays?"

"Friends mostly. Sometimes Dad. Nothing even close to the ritual of Christmas. After Pat was killed, we kept everything the same, only now it was just the three of us until Stan came along, and then there were four. If Ben had somebody, they always came, too.

"I didn't realize Ben and Molly had that much exposure to Catholicism."

"They didn't. They went to Mass for my father. He started getting on me and Pat about it when the kids were young, but he backed off. He needed us. And that would have been a sure way to create distance. I'll hand that to him. Other than a caustic comment once in a while, he kept out of it. Molly flirted with it when she was a teenager. Ben never."

"And you, Francis Xavier Kelly, are an unchurched spiritual-but-not-religious man who meditates daily and pursues cosmic consciousness with an emotional and intellectual ease that would put most Jesuits to shame. I know what's in your library."

"Yeah, right."

"That's exactly what I mean. And you and your children go to midnight Mass every year."

"We do."

"Like we did this year."

"Like we did this year."

"And Christmas is like it was this year."

"Like it is every year."

"And this house, this is home. This is the castle that protects the Kelly family from harm, and I come along and want to get rid of it. I truly am the wicked stepmother, and we aren't even married yet. You should call her, Frank, and Ben, too."

"She will have already called him."

"Of course. I'm sorry, Frank. Deeply sorry."

"I'm the idiot here, not you."

"Please call."

"I don't think I'll have to."

"Why?"

"She'll call me."

"Are you sure?"

"Yes. Or Ben will. If they don't, I will."

"What will you tell them?" Eve asked.

"The Christmas boxes are coming with us, all ten of them, wherever we move. They're welcome to go through them if they want anything, but they will have to agree on what goes to whose house."

"You do have a lot of Christmas decorations. I've never even had a tree. I would just put some things around the condominium to make it Christmassy, but nothing elaborate. One box. That's it"

"We may have to get some together then. Any chance we can get your family to come up some Christmas?"

"Absolutely. Maybe Christmas afternoon, but what about the Christmas afternoon movie?"

"I think we can handle that."

Molly did call, the next day, Sunday. She asked if she could stop by that evening and we were not to cook. When she arrived, she was carrying a bouquet of flowers. Stan was with her.

"I got these at Stop and Shop. They were the only place open. Ben's on his way. He has dinner. Can we talk?"

Chapter 16: Data and Details

"You okay? You look exhausted," Claire said as I poured coffee into my Nutmeg mug. She was cutting up fresh fruit into a bowl, a joint effort with Meg to wean Sam and me, mostly Sam, away from the more typical carbo loading of baked goods that he would bring in. Weaning Sam was working as long as Sam was in the office. Outside was another story. The man did love his donuts.

"It was a long night," I told her. "Family stuff. Productive, but long. Sam get in yet?"

"His office."

I went to my office first. Blackie strolled along beside me. It had taken some time to train everyone at the office that Blackie was not allowed to share in either the fruit or the carbo flow that entered the office every morning, nor was it permissible to give him treats. I was called a grouch, mean, and probably other names behind my back for my insistence on these boundaries. Eventually people got the message that I was serious about this. Fortunately, Blackie had been trained not to counter surf, steal food, or beg, all behaviors that other dogs I had lived with had excelled at.

I put my computer into its docking station and turned it on. There was an email from Vidal Banks: *I understand you spoke with Carlos yesterday. Can you do a catch up call this afternoon? Are you free?*

I responded: *Yes. What time would be best for you?*

There was an email from Molly: *Dad, I love you. And I am really happy Eve is in your life. She is a wonderful person. I'm glad we talked last night and, yes, Stan and I would love to have some of the decorations, and Ben does not get to pull older brother rank about which ones. Only kidding. I've started making a list. I'll clear it with you first before I talk to Ben.*

I responded: *Love you, too. I'm glad we got together last night. All good. Remember to leave us some decorations.*

I was still scrolling through email when Sam walked in with a cup of coffee in one hand and an apple in the other. "Claire said you wanted to see me."

"Got a couple of minutes? Wanted to catch you up on the Nunnely case."

"Sure. You okay? You look beat."

"I am. Late night. Molly had a meltdown about Eve and me possibly moving. Family meeting last night until one in the morning. Everybody: Molly. Ben, Stan, Eve, and me."

"Molly doesn't want you to move?"

"Nope. By the time we finished she was starting to come around to that it might be a good idea. There was a lot of stuff though."

"I'll bet. Losing her mom. She and Stan getting married. You getting together with Eve, and now the two of you getting married and a move out of the house she grew up in. Change sucks."

"You sound like Eve. Empathic."

"We, of the protect and serve fraternity, are astonishingly empathic regardless of public perception. The reality, if home has been good to you, no one wants to totally leave, ever. Look at my damned garage and Tony's stuff in it. Vicki still refers to our guest room as her room."

"Tell me about it. Actually, even though Eve and I should have thought through how we were going to tell them, I think it finally turned out pretty good. Hugs all around. I think Molly is beginning to realize that she may be gaining a lot more than she had anticipated by having Eve in her life. I think Ben intuited it."

"They're wonderful kids, Frank."

"Yeah, they are."

"So, Nunnely. Fill me in."

"Well, starting with Vidal, she lied to me about her relationship with her father and how much time she'd been spending with him before he was killed. She was seeing and talking to him, a lot. Don't know what that's all about yet. I'm talking to her this afternoon.

"Carlos Barlotti. He's a piece of work. He worked for Arnie for a long time and they were friends as well as workmates. He's sure Arnie was killed. I like the guy. Tough, but I think honest. The big thing I learned from Carlos was about the data. Arnie was a collector of data on everybody. Carlos compared him to Hoover."

"To J. Edgar. No shit. That creep had a file on everybody."

"So did Arnie. He'd developed this program he called *Secrets* to store information and manipulate it in any way he wanted. I'm hoping that we have it in the box I retrieved from Vidal.

"Also, Carlos thinks there was something strange in Thurman's election and it's possible Arnie knew about it and that's what got him killed. And then there's Thurman's opponent."

"Gene Douglas. I voted for him. If he would have kept his pecker in his pants, probably would have been elected."

"Maybe. Carlos said Arnie destroyed Douglas. Not just his chances of getting elected, his life."

I continued to fill Sam in on my visits with Carlos and Vidal, along with what my current thinking was, which was pretty meager. So, Vidal lied to me. Maybe nothing to it because she knew I would probably talk to her mother. But she also said her mother had gotten over her bitterness about Arnie. Gary, the stepfather, though, was still pissed at Arnie. Why?

And Arnie. Carlos said he was more than a professional; he was a warrior out to destroy Democrats. Douglas wouldn't have been the only politician who would have been on the receiving end. And then there was his work on the Thurman campaign and all the money and the possibility of election finance problems.

I needed a break. I called Molly, "Sweetie, thanks for your email this morning."

"Dad, I'm so sorry. I was totally out of control and I know it. I was horrible. Will Eve ever forgive me?"

"Excuse me. Were you in the same room I was in last night until one-o-clock in the morning?"

"I know, but…"

"No buts. Trust me. Eve is not holding onto anything."

"I hope not. I want her to like me."

"Oh, Mol. She does, honey, and it's more than like. She's coming to love you."

"I hope so. It's like I have a brand-new family and I'm not very good at it. I told Stan that last night and he laughed and said, 'What about me? Aren't I your family?'"

"To which you replied?"

"I told him to go do something unmentionable to himself."

"And he said?"

"Nothing I'm going to tell you."

"Good. Now, can I tell you the reason I called?"

"I'm sorry, go ahead."

"I may need your expertise."

"Trouble with your cellphone again? I thought that Nutmeg had a person. I met her, Jackie Forrest."

"No. It's about the case I'm working on."

"Super. I love it. What do you need?"

"Do you know anything about this program called Oracle?"

"You're joking? Right? Dad, I do big data. Oracle is like the grandfather, or great-grandfather program of big data. It was the first really useful relational database, and if you know what you're doing, which I do, you can make it sing, dance, and do cartwheels. There are a ton of programs out there now, but it really all started with Oracle. I'm doing something with Big Data SQL right now on a project."

"What I'm interested in is an Oracle program."

"Big Data SQL is Oracle."

"Oh."

"What do you need?"

"Not sure yet. But you'd be willing to help?"

"Absolutely. I'm bored silly with these dissertation revisions. You know Jackie is really good at this stuff too. She's just doing your

Nutmeg work part time until she gets out of school. Actually, I think she's a hacker."

"Oh, great."

"Relax. She's cool."

My next call was to Ben. "I'm glad you came over last night."

"I'm glad I could be there. You know it was just Molly being Molly. Eve is great, and you guys should definitely move and get a dock and a boat so I can borrow it."

"You…"

"I'm teasing. Well, not about the boat. You definitely should get a boat."

"Where did I go wrong?"

"Independent critical thinking with compassion I believe was what you once told me you hoped for your children."

"And you remembered."

"Mind like a steel trap. I remember everything."

"Can I ask you a professional question?"

"Is my meter running or not?"

"Not quite yet."

"Okay, go for it."

"I told you briefly about the Nunnely case last night. We now have all of this data that he's been gathering over the years. He gave it to Vidal for safe keeping. Do we have any legal problem opening it up and going through it, assuming we can open it up?"

"He gave it to her before he was killed?"

"Yes."

"He asked her to hold onto it?"

"Yes."

"Okay. I'm thinking out loud here. So, don't hold me to anything. Nunnely was an attorney, right? Still admitted to the bar?"

"Don't know."

"If he was, and if this data could be considered as work product, then privilege survives death and no, you can't open it and look at it. He also should not have given it to his daughter. If he was not performing as an attorney for his clients, he may have had, probably would have had, a non-disclosure agreement with his clients as part of a consulting agreement. If his daughter was in business with him, then she could open it and she could give you, as a vendor, access to it as well if she granted you permission and had an N.D.A. agreement with you."

"What if this was data he was collecting on his own?"

"Not for a client?"

"Yes."

"Then that would be up to his daughter, but Dad…"

"I know. Probably not the case and probably the data's all in the same database, client data and stuff he collected on his own."

"Probably."

"Shit."

"There's another out, but it would involve the Boston Police. This is a capital case. The police could go to a judge and try and get a judge to give the police permission to forget about work product and N.D.A. agreements and regulations. My hunch is that would be a non-starter unless you had specific information the police would be asking for and had a good case that it was there in the data, relevant to the crime, and essential to the investigation.

"Shit."

"Or, we never had this conversation and you are just a private investigator ignorant of these matters. Again, I'm just thinking out loud."

"Thanks, I guess."

"Sorry."

"No, I asked the question."

"Now, on the other hand…"

"What?"

"Well. If what he was collecting, and what is in the information he gave his daughter, is the raw data he had been collecting, and if it was primarily public record information, then there is absolutely no problem. You or I could get that information today."

"What about recordings done on the sly, the eavesdropping stuff."

"Still no problem in most cases. You can't expect privacy if you're talking at a campaign event, even if the cameras aren't rolling. Look at how many idiots were caught saying things because microphones were still on and they didn't realize it and just kept talking."

"So, you're saying there's no problem?"

"No, I'm saying you won't know until you see what's there."

"But you also said that if it's work product or covered by a N.D.A., and it might be, we can't find out what's there."

"Don't you love the law?"

"Only sometimes.

"Now for the really important question. How big is the dock and what kind of boat are you thinking about getting?"

"Jesus."

"Mary and Joseph. Bye. Love you."

Chapter 17: A Decent Man

Henry Gore had called Gene Douglas "a decent man." Carlos had said Arnie destroyed him and that Douglas would know how to hire somebody if he had wanted to kill Arnie. How do you destroy a decent man? I called Gore and got one of his graduate assistants. "Professor Gore is not on campus today."

"Do you know how I can reach him?"

"Not really. He's guest lecturing someplace."

"Do you know where?"

"Let me look. Do you want to hold?"

"Sure." The line went dead.

I called back. "This is Dr. Kelly. You were going to check on Professor Gore's whereabouts."

"Sorry about that. I hit the wrong button. Give me a sec. I think he gave me access to his calendar but I've never used it."

I waited. I could tell that this time he had put the phone down.

"Got it. He's not giving a lecture. He's in New Haven. Some interview show."

"Television? Radio?"

"I don't know. WTHN, whatever that is."

"Do you have a time?"

"Five o'clock."

"Thank you."

I hung up thinking that the quality of graduate students had diminished since I was one. WTHN was the ABC affiliated New Haven television station. I called Eve. "Henry Gore is in New Haven giving an interview on WTHN at five o'clock. Do you have his mobile number? I'd like to talk to him again. You free for dinner, hon?"

"No, I'm swamped with papers to correct, but you two go ahead."

I got his number from Eve and called Henry. He said he couldn't meet me for dinner. He planned on heading back to UConn for an evening meeting right after the interview, but he could meet me for a drink if I wanted. I said yes, and we agreed to meet at Christy's Irish Pub at six. I called Eve and told her I would be late for dinner. Since it was close to the Nutmeg office, I asked Sam if he wanted to join us. He said he'd like to but it was his poker night. He was definitely moving into retirement mode.

I called Christy's to see if I could reserve a table. The bartender laughed. I asked if I could bring Blackie and told him he was a service dog. It was a lie, or perhaps a stretch, but I didn't want to leave Blackie in the car. It was below freezing. The bartender said, "Sure, but I won't serve him." The bartender thought that was hilarious.

I walked Blackie on the New Haven Green and meandered over to Orange Street and Christy's. I was able to get a table. Blackie got his share of quick looks as we walked in, but since we weren't taking up any of the premium after-work bar space, no one seemed to mind. I was one of the oldest people, if not the oldest, in the place.

Henry walked in a few minutes after I did, went right to the bar, appropriated an Irish accent, and said, "Would you be so kind as to build two pints of Murphy's for me and my friend and have them brought over?"

"Run a tab?" the bartender asked.

"Not tonight, unfortunately." Henry laid a twenty-dollar bill on the bar and joined me.

He offered a critique. "This place is faux Irish, but it's close to the THN studio." He looked around and pointed at the walls. "They're really trying much too hard. Look at these posters. Quotes from the great Irish poets, but I'll wager that not more than a handful of people in here have read any of their poems. On a cold night like tonight, though, it's a brilliant place to be, a brilliant place." Henry had not dropped his faux accent and had appropriated the Irish penchant for applying the word *brilliant* to everything he approved of.

A red-haired waitress in her early twenties appeared. Her accent was real. So Henry had to ask, "Where are you from, my dear?"

"West Cork. Glengarriff," she said.

"Beara Peninsula," I said.

"You've been there?" she asked me.

"Just for a few days."

"Brilliant. What can I get you? Are you eating and drinking or one or the other?"

"Ordered at the bar," Henry said. His accent had disappeared in the presence of a real one.

"I'll grab them for you if they're ready." And off she went.

"Oh, to be young again," Henry said, watching her walk away. "To what do I owe the pleasure of buying a pint for the future Mr. Karam?"

I smiled and shook my head. "I think Eve and I will both keep the names we were born with."

"Boring. You should decide on a name for this new union that is unique and appropriate."

"Did you and your wife do that?"

"Of course not. We succumbed to the societal norms that proclaimed she was my property and should be named as such. Of course, if you met her, and I hope in the near future you do, you will see how absolutely absurd that is. I belong to her, not the other way around."

I knew I had best get to the reason why I called him or we would banter until he had to leave to head back to UConn. Henry was an entertainer, and I was beginning to appreciate just how much fun he could be.

"I need your help, Henry. When we got together for dinner in Hartford, you called Gene Douglas 'a decent man.' Today I met with one of Arnold Nunnely's former colleagues. He told me that Nunnely destroyed Douglas and, in his opinion, if Douglas wanted to, he, Douglas, would have known how to go about having Nunnely killed."

"Never. Yes, he certainly had reason to, but I know this man. He would never hurt someone, kill someone, or have them killed. That's not who he is. He's infinitely more accepting of political bloodletting than I am."

141

"You sound absolutely sure."

"I am. I know this man."

"Okay. But nevertheless, fill me in. Just for background. Perhaps someone close to Douglas…"

"No. No one. I know the people in that campaign."

We sat in silence for a minute while the young lady from Glengarriff placed the pints in front of us. There was change on her tray. Henry indicated it was for her. He used the interlude to dial back his irritation at my questions. Each of us took a long drink of our stouts. Henry was very careful to avoid leaving any remnant of the three quarters inch head as a mustache on his upper lip.

He looked at me as if to assess whether or not he could trust me before he began. He made a decision and started. "Gene was somewhat of a lost kid growing up. Waterbury's a tough town. He got in some scrapes, nothing serious, but enough so his uncle talked him into going into the Marines straight out of high school. Gene never knew his father. Gene was one of the cases where the service really did straighten someone out. He did four years in the Marines. By the time he got out, he knew he wanted to go to college. He had decided he wanted to teach. Worked his way through New Britain State and graduated with high honors. While he was in school, he also got involved in school politics – student council and all that jazz. He loved it.

"At the time, Carolyn Wilkins was the State Senator from New Britain and she was one of the speakers at Gene's graduation. There was a dinner for the student speakers and honored guests the night before graduation and, as president of the Student Government Association, Gene wound up sitting next to Carolyn. Gene had a teaching job lined up, but no contract yet. Carolyn was very much taken with Gene and he was with her. She had an opening in her office in Hartford and offered it to him. In his mind, he thought having the experience working in government would make him a better social studies teacher, so he accepted.

"Carolyn was coming out of a nasty prolonged divorce. Even though she was fifteen years older than Gene, there were long nights working together, shared values, and it wasn't long before Carolyn offered herself, body and soul, to Gene. He wasn't seeing anyone and he willingly responded. I think she loved him. Anyway, they had an affair. Gene and I talked about it once when we were both more than slightly lubricated. He said he liked being close to power, figuratively and literally, and she provided both. He also admired her and, don't you dare repeat this, he said she was a fantastic lover.

"Three years later, he decided to run for an open State Rep seat from Waterbury where he had grown up. Black man, hometown boy, former Marine, working in the state legislature for a powerful woman. Shit, he won without breaking a sweat."

"And his relationship with Carolyn Wilkins?" I asked.

"They both knew they had to end it. Which they did. Most of the time. It was the 'most of the time' that created the problem."

"How?"

"There had been some rumors before, but there were times they were not as discrete as they might have been, even after he won the House seat."

"What was the problem? They were both single."

"Oh, Frank. Come on. You're not that bloody naïve. Black man. White woman. She was fifteen years older, and here she was helping him in his career. The optics could not have been worse.

"And they were both very ambitious. Carolyn wanted to be president of the Senate. Possibly governor. She did make it to become president of the Senate. Gene wanted to get into a leadership position in the House, which he did, eventually."

"Got it."

"So, after a couple of years they did end their May-December fun and games and both moved on romantically, but politically, they remained symbiotic. He helped her get legislation through the House. She worked on his priorities in the Senate. The fact that he was black, from shit-poor Waterbury, and had been raised in the projects, and she

143

was moneyed from the time she was born just added to the mystery of their relationship. Some people referred to them as Caro-Gene.

"Carolyn helped fundraise for Gene's campaigns, although he became so ensconced no one ran against him after a few years. He showed up at every committee meeting and event where she needed him. And then she resigned. She met and married a fucking K Street lobbyist and moved to Alexandria. Became a Washington matron and fundraiser for all kinds of causes and liberal candidates."

"What did that mean for him?"

"It was the best thing that could have happened to him. Our Gene became his own person. He could appear compliant when he needed to be and would then out maneuver anyone who would get in his way. He could put a shiv in your back and you would thank him for scratching it. He was a natural to begin with and had studied and slept with a master."

"You know you're not painting him as such a decent person."

"He became an effective politician, Frank. He had power and used it to help people. He was more progressive than most of his Democratic colleagues, and he made things happen. Eventually he wound up chairing the House Ways and Means Committee. He needed the power to get things done, Frank. Gene became Mr. Douglas."

"And personally...?"

"Married a wonderful woman, they have two great kids, a son and a daughter. Son's been somewhat of a handful, but basically a good kid. Typical teenage battles, especially with his dad because he's just like him. Kid thinks dad isn't black enough, not radical enough. Daughter is more like her mom. Somewhat shy and retiring. Good kids. Great wife. Poster stuff.

"So, when old Ray Walcott's wife became ill and he announced he was not going to run again, no one was surprised when Gene decided to go for Walcott's Senate seat. I was thrilled. Gene Douglas, United States Senator from the great state of Connecticut. I loved it.

"Of course, not everyone agreed. Dems came out of the woodwork thinking they should be the one. Five of them were sure they would each make an extraordinary senator. So, we had a primary the likes of which Connecticut had never seen before: six narcissists all in a row; one would stay and the rest would go.

"Only the mayor of New London was any real competition for Gene, but his pay to play tendencies while mayor erupted into a major scandal with a little help from Gene. Only two others stood a chance against Gene, a former governor, who was too damned old, and a state representative who thought being female and a soccer mom was the road to glory.

"Thanks to Carolyn's efforts with the Democratic establishment, Gene had the money he needed. He also had the name recognition, the smarts, the personality, and was squeaky clean with his beautiful wife, photogenic children, rags-to-riches background, and clarity on the issues. He was no flame thrower, but the progressives were okay with him, and they were not about to give up the seat to a Republican from Greenwich."

"Yeah, that's the way I saw him," I said.

"Of course you did. You were supposed to."

"Well, you know what happened. Gene screamed through the primaries and, once he won, the polls showed him clobbering Thurman. Actually, the polls showed just about any of the Dems beating the rich prick from Greenwich. This was going to be sweet Democratic continuity from one long-term Democratic Senator to another."

"So, what went wrong? The rumors?"

"Not at first. The first wave of shit was money. I have to hand it to Thurman. I don't know who was advising him at first, but he must have hired really good people, and they spent a fortune getting two messages out.

"Message one: Thurman, the self-made millionaire, understood the world because of his business experience around the globe and being a Senator required that you be a man of the world, not a parochial politician who had spent his political life wallowing in small time

Connecticut politics. What was clever about this message was that, as a Senator, Ray Walcott had been a world figure. He had been on the Senate Foreign Relations Committee for years. People saw Walcott as sophisticated and worldly. So, this damned Republican, Thurman, was positioning himself as the natural successor to Walcott.

"The second message was that Thurman was presidential material. Frank, they ran this poseur as though he was a future President, and I think he does want to be President. They brought in all of the big, but semi-moderate, Republicans, if there is any such an animal left. The Bush clan showed up. If his backers could have, they would have dug Ronnie Reagan up and marched him around smiling his most ingratiating smile.

"There was nothing subtle about these messages. Basically, this black guy from Waterbury who went to New Britain State was not Senate material. Gene worked his ass off campaigning. But by the midpoint of the campaign, the polls were getting closer and then they stalled with Gene a little bit ahead. So, what does Thurman do? He demotes his campaign manager and brings in a guy who has never actually run a campaign before but is very sharp, part of the Republican establishment, and has been everything from a lobbyist to a Presidential advisor. Very high energy. Street fighter type. Some people think he may have been one of the guiding pukes behind the swift-boating of Kerry."

"Jason McCloud."

"You know about him?"

"Carlos Barlotti, Nunnely's lawyer, mentioned him."

"Up until then, Thurman had been going positive. I don't know if Nunnely was working for him or not at that point."

"According to Barlotti, he was."

"Makes sense. If that's the case, McCloud let Nunnely loose to do his thing. History's a bitch. Nunnely launched an internet offensive. Within a week, Gene's affair with Carolyn Wilkins became a sordid internet fascination.

"Thurman's campaign acted as if they had nothing to do with all of the internet chatter about the scandal and, when asked, Thurman refused to comment about Gene's affair with Carolyn. Meanwhile, the super PACs supporting Thurman did all the dirty work. In its reach, this became like 'swift-boating,' version 2.0. Only it was far worse."

"How?"

"Because it was all true, and your friend Arnie the Assassin had proof. When the rumors had been flying years before, Arnie had sent his minions to tail Gene and Carolyn. My guess is that he was after Wilkins, but he got Gene as well. Arnie had pictures, dates, and all of it was factual. Once the super PACs released the shit, it stayed live on the internet. Before long the newspapers picked it up. It even went national for a while because of Carolyn's status in Washington.

"So, the message was that the golden black boy with the beautiful family had been dipping his black wick into the powerful white lady and that's how he got ahead. The racism was blatant.

"Gene's family was embarrassed. Fortunately his wife, Sandra, already knew about the relationship. But his kids didn't. Rick was off at B.U. and Viv was in her sophomore year of high school."

"Those poor kids."

"So, Gene had to deal with them, and then the money dried up. Carolyn was devastated. She had been fundraising for Gene from her perch in Alexandria and she stopped. She went into seclusion. She was hounded and went into the desert of 'no comment' land."

I said, "I never really got the uproar. They were two single people then, and it was years ago."

"Oh, come on, Frank. Why are you resisting this? Post-racial America does not exist. This is America. How many black and white couples do you know? How many are in politics? Add to that fifteen years difference in age. She's his boss and helps him get ahead. And it's all true. With everything Arnie had, Gene had to admit it. Carolyn refused to say anything. Gene's campaign tried the lonely-hearts soap opera routine, and Sandra did her 'standing by her man' bit à la Hillary.

But this is America where we cherish our mythical post-racial beliefs. That is until we have the opportunity to become judgmental racists.

"So, all of September and October Gene is on the defensive. Thurman doesn't say boo about any of this and, when he's asked, his response is a pseudo-statesmanlike, 'Let's focus on policies and qualifications, folks.'

"Qualifications. How fucking subtle is that? Schmuck. What does he do during the debates? Every damned question Thurman pivots to 'qualifications.' And then his ads change. Family man, family man, family man. White, white, white."

"I remember those."

"The stink was so great Gene's polls took a nosedive into an empty cesspool. Then in the beginning of October two bombs go off. Money had been coming into Gene's campaign from out of state, courtesy of Carolyn Wilkins. It stopped when the scandal broke and Carolyn went into hiding. However, the Thurman super PACs made it an issue: Gene's white love muffin was still pushing him up and onward to bigger things. And, as twisted as their message was, it was also true. There had been money from outside the state. Senate races raise money outside their states all the time, but in the context of the affair, the Thurman super PACs made it seem as though the affair was still going on.

"Gene was again on the defensive. Of course the Thurman super PACs could spend as much money as they could get, and, using a bunch of back door accounting, you never knew where the money was coming from. In addition, since Thurman was doing a lot of self-funding, most people could care less about where his money was coming from. They knew he was rich.

"And then came the second bomb, middle of October. Gene was alleged to have had affairs with two unnamed women during the campaign. No names. No proof. But because of the Carolyn Wilkins affair – which, since they were both at least semi-single, wasn't really what most people would call an affair, people were primed to believe it. Now every paper was on it and every damned reporter was digging in and wanting to be the one who broke the story open with the names of these two women. Every woman who had ever met Gene was a potential lover of the black stud, and names were thrown around like confetti. Arnie followed that, or should I say the PACs did, with a push poll: 'Would you be more or less likely to vote for Gene Douglas if you knew that he was having affairs with two different women?' Basic Republican playbook.

"Of course there were no names because it never happened. The timing, though, was perfect. Nunnely was good. Everywhere Gene went, that's what people asked about.

"Thurman ads shifted again. Now he was the independent self-made man not beholding to anyone. There was no Carolyn Wilkins helping him get ahead. The message: don't worry about the Republican label folks, I'm really an independent. Of course, in Connecticut voter registration, registered independents out-number both Democrats and Republicans. Thurman made 'independent' sound like it was a separate party. I have to admit, it was brilliant."

"Obviously it worked. I was surprised Douglas lost so badly," I said.

"And all because a couple of decent but needy human beings worked together and helped each other out in multiple ways years ago." Henry paused and took a very long drink of his stout.

I said, "That it took place a long time ago and they were both single at the time didn't matter."

He slammed his glass onto the table. "Not when you're a young black male and your lover is an older white woman.

"And now Gene is finished in politics, the only career he's ever known. His family is in disgrace and shambles. I don't know if his marriage will survive these alleged affairs he's supposed to have just had. Sandra's tough, but that level of doubt would be tough for anyone. Vivian has had it the worst. High school sucks to begin with. And now this shit. She's started catching all sorts of cyberbullying and worse."

"Worse?"

149

"Comments in the halls. Boyfriend dropped her. She hit the skids. Started cutting herself. They sent her for therapy, had her drop out of school and enrolled her in a private school, but guess what?"

"What?"

"They're broke. Not totally. Sandra still has her job, but Gene has decided he's resigning from the state legislature. He believes he will have lost any effectiveness he had. And then there's Rick. He's pulled away from everyone in the family but his sister. Who knows what's going on in his head?"

"Nunnely really was an assassin."

"Nunnely? Yeah. He earned his nickname. And Gene Douglas, the best person to pursue the common good, the commonweal, will be lucky if he can find a teaching job."

"Would Gene kill Arnie?"

"No."

"Would he know how to?"

"Of course."

"Would he talk to me?"

"I seriously doubt it."

"If you asked him to?"

"Maybe."

"Would you?"

"Why would I?"

"Because you don't think he had anything to do with it and because he might know something that could prove useful in finding out who did kill Nunnely. Ruling him out would also be a good thing."

"For you."

"Yes. And his family."

"You do understand what you're asking."

"Yes. Even bringing it up is going to be hurtful to him and his family. Would you be willing to think about an introduction?"

"Think. Yeah, I'll think about it. Maybe."

Henry finished off his stout and got up. Without saying a word, he put his coat and hat on and turned to head towards the door. He stopped, turned back to me and said, "He's one of the good guys, Frank, one of the good guys," and left.

Chapter 18: The Real Republican

When I got home from meeting with Henry, Eve was waiting for me in the dining room. There were three separate piles of student examination "blue books" on the table in front of her. She didn't look up when I came in. "Do you need a drink? Henry just called. I gather he left in a bit of a snit."

"What did he say?"

"He said you are hopelessly naïve, have no understanding whatsoever of Connecticut politics, and are engaging in an absurdist fantasy to think that Gene Douglas could possibly have anything to do with the murder of Arnold Nunnely."

"That's all?"

"No. He said I had a challenging job of education ahead of me, but he knew I was up to the task."

I went over to where she was sitting and kissed her on top of the head. "And what do you think?"

She looked up in response to my kiss. "Several things. First, you're doing your job and that means entertaining all possibilities. Second, he's right about your naiveté, but there's no reason why you should be a student of Connecticut politics. Third, no way in hell am I going to be your tutor. And finally, someone did shoot Nunnely and he was not an innocent bystander to a gang hit, and you're going to find out who did it."

"You neatly avoided saying anything specific about Gene Douglas." I sat down at the other end of the table.

Eve took her reading glasses off and let them dangle from the chain she wore around her neck. "I've only met Gene in person a few times. I like him, but I don't know him the way Henry does, but Henry's a pretty good judge of character."

She held up her glass of wine, tilted her head, and raised her

152

eyebrows in an invitation to join her. I shook my head no. "You sure?" she asked.

I nodded yes. She took a sip and continued. "Frank, I have a hard time imagining Gene Douglas as a cold-blooded killer. Whoever did this set Nunnely up. This was well planned and executed down to making it look like it was something other than what it was. I cannot get my head around the idea that Gene would do something like that."

"Maybe I will have a beer." I got up and went to the refrigerator, opened it, looked in, and called back into the other room, "We have any more Guinness left? Your friend Henry claims it's not as good as Murphy's. I don't think I could tell the difference."

"On its side, top shelf, back left."

Retrieving the bottle from the exact location in the refrigerator Eve said I would find it, I closed the door, opened the bottle, and headed back to my seat.

"No you don't. Get over here. I want a proper kiss."

I did as I was told, leaned down, and kissed her.

"Now we can continue," she advised.

I sat down and took a fairly hefty pull on the bottle and said, "Gene Douglas has several good reasons to be delighted that Arnold Nunnely is dead."

"I don't disagree with you that he wouldn't be unhappy that he's dead, but that doesn't mean he killed him. He wouldn't have anything to gain at this point. What about the Thurman crowd? Didn't Vidal say that her father was scared and that things had gone too far in the campaign, even for him. He may have known things that could have been damaging to the campaign and might even stop Thurman from getting elected. Look at when he was killed. If he knew something and let it out just before the election, wouldn't that be enough reason…"

"To have someone killed?" I interrupted.

"Yes," Eve answered. "To have someone killed. There are millions of dollars on the table in every election, Frank. Not just donors, but money to be made. Not just by the candidate, but by what the candidate is able to do if elected. There was even talk about Thurman being groomed for an eventual Presidential run. Power, Frank. Think power. We've had this discussion before. This is not a television series where love, money, and revenge are the only motives. Power may be more important, much more important."

She may not have been tutoring me, but she was definitely in lecture mode. She continued, "There's a cultural battle taking place in this country for values and it's not just between the two parties. It is within each of the parties and the outcomes that are at stake are enormous. The odds are so close that one vote can make all the difference in the world. Look at what happened when John McCain dramatically turned thumbs down on repealing Obamacare. That one vote affected the lives of millions of people and millions of dollars were at stake as well. Frank, Connecticut has had a Democratic Senator for years. One more Republican Senator, a Lee Thurman in the Senate, could change lives, not just here in Connecticut, but in the country, and like it or not, even in the world."

We had had this discussion before. Molly and Eve believed there was a battle for values taking place in the country that was even more intense and more important than what had happened during the Nixon years and the Vietnam War. They were convinced that the America they believed in was in enormous jeopardy of being transformed into an oligarchy where money became the sole measure of value.

"He who has the most toys wins" was, in Molly's eyes, the perfect expression to capture the value system of the white patriarchy that sought not simply to maintain control, but to extend it. Would somebody kill for toys?

I knew that the use of "toys" was a metaphor and that the real toy was power. Political power was a "toy" that could be wielded with enormous consequences. Would a drive-by shooting in a poor neighborhood in Boston possibly be part of this much larger war that was taking place? I had a hard time getting my head around that. Maybe I was falling into the same trap as I thought the Boston police were.

Were the limits of my own imagination and world view creating tunnel vision? Perhaps it was easier for me to imagine Gene Douglas as a killer than a cabal of some kind. Then there were the gangs. They were fighting it out for power and influence and money. The scale was smaller and murder was certainly more open and expected, but wasn't the dynamic the same? Gangs provided membership. More than one political analyst had referred to our current politics as tribal warfare. Some even used the word "cult." Was I just struggling with seeing the political process in the United States as parallel to gangs? But what if I did think about it that way? I knew about gangs. Maybe Eve didn't have to tutor me after all.

It was only eight o'clock. I had finished stacking the dishwasher and Eve was back at her stack of blue books. On a whim I called Norm Burchill. "Hi Norm. You busy?"

He said, "Actually, I was trying to figure out a way I could escape watching one of those boring English murder mysteries on PBS that Nancy is addicted to. What's up?"

"I'm involved in a case you might be able to help me with. Some background information. I know it's late, but I thought I'd..."

"A real mystery. Are you kidding? Absolutely. Do you want to come over here? This calls for my best bourbon."

I told Eve that I was going next door to talk to Norm. She gave me a polite, less than half-hearted, "Enjoy." I threw my coat on and walked over to Norm's. After my conversation with Eve and my musings about toys, I was aware of the addition to Norm and Nancy's house and the Mercedes sedan I knew lived behind the closed garage doors along with Nancy's Lexus SUV. Norm's insurance agency now had offices in all of the larger towns in Fairfield County.

During the summer Nancy would leave Fairfield and settle in at their cottage on Lake Candlewood. Norm would commute to his offices from there, and I would rarely see them. Norm had done well for himself, and his decision to go into business with his father right out of college had paid off for him. Insurance was his work; politics was his

155

hobby.

He opened the door as I came up the steps. "Come on in. It's like the North Pole out there."

"And you would know that because…"

"I'm a man of the world and have had many experiences that I have never told you about."

I laughed and said, "I guess so."

"Here, give me your coat. Let's go into the den. I have the bottle and glasses out and I can't wait to hear all about your case."

We settled down in leather chairs. A television set of immense proportions dominated one wall. Apparently Nancy was watching her show someplace else in the house or had been temporarily evicted from the den.

"Ice?" Norm asked.

"Please," I responded.

Drinks in hand, Norm said, "So tell me. This is exciting."

"There are some things I can't tell you."

"Confidentiality, huh?"

"Yeah. However, I do have some things I thought you might be able to help me with, if you'd be willing."

"Sure. Just ask."

"It's about politics, the Thurman campaign and the election. I know you were very involved. Did you ever meet Arnold Nunnely?"

"The Assassin? No. I knew he was working for Lee, but I never met him. Shame what happened to him. Drive-by shooting in Boston, for God's sake. Waiting for a bus. Everyone was shocked. What about him?"

"Well, there may be some question as to whether or not he just happened to be in the wrong place at the wrong time or whether he was targeted."

"No shit. Do the cops think Nunnely was targeted? Wow."

"I don't really know what the police think at this point. I'm doing a little bit of background research for a client on the election though, to see if it is at all possible that it might have something to do with it."

Norm leaned forward excited. "Douglas. You think Douglas did it? He got beat up pretty bad. I would never have figured him to be a killer, though. I don't know. I guess everyone has a breaking point."

I took a sip of my drink. Norm was right. It was very good bourbon. I didn't want this conversation running away from me, personally or professionally. I held the glass up and twirled the liquid around. "This is really good."

"Told you. Not outrageously expensive either. Sixty bucks a bottle. Willett Pot Still. Nancy gave it to me because she liked the shape of the bottle."

"It is unique." I took another sip. I needed to slow things down. "My memory is you were really excited about Lee Thurman."

"Absolutely! He's a real Republican. Mode of Romney, McCain, guys like that. I wish that Paul Ryan had stayed in the House. We need people like that, not this current crowd of isolationist assholes who have no understanding of economics. Thurman could be President someday. I'd love that."

"So, you don't approve of our current President?

"I didn't say that. He's done some great stuff. Someone had to deal with our ridiculous taxes and immigration. You have to understand something, Frank. Both parties are split in two and both are in trouble. It's why so many people are registering as undeclared."

"What's the split for the Republicans and how does Thurman fit into it?" I asked.

"Okay. Now understand. I'm going to exaggerate. Basically, there are the social conservative isolationist types that came to power with the Tea Party and learned how to get power, the Freedom Caucus in the House. They caused John Boehner and Paul Ryan fits. Republicans controlled both houses and still couldn't pass diddly shit. I know I'm biased, but these guys are slightly nuts and definitely myopic. Then there are the people like Lee who know the world is interdependent and you can't go about threatening tariffs on everybody. Let me give you

157

an example. Question. American cars. What cars are made in the United States? By that I mean manufactured and assembled?"

"No idea. I assume…"

"Jeep Cherokee is first, but then it's three models of Hondas. Not Fords. Not Chevies. Hondas. That's how global we are. Lee gets this. Lee's smart. He knows how the world works. And people like me want him in office, not these other loonies."

"Eve keeps telling me how high the stakes are."

"She's absolutely right. Young people don't get it. You hear them whine that their vote doesn't matter, that nothing changes. That's why they don't vote. Bullshit. They just never lived through something that caused them pain because of an election.

"A military base closing can cause a town to go under and the value of people's homes goes into the toilet. That's real pain."

Norm was worked up. I guessed the bottle of bourbon may have already been out before I arrived. I said, "Would someone kill because of this?"

"Of course. Look at the Clintons. They did."

"What are you talking about?"

"You don't really think Vince Foster committed suicide, do you? And then there was Seth Rich, the guy who worked as a computer nerd for the Democratic National Committee. Two shots to the back and the police say it was a robbery gone bad. In the back. Who are they kidding? Nothing was stolen. He was killed just days before Wikileaks released all of those emails from the Democratic campaign. You figure it out."

We talked for another hour. Rather, Norm talked and I listened. He was fascinated with politics and power, and as absurd as I found many of his conspiracy theories, he clearly believed them. I kept asking him about the Thurman campaign.

"Beautiful campaign. Lots of money, and when Lee brought Jason McCloud on board to run the campaign, McCloud really made things happen."

"Is that who Nunnely would have reported to?"

"I wouldn't say reported. From what I have heard about Nunnely, he didn't report to anybody. But yeah. Nunnely would have worked closely with McCloud and his assistant campaign manager, Sheila Neverdowski."

"Do you know them?"

"Yeah. I've met Jason a few times. Spent more time with Sheila. She had more to do with the ground game, and that's where the locals like me fit in."

"Any chance you could introduce me to either one of them? I'd love to get their take on Nunnely's death."

"I think I probably could. How'd you get involved anyway?"

"Sorry."

"Confidentiality?"

"Yep."

I finished my bourbon and declined the offer of a second. I agreed we would all have to get together for dinner sometime soon and welcomed the cold night air.

Chapter 19: The File Maker

Vidal had not gotten back to me. I wanted to talk to her about the discrepancy between her report that she had very little contact with her father and what Carlos Barlotti had told me. According to Carlos, Vidal and her father had talked to each other frequently during the Thurman campaign.

I hadn't yet opened the box that Vidal had given me. I wanted to talk to her about the legal issues of who owned the data and her comfort level with her rights to whatever information her father had passed on to her. In addition, I was working under the assumption that there would be all kinds of passwords and codes and things that would be absolutely meaningless to me. I was going to have to rely upon our Nutmeg computer guru, Jackie Forrest. Sam, Meg, and Molly had all assured me that Jackie was capable of doing whatever needed to be done to examine the Nunnely files.

However, after talking with Norm, I became more anxious to see what was in the Nunnely files, especially the most recent ones. Although it was late, I called Sam after my visit with Norm. I told him my thoughts and his response was immediate. "The hell with the legal stuff, just go ahead. Her father sent it to her. We have proof of that. She gave it to you. The legal issues may be a bit iffy, but we have a job to do. If someone complains, it's Vidal's problem, not ours."

I wasn't sure I agreed with Sam, or that a lawyer would, but there was something in my conversation with Norm that I had found deeply disturbing. He had immediately assumed I was interested in Gene Douglas. So, regardless of my concerns about legality, I decided to follow Sam's lead.

Sam arranged for Jackie to be at the Nutmeg office first thing Tuesday morning. When I arrived, she was waiting for me in the small conference room that we had now dubbed "The Nunnely Room."

Jackie was wearing a Boston Bruins cap, boots, pajama bottoms, and a heavy sweater. Three laptop computers were on the table in front of her. There were wires running from one computer to another and then to external drives. I had absolutely no idea what she was doing, but her fingers were moving quickly from one computer to another.

Hearing me come in she said, "I'm ganging these. Don't know how much power and band width we'll need, so I wanted to be ready."

"Have you been here long?" I asked.

She didn't look up from her computers. "I don't know. Maybe an hour. Mr. DeRosa had Claire let me in. I've got a class at one so I'll have to leave about eleven. He asked me not to load anything until you got here. You tell me when you're ready."

"Do you want some coffee?" I asked.

"No thanks, I'm all set," Jackie said and pointed to a large black travel mug with the brand name *Aladdin* on the bottom. Fitting, I thought. Were we about to release something powerful when we opened these files? "You ready to do this?"

"Yes, let's get started."

"First, this Nunnely guy knew what he was doing. He was storing in the cloud and on discs. He wasn't taking any chances."

She held up one of the discs, careful to hold it by the edges. "These are 100 GB M BD-R discs. You can put over a hundred movies on one of these babies and they'll last forever with no degradation. There are hundreds here. To make life easy, he left a complete manual with access information, file structures, the complete works. He wanted to make it simple for someone."

"His daughter."

Jackie turned around. "These aren't yours?"

"No, but his daughter gave them to us."

"No matter. You want to start with the most recent ones?"

"Please."

Jackie started loading discs into the peripheral drives and they started whirring away. She pointed to one of the computers. "I'm loading everything up onto our server with this guy." She pointed to the other two laptops. "We'll use these two to pull data down and view it. I'm loading the most current and will work backwards from there."

After loading the discs, Jackie turned to me. "This guy was anal. His paper manual is really intense. Every file name includes time, date, source, type, and multiple key words. He also did something really weird. Every file was given a color code from blue to red. According to his manual, it's a classification system indicating the level of potential damage that the information could cause someone if it was made public. Blue indicates, now these are my words, *who cares* all the way up to a hot red which sounds like it means *complete destruction.* Nunnely called his color code system, *potential*, I guess as in potentially useful. Files that aren't given a color code he called *personal*. You want to see those too?"

"Yeah."

After the first several discs were loaded on to the Nutmeg server, we began to look at what was included. As Carlos Barlotti had told me at lunch, Arnie was meticulous. There were videos of speeches by Gene Douglas and Lee Thurman that had been downloaded from media outlets. There were videos taken on the sly by trackers with cellphones. There were audio recordings as well. Thousands of emails between Arnie and the Thurman campaign staff and Arnie and his trackers had been labeled and filed. What I was not prepared for were the memos that Arnie wrote to himself. Some of these were musings, almost like private journal entries. Others were strategic in nature. Sometimes they raised questions that he felt needed to be answered.

At first, I asked Jackie to skip around among video, audio, and text so I could get some sense of what was there. Then we went to the last entries on the final disc and started working backwards. Fifteen minutes later I stopped Jackie and called Sam on the intercom. "Can you come in right away, and perhaps clear your schedule for the day? It's the Nunnely case."

"No problem. I'll tell Claire my schedule just came down with a cold."

A couple of minutes later Sam opened the door, came in, and sat down facing the two of us, "What's up?"

"This stuff is dynamite, Sam. I don't know the legalities of all that's here but, just for starters, it looks to me like campaign finance laws were broken. I have multiple concerns."

"Such as?" Sam asked.

"First, I'm worried about Jackie's involvement." I turned to Jackie and said. "Sorry, but I'm concerned that there's material here that is really flammable, and I don't think it's fair to involve you. This could easily wind up in very nasty court cases and that could be the least of it. Nunnely may have been killed because of this information. I don't want to put you into a dangerous situation."

Jackie immediately responded, "I'm an adult. I'm twenty-one and that decision should be mine. If this was the Marines, you wouldn't be worrying about putting me in harm's way. You'd just do it."

Sam quickly responded, "This is not the Marines and you did not enlist at Nutmeg. We hired you, part-time."

"Come on, Mr. DeRosa. You need me on this. I can make this data…"

Sam said, "I'll think about it, Jackie, but no guarantees. For right now, until I know more, I'm going to ask you to leave the room. I've heard you, and I appreciate that this could be exciting. And I know you could be helpful, but there's a lot going on here. Sorry. And remember, you've signed a blanket confidentiality agreement with Nutmeg and it's clear that this is very sensitive material. You cannot, and you will not, talk to anyone about it. Friends, family, no one. Understand?"

"Yes, sir. What about the gear?"

"Whose is it?"

"Laptops are yours. Some of the peripherals and cabling is mine, some yours."

"You okay with leaving your stuff with us for right now? Actually, let us just buy it from you. I haven't made any decision yet. I want to think about it. And this has nothing to do with you personally, you understand that?"

163

"Yeah. I get it." A very dejected but polite Jackie left the room.

When the door closed, I asked, "What was that Marines stuff about?"

"Her older sister's in the Marines. Helicopter pilot. She's done something like three tours in Afghanistan."

"Oh," I said.

When the door closed, Sam turned to me. "So what did you find?"

"In one of his file memos Nunnely said large amounts of money were flowing from various Saudi groups, possibly even the Saudi government, into the super PACs that were supporting Thurman. Arnie believed that Thurman's campaign manager, Jason McCloud, was being paid by the Saudis to create the mechanisms for the money transfers."

Sam said, "Money laundering. Whoa, McCloud was taking a cut!"

"Something like that. Here's the kicker. Arnie talked to McCloud's assistant, Sheila Neverdowski, about his suspicions. Neverdowski told him she didn't know anything about it. A week after that conversation, Arnie was killed. Somewhere during that time period, Arnie implied to both Vidal and Carlos Barlotti that he might be in danger.

"It also appears that Arnie was not responsible for the stories about Gene Douglas's affairs with the two mystery women. Those came from McCloud and Neverdowski over Arnie's objections. Arnie felt they had already done enough damage to Douglas; this was overkill and could be dangerous if they got caught. Arnie was furious about it and McCloud told him, according to Arnie's file memo, to get on board or he would be replaced."

"And you're thinking…"

"I'm wondering if Arnie was ready to go public with all of this."

"And Thurman killed him or had him killed?"

"Or McCloud, or Neverdowski, or someone from the Saudi involvement."

"You mean like they did to Khashoggi?"

"Came to mind. If a Saudi Prince can get away with killing an American reporter in the Saudi consulate in Turkey, having someone like Arnie killed and make the killing look like a gang shooting would be child's play."

"Did Arnie say how they did the money laundering?"

"Easy. At least according to Arnie, it was easy. Money goes from the Saudis to Thurman supporters who then maneuver it into the super PACs. They'd shift the money around through three or four shell companies or donors before it would wind up in the super PACs. They made it look like there were only a handful of rich supporters involved.

"In Arnie's file memo he wrote that McCloud got a percentage of the money for helping to arrange the transfers. I think Arnie may have actually gotten into McCloud's email account because his memos are very specific about how McCloud was doing it and what McCloud received as compensation for his efforts. I seriously doubt McCloud would have volunteered that."

"Does Nunnely say he confronted McCloud about the money laundering?" Sam asked.

"No. That's also interesting. His memos don't say how he knew or that he ever talked to McCloud about it. And there's something else."

"What?"

"Two days before Nunnely was killed, he got a telephone call asking him to go to that bus stop in Boston. According to his note, the caller told him that there was information on both Douglas and Thurman that would be game changers in the campaign. The caller told him to take the train from Stamford, then an Uber to the bus stop at Humboldt and Homestead, and to wait there. He was given a date and a time."

"Did he say who the caller was? Did he save the message?"

"No and no. Just two sentences in his daily diary. I do think it totally disproves the Boston Police contention that he was a victim of a drive-by. There's no way those detectives can hold onto that myth given this information.

"Sam, I'm just starting to look at these files. This could wind up being much bigger than I ever imagined."

Sam said, "And very messy. We're going to need help."

165

Chapter 20: Thurman

We did need help. There were numerous questions that had to be answered and there were a lot of people I should interview to get answers to those questions. I started to make a list. First there were the Thurman people: Lee Thurman, Jason McCloud, Sheila Neverdowski.

Next, I needed to follow up with Gore. I still hadn't heard from him about the Douglas people. I jotted down questions on my mind: Would Douglas talk to me? Would his campaign staff? And then there were his family and friends. Didn't Gore say his son went to school in Boston? I needed to follow up on the Douglas people regardless of Henry Gore's beliefs about how *wonderful* they were.

Third, I still hadn't spoken with Nunnely's secretary, Leslie Cahill. I also had to get back to Joe Lewis so I could ask him how many cars had stopped in front of that bus stop. What did that differing information mean, if anything?

I continued writing. There was another discrepancy. Had Vidal lied to me? Or had Carlos Barlotti misrepresented Vidal's involvement with her father based on something Arnie had said? What did Barlotti actually know versus what he surmised?

The legal situation was also getting very complicated. It went beyond the question of who owned these files and were they protected by non-disclosure agreements or legal work product regulations. Should we notify the FBI about the information we found in Arnie's files now, or should we wait until we had gone through all of the files related to the Thurman campaign? Campaign finance abuse was the FBI's responsibility. How would this affect Vidal? And what were our obligations, legally and ethically, to her?

I continued making my to-do list when Sam left for a client appointment. Then, before I went back to examining files, I googled the Federal Election Commission and researched their definitions for foreign nationals.

Foreign nationals

Campaigns may not solicit or accept contributions from foreign nationals. Federal law prohibits contributions, donations, expenditures and disbursements solicited, directed, received or made directly or indirectly by or from foreign nationals in connection with any election — federal, state or local. This prohibition includes contributions or donations made to political committees and building funds and to make electioneering communications. Furthermore, it is a violation of federal law to knowingly provide substantial assistance in the making, acceptance or receipt of contributions or donations in connection with federal and nonfederal elections to a political committee, or for the purchase or construction of an office building. This prohibition includes, but is not limited to, acting as a conduit or intermediary for foreign national contributions and donations.

A person acts knowingly for the purposes of this section when he or she has:

- Actual knowledge that the funds have come from a foreign national;
- Awareness of certain facts that would lead a reasonable person to believe that there is a substantial probability that the money is from a foreign national; or
- Awareness of facts that should have prompted a reasonable inquiry into whether the source of funds is a foreign national.

Pertinent facts that satisfy the "knowing" requirement include knowledge of:

- Use of a foreign passport or passport number;
- Use of a foreign address;
- A check or other written instrument drawn on an account or wire transfer from a foreign bank; or
- Contributor or donor living abroad.

167

Definition of foreign national

A foreign national is:

- An individual who is not a citizen of the United States, and not lawfully admitted for permanent residence (as defined in 8 U.S.C. § 1101(a)(20)); or
- A foreign principal, as defined in 22 U.S.C. § 611(b). Section 611 defines a foreign principal as a group organized under the laws of a foreign country or having its principal place of business in a foreign country. The statute specifically mentions foreign governments, political parties, partnerships, associations and corporations.

That could not be clearer. If Thurman, or McCloud, or Neverdowski, or any others, including Arnie, facilitated Saudi money flowing into the super PACs, benefited from it, or knew about it, they had broken the law. It didn't matter if the money came from individuals or "foreign governments, political parties, partnerships, associations and corporations." We had to turn over the information to the FBI, but when? The election had already taken place, and Thurman had been sworn in as a United States Senator.

I went back to the files that were already up on our server. Fortunately Jackie had loaded all of the discs from the beginning of the Thurman campaign, and those were the ones I was most interested in. I spent the rest of the morning working backwards. Nunnely's file labeling system made it easy. I found myself becoming more and more interested in the memos that Arnie had written to himself.

As the campaign had moved forward, he had become more and more uneasy with Thurman and McCloud. In one early memo he wrote, "Thurman may understand stocks, but he hasn't a clue about government. This is an ego trip for him." After Jason McCloud came on board as the campaign manager, he wrote, "JM doesn't have an ethical bone in his body. He's working for Thurman on the surface, but there's something else going on." In another memo he wrote about Sheila Neverdowski, "SN is okay. I like her. If I was younger or she was older, I could see something happening between the two of us. I'm old enough to be her father. Oh, well."

I started cutting and pasting pieces that I wanted to show Sam, and possibly Vidal, and possibly Dolan, Malone, and Galvin in Boston.

One memo revealed how low the Thurman campaign would go. Arnie wrote, "One of the super PACs set up a mimic website. JM's idea. People google *Gene Douglas* and one of the options is *Gene Douglas for United States Senate*. When people go there, what they see are photoshopped pictures of Douglas with two women, one black and one white. The women have captions. They talk about what a stud Douglas is. JM's prediction when he brought it up was right. It went viral. The site was only up for three days but the damage had been done. JM has a list of three more site names he's going to roll out."

Arnie wrote this memo soon after McCloud joined the campaign: "I overheard JM giving someone shit about a delay in the Saudi money getting into someone's bank account. I have no idea what's going on. Has to be the super PAC on Senate Leadership. It's not coming into the campaign account. I looked."

In another memo Arnie wrote, "JM wanted to start a whisper campaign about GD's son being a radical. There's a picture of son at a *Black Lives Matter* rally in Boston. I said no way. Thurman and Neverdowski agreed. JM really pissed."

A week later he wrote: "JM is spending money like mad. Not coming from campaign account. He's got a driver now and doesn't use his own car. What the fuck is going on?"

I decided to become more methodical about the data. Gore had told me about the issues that had been used against Gene Douglas. Nunnely would have investigated his own client as well. I knew nothing about Lee Thurman. I found an early memo Nunnely had written about Thurman. Some of it was straight biography.

> To: File
> Lee Thurman was born in Greenwich Hospital to Richard and
> Leila Thurman on March 12, 1967. He has a brother Richard

169

(Richard Wilson Thurman, Jr.) who is three years older. Lee has lived in Greenwich his entire life.

His father worked for several banks before he retired. His mother was trained as a nurse and stopped working when Richard was born. She returned to work when Lee went away to Kent School in Northwest Connecticut.

Brother Richard became a banker like his father. No arrests, divorces, scandals. No one is gay, or at least openly so. Nothing about the Thurman family that should be troubling for the candidate.

After graduating from Kent, Thurman went to Princeton for a year and then dropped out. Why? I haven't found anything about what he did that year. A year later he started up again, but at Yale where his father had gone and where his brother was a senior. Legacy? Did his brother need to keep watch over him? Lee didn't get into any trouble at Yale and did okay as a student. Economics major. A- student. Played intramural lacrosse and some club stuff. No arrests.

After graduation from Yale, he spent a year working at daddy's bank, and then there's another blank year. Then off to UCLA for B School (get away from home?). Meets Judy Tepper who's an undergrad in communications. Gets his MBA. Stays in LA for a year working for a brokerage house (waiting for Judy to graduate?) She graduates. They get married. He comes back to NYC. She gets a job as a secretary at NBC. He goes to work for Lehman Bros. They live in New Rochelle. He does well at Lehman. Dad dies and leaves him some money so he decides he's going to be a day trader. Then he goes on to using other people's money and the world of the Hedge Fund. Bounces from one firm to another before striking out on his own. Makes it big.

The Lee and Judy Thurmans move to Greenwich, have two kids, and live happily ever after. Thurman makes oodles of money on technology stocks, a sector in which he features himself an expert. He becomes politically active, mostly as a donor, decides he's a genius compared with people in politics, and he should run the country.

Big ego, but nothing for the opposition to use unless it lives in the blank years. The guy is so white bread he probably eats Peter Pan smooth peanut butter. No crunchy for this guy. Yet, what were those two blank years about? Ask?

I took a guess and searched for "blank year." A fairly long entry came up. Nunnely had spoken with several people about those two years and was able to patch together what Thurman's life had been about. During the first, between Princeton and Yale, he had gone to live with his grandparents who had retired to Naples, Florida. The family conclusion was that he was simply not ready for college when he went off to Princeton. He had not done well and had become alienated from his family, especially his father, who saw him as a disappointment. His grandfather helped him get a job as a teller at a local bank and he enjoyed it. Apparently, his grandparents were both loving and good about setting boundaries.

Nunnely had asked Thurman about that year and Thurman told him that he considered his grandfather to be his mentor. It was during his time with his grandfather that finances moved from being the "family business" to becoming something fascinating. So when he returned to Yale his decision to major in economics was his. He loved his economic courses. Thurman remained close to his grandparents and when his grandfather died, Thurman said it was the biggest loss of his life.

The second blank year was entirely different. Thurman wouldn't talk about it. But his wife, Judy, did. After Yale, Thurman worked at a bank where his father, Richard Sr., was CEO. The bank was bought out by a larger bank and there was no place for Richard Sr. Pushed out, Richard Sr. became CEO of a different bank where he shepherded through a merger of three different banks and eventually became the CEO of the newly merged entity.

171

Lee Thurman, however, had been left behind and began to hear a lot of stories about his father's management style. Some of the decisions that his father had made were labeled as close to unethical or actually unethical. The CEO who had taken over from Thurman's father made it obvious that there was not going to be a place for Lee, so Lee left. Where once his father had been disappointed in Lee, Lee was now disappointed in his father.

Lee left and wanted to get as far away from his father as he could. He moved to Seattle, got a job with a startup tech firm, and moved into a whole different life that included recreational drugs and three different jobs in a year, as he kept seeing bigger opportunities in different startups. He had several girlfriends, some at the same time. He was buzzed much of the time, according to his wife, but never got arrested. Sowing his wild oaks was how Judy described the Seattle time.

According to brother Richard, it came crashing down when his girlfriend became pregnant and the startup he was working for went belly up because of lack of capital and a lawsuit for patent infringement. Lee bailed on both and, according to Richard, escaped to grad school. The girlfriend back in Seattle immediately found another boyfriend and had an abortion. Paternity was questionable according to Richard.

Richard said that he and Lee became close during that time. "Older brother looking out for younger brother stuff," according to Richard.

Nunnely's conclusion: "Nothing of concern. Relationship to grandfather spins as positive. Time in Seattle is consistent with interest in technology. No arrests. He can admit to illicit drug use as a youthful error in judgment if discovered. Abortion a consequence of other boyfriend. Peter Pan Peanut Butter is intact."

It was four o'clock when Meg walked into the conference room and sat down opposite me. "I want to talk to you about Jackie."

"What's up?"

"I think you and Sam made a caring but rash decision."

"She's been to see you."

"Yes. And as jack-of-all-trades, including human resources, I think she was right to do so. We've been talking with her about coming on fulltime when she graduates in the Spring. Cybersecurity is going to be a growing part of our, your, business, and Jackie is and will be a real asset."

"You're building a case for allowing her to work with the Nunnely files."

"I am."

"Sam?"

"Says it's your case and it's up to you."

"She's so young, and this could get really hairy."

"Come on, Frank. There will always be some danger in what we do. She knows this. It's one of the reasons she's interested in us. It's exciting. It seems to run in the family. Her sister..."

"Is a helicopter pilot in Afghanistan. I know. Sam told me."

"So."

"Okay, but I want to reinforce everything Sam has talked to her about regarding confidentiality."

"I've spent time with her about that as well."

"You're comfortable with this?"

"More than comfortable. I think it's the right thing to do."

"She's just so young, and there's the chance this could become dangerous."

"Are we talking about Jackie or Molly, Frank?"

"I..."

"And Frank, would you be feeling the same way if Jackie were a he?"

"Oh, shit." Sudden awareness is never terribly pleasant. I looked at Meg, shook my head, and sheepishly said, "Do you want me to call her?"

"No need. She's in my office."

Chapter 21: Dinner in Westport

Thirty-six Railroad Place in Westport, Connecticut, used to be the home of Mario's Restaurant. Now it's The Harvest Wine Bar. The difference between the two could not be more dramatic. Mario's was moderately priced with big dishes of great food. People who'd known each other since kindergarten hung out at the bar on weekend afternoons watching sports. On weekday evenings commuters came off the trains from New York City and met their spouses for dinner or grabbed a drink before heading home.

The Harvest Wine Bar is part of a chain with high prices and menu descriptions like "Wood Fired Prime Angus Hanger Steak, truffle parmesan fries, green beans, chimichurri sauce." Their website proudly proclaims, "The landmark building is transformed to a modern space through its use of concrete, hand-hued reclaimed wood, metal, and glass elements." I knew Vidal Banks would be comfortable there. I miss Mario's.

When I called Vidal, I said it was essential that we get together that evening. "We've started going through your father's files and we've discovered some information that you need to know about. We have some decisions to make."

"Can't you tell me over the phone?" was her response.

"I'd rather not. This is very important, Vidal."

"I'm in New York."

I became patiently paternal. "Why don't you take the train to Westport? We can have dinner at the Harvest Wine Bar right on Railroad Place. It's directly across the street from the station."

"I know where it is."

"Good. I'll drive you back to Stamford after dinner."

"Why don't you just come to Stamford?" She was becoming impatient.

"Sam DeRosa is going to join us and possibly one or two others. It's a matter of getting everyone together, and Westport is an easy meeting place. It's only another ten or fifteen minutes for you on the train."

"You're sure this is necessary?"

"I am. What train will you be getting? The earlier the better."

"Well, if I rush my last meeting, I can probably make the 6:13."

"We will be waiting for you at the restaurant."

I didn't understand her hesitation. I told her we had found important information in the files and that did not seem to either impress her or make her curious. She didn't even ask what it was. If I gave her the benefit of the doubt, perhaps she was just exhausted after a bad work day. Or, was she avoiding me for some reason?

Sam agreed with me that one of the people we were going to invite was Carlos Barlotti. I had two reasons. First, I wanted to get at the truth. Vidal's and Carlos's stories were completely different. What was the frequency of contact between Vidal and her father before he was killed? I knew this might not matter in the long run, however I wanted to make it clear to both of them that I was not going to play games with lies or half-truths. Second, I wanted them both to know about the campaign finance issues and to see if Nunnely had spoken to either one of them about them and what, if anything, they had done with the information. I also wanted to know if Nunnely had hinted in any way about why he was in danger or who might be interested in harming him.

Sam and I also decided to invite Jackie. Our if-then thinking about the invitation, prompted by Meg, may have been a little bit convoluted, but we felt comfortable with it. It went like this: if Jackie was going to be joining the staff in a few months, and if she was going to be working on the Nunnely case, and if she was going to play a key role in massaging the Nunnely data, then she should meet the key players and begin to experience the weightiness of what we were dealing with. When I told Jackie she was invited, she was surprised, delighted, and anxious in that order. I told her business casual when she asked me what she should wear. Sam told me later that she immediately called Meg to find out what that meant.

We drove down in two cars because I would be driving Vidal back to Stamford. Jackie drove down with me, and I briefed her on the plan for the meeting that Sam and I had developed.

Vidal's train was due in at 7:19. I told Barlotti to arrive at 7:30. Sam, Jackie, and I arrived at 7:10 and got a table for five away from the major traffic of the restaurant. Vidal walked in the door at 7:25 and came over to us. She looked a bit disheveled. I introduced Sam and Jackie and described their roles at Nutmeg and told her that I had also invited Barlotti.

Surprised, she asked, "Carlos? Why?"

"I think you'll understand when he gets here."

Barlotti arrived a minute later. He gave Vidal a hug, greeted me, and shook hands with Sam and Jackie when I introduced them. Then he said, "This used to be Mario's. When the hell did this shit happen?"

"It's been a couple of years," I answered.

"Jees. I'm out of it," he said. "What a difference. Mario's was great. I guess this is Westport now."

A waiter came to take our drink orders. Carlos and Vidal bowed their heads into the drink menu. When Carlos popped up, he ordered a Sicilian Manhattan, Sam and I ordered Heineken Lights, Vidal took her time studying the wine menu before ordering a Cakebread Napa Chardonnay at nineteen dollars a glass.

Finally, Jackie ordered. "A Frank Sinatra please." Seeing a hesitation on the waiter's face she quickly added, "Two fingers of Jack Daniels, two of water, and four ice cubes."

We all looked at her surprised.

The waiter said, "May I see some identification, mam?"

Jackie was ready for the request and had her driver's license out and in her hand. She gave it to the waiter for inspection. Turning to the rest of us she said, "I'm used to it."

Smiling at Jackie, Vidal said, "Sometimes I still get carded. I like it, most of the time. I've never heard of a Frank Sinatra."

Jackie was eager to explain. "I'm a Sinatra freak. My mom has every record he ever made. Some are on CD when she couldn't find an old vinyl. Only the albums, not the singles. I fell in love with him when I was a kid. Maybe its genetic. It's that voice.

"The story about the drink is that at some point Sinatra was really down and wanted to drown his troubles. Probably after he split up with Ava Gardner. Anyway, he was with Jackie Gleason and he asked Gleason what he should drink to get rid of his troubles. Gleason told him, Jack Daniels. Over time it became two fingers of Jack, two fingers of water, and four ice cubes.

"Well, one night a group of us were talking about how we each needed a signature drink, sort of our "go to" drink. I remembered the Sinatra story, so I thought, okay, Jackie Gleason, Jack Daniels and Jackie Forrest. I know, it's really hokey. I had never had a Frank Sinatra, so I tried one and really liked it. A lot of bartenders know the exact proportions, so it's always the same."

"So, a Frank Sinatra is your signature drink. I totally get it," Vidal said. "I only drink chardonnay, and I'm still looking for the perfect one. Never thought about it as my signature drink, but I guess it is."

I wondered at the bonding taking place in front of me. These two young women, separated in age by a little more than a decade, were bonding over booze. I was also aware of how relaxed Vidal had become talking to Jackie, and how relaxed Jackie was talking to Vidal. Big sister, little sister?

We chitchatted waiting for our drinks to arrive. Sam and I had orchestrated the meeting before we left New Haven for Westport. Jackie was to begin by describing the files, the labeling system, and how we were going through them. Sam would then give the highlights of what we had found so far. He would emphasize the federal campaign funding violations and the creation of the false narrative about Gene Douglas and the two women he was supposed to be involved with. He would report that the narrative was created by the Thurman campaign manager, Jason McCloud, and not by Vidal's father. Sam would let them know that, from Nunnely's file memos, it was clear that Arnie was very upset by what was happening during the campaign. Sam would also let them know about the telephone call Arnie had received asking him to go to the bus stop in the H block.

When our drinks arrived, I turned to Jackie and asked her to begin. The three of us stayed on script. When Sam finished, we didn't give them an opportunity to respond or ask questions. It was my turn. I showed them a photograph I had downloaded from the internet. "Do either of you know this woman?"

Carlos said, "I recognize her, but I don't know from where."

"Isn't that the woman who was at Dad's funeral?" Vidal asked.

Carlos said, "That's where I know the face. I never talked with her, though."

"Neither did I. I don't think she talked to anyone."

I said, "So, neither of you know her or have ever talked to her. In that case, meet Sheila Neverdowski, assistant campaign manager. Your father was very fond of her. Since she showed up at the funeral, it's possible she liked him as well."

The waiter arrived again, this time asking for our food orders. When he left, I continued with what was as much an interrogation as an interview.

Chapter 22: Main Course

"I need your help to clear something up." I looked from Vidal to Carlos and then back to Vidal again.

"Sure. Anything," Carlos said.

Vidal nodded her assent.

"There's a contradiction between what the two of you have told me about Vidal's relationship with her father."

I turned and looked directly at Vidal. "It's about the frequency with which you interacted with your father. I know you and Carlos understand the stakes here are very high. Two people have been killed. We don't know why, and it's possible that other people may be in danger, and that includes both of you. I can't be worrying about conflicting stories from people who are interested in helping me find out who killed Arnie. I need accuracy, completeness, and no exaggeration in any direction."

"I don't know what you're talking about," Vidal said.

"Carlos, would you help her out here?"

Carlos looked across the table, leaned forward, and spoke directly to Vidal. "Sure. Glad to. Apparently, you told Frank you had only met with your dad once in several years, but your dad told me you were getting together on a fairly regular basis during the Thurman campaign. He told me you wanted introductions to some of Thurman's supporters. He thought you were after clients."

Vidal didn't say anything. She pulled her chair back and got up. I thought she was going to walk out. Instead, she said, "I'll be back in a minute." She looked around, found the sign for the restrooms, and headed in that direction.

Jackie looked at Sam and then at me and said, "She's really upset. I'd better go with her." She got up and followed Vidal.

"Did I say something wrong?" Carlos asked.

"No," I responded.

"Think she'll stay?" Sam asked.

"Probably." I answered. "Jackie is…"

"Full of surprises," Sam finished my sentence.

A few minutes later our meals arrived along with Vidal and Jackie. They both sat down. I don't know what Jackie and Vidal talked about, but there was no preamble. Vidal said, "Yes, I did want to get access to potential clients, but Dad offered. It was his idea. I'm under a great deal of pressure to bring in new clients as a condition of becoming a partner. He wanted to help. I didn't tell you about the meetings because I didn't want my stepfather to find out. Gary gets crazy about my father. I think even my mother would be upset if she thought Dad was helping me. I didn't think not telling you would matter. The only important thing is that my father was worried, so I didn't mention the other times we got together."

"Anything else?" I asked.

Vidal looked at me. At first I thought it was anger or even hate. Then she took a breath. "I was ashamed of my father and what he did. I didn't want you to think I condoned it or was using him in spite of how I felt about it. I guess I am ashamed of myself for having done that."

She turned to Carlos. "We talked on the phone, but there were only three meetings, by the way. He started it. He called me, and that was out of the blue, and it was just coffee the first time. It was the last time we got together that he told me about the files and that something was going wrong in the campaign."

I asked, "Do you understand why your omission is important?"

"Not really," she said.

Carlos said, "Jesus, Vidal. He's got to be able to trust you."

"Let me make it simple," Sam offered. "If you want us to help you, we determine what's relevant together. We're talking with several people, so we will see connections you can't."

I added, "Also, I was surprised at your hesitation about getting together tonight here in Westport."

Vidal took a deep breath. "Okay. I didn't want to come here. There's someone I didn't want to run into, but it has nothing to do with my father. It's a former boyfriend. He lives in Westport, and we used to come here all the time."

"Vidal, why didn't you just…"

"I get it, Frank. Please don't lecture me."

"Let's eat," Sam said and broke the tension.

We ate in silence. Within a few minutes, comments were made about the food. Finally, Vidal asked me, "What else did you want to talk about?"

"Sam and I are concerned about the ownership of the information in the files and whether you, or we, had the legal right to be looking at them. We know that your father had a non-disclosure agreement with every campaign he worked on, including the Thurman campaign. There is a copy in his files."

"Goes without saying," Carlos said. "There was always an airtight NDA."

"So," I continued, "I called my son who's a lawyer with Lawton, Chase, and Harrison in New Haven and I asked him to do a little digging. He talked with some of his colleagues. I'd like to read you the email he sent me if that would be okay? I'll also give you a copy."

"Yes," Vidal said.

I pulled a copy of Ben's email from my briefcase and read it to the group:

> *Here is hallway thinking from me and Emily.*
> * *Arnold Nunnely was a member of the Connecticut Bar while he was employed as a consultant by the Lee Thurman for Senate Campaign. However, he was not functioning as a lawyer. The campaign was not anticipating or preparing for any litigation that we know of. It is doubtful that he would be representing them anyway since he hadn't functioned as a lawyer in years. While attorney-client privilege does survive death, this may not*

be an issue because there is no litigation involved. For the same reason, "Work Product" does not attach.

- *The Non Disclosure Agreement (NDA) that you found in his files is comprehensive and is applicable. However, Ms. Banks was not a party to the agreement and neither was Nutmeg.*

- *If the Lee Thurman for Senate Campaign engaged in any illegal activities, and if the people, or the campaign, were prosecuted and the information from the Nunnely files was used in the prosecution, the campaign could sue Vidal Banks and possibly Nutmeg, but the suit would likely be thrown out. Admissibility of the information battle would be between the campaign and the prosecutors. However, if the defendants were found innocent, a suit could go forward, but if it is a close call, and your intentions and those of the prosecutors were on the side of the angels, it is doubtful they would win, but, you would have the expense of defending yourselves.*

- *From what you said, the two super PACs who are involved, Moving Connecticut Forward and A Prosperous Connecticut, may be the organizations who were involved in the criminal behavior. However, if there was any direct relationship between these two super PACs and the Thurman campaign, that would be illegal. If Nunnely had no formal relationship with the super PACs, and no agreement with them, everyone is in the free on this.*

- *Vidal Banks, the recipient of the files, is an innocent recipient of information she did not know existed, did not request, and had no knowledge of what was in the files. Neither did Nutmeg. Nunnely was deceased. The NDA would not carry forward outside of his firm and firm's employees and/or sub-contractors. Vidal was neither. Nutmeg was neither. Nutmeg's relationship is with Vidal Banks, not Nunnely, and Nunnely was already deceased at the time you were employed by Vidal Banks. Bottom line, we think you are free to use the data and to turn it over to federal and state prosecutors with no liability on her part or yours. As always, anyone can sue about anything. Winning is a different question.*

If you want us to take this out of the hallway into an opinion memo, the meter will have to start running. Let me know.

When I finished reading, Sam said to Vidal, "Given this, we at Nutmeg are fine with using the files in our investigation. Are you? Or would you like to have an opinion memo either from Ben's firm or a firm of your own choosing?"

Vidal looked at Carlos to see if he had any objections. When he didn't, she said, "No, I'm comfortable with this."

"Okay. Sam, Jackie, and I will keep going through the files. As Jackie told you, we are moving from current to older files. Our assumption is his sense of threat had more to do with the current campaign than with previous ones."

"Absolutely," Carlos said.

"However," Sam warned, "that sense of threat does not necessarily mean that the murder emanated from this campaign. He probably had hundreds, maybe thousands, of people who would have been happy to see him dead."

"Of course, but respectfully, I disagree," Carlos said. "I've known that man for years. Sure, people got mad at him, threatened to sue him, and probably threatened him once or twice, but this was different. He was scared. Real scared."

"Carlos," I asked, "Was he ever specific? Did he name any names or hint at anything?"

"No, but it was this campaign. I'm sure of it. You ask me, I think it was something to do with the super PACs and people getting scared he would turn into a whistleblower. This was going to be it for Arnie. He told me that. No more. If he told people in the campaign that he was going to retire, they might figure that he wouldn't care anymore about his reputation for keeping his mouth shut. I don't know. He even talked about writing a book."

"A book?" Vidal said. "He never said anything to me about writing a book."

"Look, I don't know if he ever talked to any agents or publishers," Carlos said. "He was definitely thinking about it though. Said he had an outline and everything. Can you imagine? A book about political campaigns by the dean of oppositional research, Arnold 'The Assassin' Nunnely. Immediate best seller."

I turned and looked at Jackie. Her thumbs were flying on her smart phone. She sensed my looking at her and looked up. "Making a note to look for the book outline in the morning."

"What do you think, Vidal? Someone or someones in the campaign get scared enough to kill him or have him killed?" Sam asked.

"I thought he was upset because he had crossed the line with the way he was treating Gene Douglas," Vidal said. "Even if he hadn't planted the stories about those other women, the Douglas people wouldn't have known that, and he couldn't very well go and tell them.'"

"Did he say anything specific?" I asked.

"Not really. He just said he was tired of messing with the lives of people who were basically good."

"Do you think he was afraid of any repercussions from the Douglas campaign? Did he receive any threats?"

"Not that he told me about."

I turned to Carlos. "What do you think about the possibility of someone associated with the Douglas campaign?"

"No way. Gene Douglas is a big boy. He's been around a long time. The stuff about him and Wilkins was true. The stuff about these alleged current affairs? Damaging as hell in the campaign, but something to kill over? Nah. Given what you guys have turned up so far, I'm betting on the Saudis."

"You sound convinced."

"The more I think about it, the more I am. They're pumping money into getting this guy elected. Arnie did tell me that in the campaign there was talk about running Thurman for President some day. Maybe they're buying themselves a President, illegally mind you, and here's Arnie, this little Jewish guy who is retiring and isn't going to give a shit. That might have scared the hell out of them."

Sam said, "A lot of suppositions."

Carlos answered, "Yes, but it makes sense. More sense than most anything else at this point."

Jackie was thumbing away as she said, "I can search through all of the file memos tomorrow and see if there is anything there that might be helpful."

"Okay," Sam added. "Let's see if we can get some specificity of threat. If not, there may be danger themes that he may not have put together himself."

"What do you mean?" Vidal asked.

I responded, "He may have expressed dismay, concerns, or anxieties at different times and in different ways which produced a generic feeling of unease but may have been illusive to him because he didn't have all of the dots connected. Jackie's going to see if there are dots to be connected. Sometimes a victim can unknowingly point in the direction of an assailant without knowing that they have done so. In this situation he didn't give either one of you anything specific. It doesn't mean it isn't there."

"I'm going to do some digging, too," Carlos said.

All of us looked at him.

He said, "I've got more experience with this shit than all of you put together."

Vidal said, "Please, just be careful."

"He was my friend," Carlos replied.

Driving Vidal back to Stamford, I asked her how she was doing with all of this. She said, "I'm finding it terrifying and exhausting." She was asleep by the time we got to her condominium complex.

Chapter 23: Missing Pieces

I t was Wednesday, January 16, 2019. It had been nine days since Vidal Banks walked into my office. I was supposed to know who had killed Arnold Nunnely by now, at least according to my internal evaluation system. It was snowing again, a wet sloppy snow, the kind that you skid in. Two cars had slid off the steep entrance ramp trying to get onto the Merritt Parkway in Fairfield. So I had to back up, retrace my route on Newtown Turnpike, and then get stuck in the traffic trying to get onto the Connecticut Turnpike. I was going to be late getting to the office.

Walking Blackie in the wet morning snow had already taken longer than usual as I tried hard not to fall on my butt. This morning had been an exercise in pure love and devotion and prompted me to once more think about fencing in the back yard so I could just open up the door and let him out. Or, better yet, I could install a pet door and he could come and go as he saw fit. But why would I do that if we were seriously thinking about moving? I admit I'd been thinking about fencing in the yard for a couple of years, but it somehow seemed like a lazy way out and not fitting of the devotion I felt to my furry partner.

Today, Eve was the lucky one. She was staying home to revise a paper she had submitted to *Political Theology*. One of the "blind" reviewers had commented that a couple of her paragraphs lacked clarity. Her revision efforts were conducted to the accompaniment of: "Is he an idiot?" "Ugh," and, "What the hell is he looking for?"

To dampen my spirits even more, Lee Thurman was a United States Senator, probably illegally, and I was sitting on information that I knew the FBI would want, and I knew they would be more than a little upset if they knew I had it and not given it to them. Add to that I had more information to give the Boston P.D. about Arnie's reason for being there – he was not an innocent bystander in the wrong place at the wrong time. Someone wanted him there, knew he'd be there, and had a plan.

I hoped someone would have brought in more than fruit this morning. I considered stopping at Billy's Bakery on my way, but that would have made me even later.

When I finally got to the office, Claire stopped me as I headed for the conference room. "You had three calls. I forwarded them all to your voicemail."

I headed to my office and started retrieving the messages. The first was from my neighbor, Norm Burchill. "Frank, I called Jason McCloud and left him a voicemail explaining how I knew you and that you would like to talk to him. He has not gotten back to me. I also called his assistant, Sheila Neverdowski. She said she would be glad to talk to you. I've sent you an email with her contact information. Hope this was helpful. If I hear from McCloud, I'll let you know."

The second call was from Henry Gore. "Frank, I've given this a great deal of thought. I don't want to provide you with introductions to the Douglas family. They've suffered enough. I cannot believe Gene or anyone close to him had anything to do with the unfortunate demise of the Assassin. Sorry."

"Damn it, Henry," I thought to myself. "Now how do I get into that campaign and find out what was going on there when Arnie was killed." Henry Gore was starting to really piss me off. He loved to posture, and now he was taking on the role of protector-in-chief. I wondered if Eve might be able to talk him into giving me the introductions.

The third call was from Carlos Barlotti. "Hey, Frank, like I told you last night, I'm going to do a little digging into these payouts from the Saudis to McCloud. I used to be really good at this stuff. I'll let you know if I find anything. Least I can do. Oh, and thanks for dinner last night. Not as good as Mario's, but not bad. And don't worry about Vidal. She can handle this. Basically, you get past the posturing and she's a good kid."

I called Carlos. No answer. I left him a voicemail asking him to call me as soon as he could. I sent him a text saying the same thing. The last thing I needed was Barlotti stirring things up, things that he was not prepared to handle no matter what he said.

I sent Gore a text thanking him for giving it some thought and saying I understood. Then I opened the email from Norm and transferred the Neverdowski contact information to my phone and headed for the conference room.

Jackie was buried in the computers. She had earphones on. No pajamas this morning. She had graduated to jeans. Even her Bruins cap was on the table in front of her rather than pulled down on her head. She didn't hear me come in so I walked around the table where she could see me. She stopped typing, slid the earphones down around her neck, and said, "He not only had an outline, he had written two chapters. They both pre-date the Thurman campaign, though. However, if anyone knew he was writing a book and they were in it, wow. He wasn't holding anything back. Are campaigns really this dirty?"

"I guess some are," I said. "And he specialized."

"I tried doing the kind of search you talked about to see whether he had any idea of who might harm him, but I wasn't sure what to look for. You're going to have to help me. I'm not sure what kind of search terms to use."

"I'm not sure either. We'll have to try different words and names and combinations and see what pops up. I need to make a call first. Anything to eat around here?"

"Fruit in the fridge."

I must have made a face because she smiled and said, "Eat healthy, Frank."

I went to my office and dialed the mobile number that Norm had given me for Sheila Neverdowski. She answered on the first ring. "Ms. Neverdowski, this is Frank Kelly. Norm Burchill gave me your number. He said he spoke with you yesterday."

"Yes, I was expecting your call." She sounded flat to me: no excitement, no anxiety, nothing.

"I'd like to get together if we could, to talk about the Thurman campaign and Arnold Nunnely."

"I know. That's what Burchill told me." Again, her voice was absolutely devoid of any engagement. I wondered if she was this way all the time or just being that way with me.

Then she added, "I also got a call from Mr. Nunnely's lawyer, a Mr. Barlotti. I directed him to Mr. McCloud."

I thought, *Damn it, Carlos*. I responded with a weak, "Really?"

She asked, "Do you know what he wants?"

"No, I really don't. I was wondering if you had any time, possibly even today, for the two of us to get together. I know that you and Mr. Nunnely worked with one another, and I believe that you attended his funeral."

She said, "I'm back home in New York."

I had no idea what that meant other than that New York was home. She didn't say where she had been.

"Not a problem," I said. "I'd be glad to come and see you there."

"I guess that would be okay if you don't mind making the trip." Still, no personality, no engagement.

"I'd be glad to. Norm did not provide me with your address though, or we could meet someplace else."

"When would you get here?"

"Would late afternoon work for you?"

"Yes, I can do that. How will you be coming?"

"I'll take the train." There was no way I was going to try to drive in and get caught in rush hour traffic on the way back in this weather.

She said, "Why don't we meet at the Madison Club in the Roosevelt Hotel? It's right next door to Grand Central Station?"

"That would be fine. What time would be convenient for you?"

"Shall we say four o'clock? How will I know you?" she asked.

"I'll find you. I'm sure there are pictures of you online at campaign events."

"Of course."

"I'm looking forward to meeting you. See you at four in the Madison

Club."

Carlos Barlotti did not call me back. I left another message and texted him again. I let him know that I had heard back from Neverdowski, hoping that would get him to pull back from doing anything foolish, or doing anything at all. I told him to be patient.

Jackie and I spent the rest of the morning trying all kinds of words and word combinations. I thought, "Come on, Arnie, help us out. Tell us who was scaring you."

Some things did become clear to us. He was disgusted with the Thurman campaign, and he wanted out of the business. It was also clear that he did plan a tell-all book and he had started work on it. What I found interesting in his outline was that was he going beyond a tell-all. He planned to describe how he had worked. In some ways the book was to be a combination of how to be a great oppositional researcher and stories of campaigns in which he had destroyed the opposition. Given the current political climate, I'm sure it would have been a best seller.

I finally decided to try something ridiculously simple. We put in people's names and searched for how often the names appeared in his file memos, starting with Jason McCloud's. First, we pulled out all of the paragraphs in which McCloud's name appeared. We then arranged them into a timeframe.

When McCloud first joined the Thurman campaign, Arnie was delighted: "A real pro," "hard hitter," "he'll stay out of my way." Over time his language changed: "McCloud doesn't give a shit, anything goes," "vicious," "no class," "fucking crook." A confrontation with McCloud was reported in one of the last memos: "I told him that he was not going to get away with it and if the feds found out, we were all going to serve time, including Thurman. He said Thurman didn't know anything about it and even if he did, he would be okay with it."

Look for the conflict, I told myself, and there was no escaping it – Jason McCloud and Arnie were disagreeing about the money coming into the super PACs from the Saudis. I wondered how much Sheila Neverdowski knew.

I drove back to Fairfield so I could leave my car at the station and be closer to home when I returned from New York. I planned to catch the two-nineteen which would get me into Grand Central at three fifty-five if it was on time. I texted Neverdowski my travel plans and told her I might be a few minutes late. Then I called Eve, told her my plans, and asked her if she would walk Blackie.

"Of course," she said. "But I need something from you."

"Anything."

"That, my love, is a foolish statement; just remember you said it."

"Okay, what do you need?"

"Get on one of the cars where you're allowed to use your phone. I want to read you the revised paragraphs along with the reviewer's comments. I want you to tell me if I've addressed his concerns."

"Are you sure? Political Theology is not exactly my field. I didn't even know it existed until I met you."

"That's a good thing. And by the way, I'm not sure this reviewer understands it either."

"Oh, so if I can understand it, the reviewer should be able to."

"Something like that."

"Okay, I'll do my best."

"Believe me, your best is far better than this idiot reviewer."

"I love your confidence in me."

"Call me when you get settled in your seat."

"Will do."

And I did. By the time the train arrived at Grand Central Station, I think I actually understood what she was writing about: The relationship of Reinhold Niebuhr's Christian Realism to Liberation Theology and Paulo Freire's *Pedagogy of the Oppressed*.

Chapter 24: The Madison Club

I had spent years in Manhattan and knew it well – as a student. I had received my bachelor's degree, a masters, and finally my doctorate, all from the John Jay College of Criminal Justice up on 59th Street. In all those years, I never stepped foot in the Roosevelt Hotel and certainly not the Madison Club with its stained-glass windows behind the bar, its billiard room, and its twenty-dollar hamburgers. On the other hand, I could tell you all about the Greek Kitchen on 58th street or Justino's Pizza next door.

It was ten after four when I found Sheila Neverdowski. She was in the main room of the lounge at a table as far back from the entrance as she could get.

In the internet campaign pictures I had seen of Neverdowski, she seemed to be glued to her cellphone, or, if she knew a picture was being taken, she'd be forcing a smile. I found her easily. She was a tall woman with big shoulders, lots of hair, and a long face. She looked younger in person than in the pictures I had seen. She was probably in her late twenties and wore no make-up. She wasn't smiling when she got up and extended her hand. "Thank you for making the trip."

"Thanks for taking the time," I replied.

We sat. There was a glass of white wine in front of her. She said, "I didn't know how late you might be, so I went ahead and ordered. I told the waiter to come back when he saw you arrive."

"Thank you." As if on cue, the waiter arrived. I ordered, "Sparkling water with some lime, please."

"Would you prefer Pellegrino or Saratoga, sir?"

"Let me try the Saratoga." He left.

Neverdowski asked, "Your trip in was okay?"

"No problems. Everything was on schedule."

"During the Thurman campaign, I'd take the train back and forth to

Greenwich all the time. I used to leave my car there so I'd have it when I had to drive around to different meetings and events in Connecticut. Kept me from having to fight the traffic getting in and out of the city."

"Manhattan's home for you?"

"I'm a native. I've spent my whole life here. Went to school here, from kindergarten right through to the twelfth grade at Dalton; then Cooper Union for art."

"And then…"

"Spent a year looking for work as a graphic artist." She was as wooden in person as she had been on the telephone. Still, I picked up an intensity, as if a wrong word or look would bring about some kind of explosion. I had no idea whether it would be anger or tears, running away or throwing something. With Sheila Neverdowski I sensed there was a very narrow path with an abyss on either side. If I asked the wrong question in the wrong way, she might jump up and leave. The problem was I needed her. I didn't know if she needed me.

"How did you wind up working in politics?"

"By accident. I had taken courses in the New Media and the Visual departments at Cooper. During the summer between my junior and senior years, one of the alums posted that he needed an assistant producer on a project. I responded. It turned out to be working on a political campaign, everything from video to web design and social media strategy. I enjoyed it. He asked if I would work with him during the year after school started. I did and stayed with him part-time after I graduated while I looked for work in graphic design. When that didn't pan out, I stayed with him doing political work. Eventually, my name got out and it was really just word of mouth. That's how I met Jason McCloud."

"Had you worked with him before the Thurman campaign?"

"No. I'd met him before because he had been involved in New York campaigns as a bundler and sometimes as a consultant."

"A bundler?"

"That's a person who solicits money for a campaign, stages events,

193

and primarily collects checks. It can get pretty shady at times, but every campaign has to do it. Being a bundler buys you a lot of influence and makes you a kind of network hub if the candidate wins. Officially, there's no lobbying and no one is registered as a lobbyist, but bundlers have the ear of the candidate before and after the election. Thurman was the first campaign where McCloud actually managed a campaign."

"How did McCloud get this kind of influence?"

"There's a lot of people like McCloud in politics. He called himself a public relations consultant. He had lots of clients, mostly from the Middle East from what I understand. He was a wheeler-dealer type and knew tons of people. He was connected. In Republican circles, he was the equivalent of a mafia *made man*. My mother called him a 'flasher' when she met him."

"A 'flasher'? I'm not familiar with that term, either."

"Always glad-handing, very smooth, well dressed, manicured, oily." Her woodenness was on the edge of bursting into flames.

"What did you think?"

"I was surprised when he joined the campaign, especially as manager. I was more surprised when he brought me on as his assistant."

"Why?"

"He didn't know me that well. Apparently someone recommended me. It was a good opportunity for me to get my name known, so I said yes."

"What was he like to work for?"

"At first I thought he was just a big talker."

"And then…"

"He is one of the most despicable excuses for a human being I've ever met. He lies, cheats, and all he cares about is himself."

"You had run-ins with him."

"I guess you could call it that."

"What do you mean?"

"He couldn't keep his hands to himself. He propositioned everyone under thirty."

"Including you?"

"No. I wasn't his sweet-young-thing type. Two of the women who reported to me were though. They told me what happened and when I said something to him, he just laughed and told me to stop being such an uptight prude and to go get a life."

"What did you do?"

"Nothing. I talked to Arnie about it."

"Not to Thurman."

"No. Lee was never really available for that kind of discussion. Lee thinks because he's rich, he knows everything and should be running the country. Campaigns don't have the human resources infrastructure of organizations, so there was no one I could really talk to and get any satisfaction. Anyway, it went on for months. I can only tell you that McCloud is evil, but slick. He would have talked his way out if it. Besides, Lee was full out and I didn't want to distract him."

"Any idea why Thurman hired McCloud? Did he know him?"

"Not really. The problem was the campaign's polls were stuck. They had a lot of early positive momentum and then nothing. Connecticut's a purple state leaning towards blue. If the polls had stayed where they were, Douglas would have won. People don't like change, and that Senate seat had been held by a Democrat forever."

"Whose idea was it to bring on McCloud?"

"One of Lee's business partners. He said McCloud would bring new life to the campaign and we needed to take the gloves off and go after Douglas if we wanted to win."

"So, the gloves came off?"

"Did they ever. Arnie was happy as could be. He had all the information on Douglas he needed and couldn't wait to use it. Lee had held him back while the polls were moving in his direction. When that stopped and McCloud came on board, McCloud convinced Lee that he had to hit hard and hit often."

"And then…"

"The polls moved a little; I think we would have won if we had just stayed with the old story about Douglas and that woman back when she was in the State House. Winning wasn't enough. McCloud wanted to produce an electoral mandate. He wanted Thurman to be the next big Republican hope."

"Hope?"

"Presidential. The biggy."

"What did McCloud do?"

"Spread lies and spent money. Douglas never had affairs with those women. Totally fabricated by McCloud. I was the one who had to get it out on the internet and make sure it went viral. It made me sick, literally. The push poll did the rest. I hate them. I was responsible for executing it, though: 'Would you vote for Gene Douglas if you knew he was still having affairs?' McCloud wrote it. I got it out there."

I didn't say anything. I waited for her to go on.

Finally, she said, "I know you're judging me. Your judgments can't be any worse than my own. I needed the money. I was building a career. I wanted to be the Republican Mandy Grunwald."

"Sorry, I don't know who that is."

"Democratic media person, a Clintonista. Probably the most successful female media consultant ever."

"So you were hesitant to rock the Thurman boat?"

"Arnie advised against it. His motto was: candidates come and candidates go, but we go on and on."

"Mercenaries."

"When you are in the top tier, a highly paid mercenary."

Again I didn't say anything and waited. She had become more animated, but something was still off.

"Then Arnie told me about the super PAC money, where it was coming from, and McCloud taking a 'finder's fee.' I was disgusted. I wanted to resign. Arnie begged me not to. He said it could be dangerous. He was afraid of McCloud and his international connections. I'm not entirely sure why. He told me to just ride it out. So, I did."

"When did Arnie tell you about the money?"

"About two weeks before he was shot. We were working late at the campaign office in Hartford. No one was around. Arnie had been drinking. I think he was a lonely man. He didn't want to go to the hotel where we were all staying. So he drank and talked. I listened. He kept talking about what had happened to Khashoggi and how the Saudis could get to anyone. He was also afraid of going to jail. He said if the money trail led to the campaign, we were all in jeopardy."

"And then he was killed. Yet you stayed with the campaign."

"I didn't dare leave. I stayed on and left the week before the election. My work was done. They paid me. I came back to New York and crawled into a hole."

"Tough going."

"Horrible nightmares. I feel like a coward for not blowing the whistle on the campaign finance violations."

"How are you holding up?"

"Therapy twice a week. Anti-anxiety medication. I feel like I'm sleep walking most of the time."

"Is there anything I can do to help you?"

"I don't think so. I don't know."

"I'll be glad to help if I can."

She ignored my offer and continued. "McCloud keeps calling me and wanting to get together. I've given him excuse after excuse. The last time he reminded me that I had signed a non-disclosure agreement."

"Did it sound like he was threatening you?"

"Not specifically. He was almost joking about it. I got the message, though. Then he asked me if I had another campaign lined up. I told him I didn't, that I was taking some time for myself. I don't think I'm going to relax until this is all out in the open. I worry that it might never happen. Then I worry that it will."

"Okay if I ask you some very direct questions?"

When she didn't answer me, I decided to just go ahead and ask. "Do you think Jason McCloud is responsible for Arnie's murder?"

She surprised me. She said, "No, I don't."

"You sound very certain."

"Jason was with me when Arnie was killed. We were in a campaign staff meeting."

"You're sure."

"Absolutely."

"Okay, another one. Was Arnie preparing to blow the whistle on McCloud?"

"Not that I know of, and I doubt it."

"Because?"

"Arnie was smart. He told me he was retiring and wanted to retire quietly and very rich. I can't see him jeopardizing that."

"He ever say anything about writing a book?"

She chuckled. "Everybody in this business talks about writing a book. Some do. Most don't. Arnie might if he retired and got bored. I don't know."

"Did he ever say anything to McCloud or Thurman about it?"

"I seriously doubt it, but others on the staff heard him say it one night when we were having drinks in Hartford. We all laughed."

"So it wasn't considered as a serious possibility?"

"No. Just one of those booze things that Arnie would say."

"Sheila, given what was going on in the campaign and Arnie's reactions to it, can you imagine McCloud or anyone with the campaign arranging for Arnie to be killed?"

"McCloud? Hire someone to kill Arnie? Are you serious?"

"Yes."

"Really? Now, you're scaring me."

"Sorry, I don't mean to."

"I don't know. I really don't."

"You said Arnie was scared? Of McCloud? What was he scared of?"

"All of it. He was just scared."

"Sheila, I don't know quite how to ask this because it's so general, but do you have any information that you think might help me find out who killed Arnie?"

"No."

There was nothing else to say. I thanked her for the time, paid the tab, and was just able to make the five twenty-eight which would get me into Fairfield at six forty-six. I called Eve and let her know what train I'd be on. Then I tried Carlos again. Once more it went to voicemail. I had been leaving messages on his mobile number. I called the home number that Vidal's mother had given me. His wife answered.

"Ms. Barlotti, my name is Frank Kelly. I was wondering if Carlos was in."

"No, I'm sorry. He isn't."

"Would you mind telling him I am trying to reach him when you see him.?"

"Not at all. I thought he might be with you."

"Why is that?"

"He said he was working with you on something to do with Arnie Nunnely."

I felt on the spot. We had met. We weren't working together. I fudged, "Yes, we have met a couple of times, but I haven't seen Carlos today."

"Oh. Well, if you hear from Carlos would you tell him to call me. I thought he'd be home by five."

"Certainly."

When I hung up, I called Sam and told him about my meeting with Neverdowski. When I finished, I added, "Not one piece of information that is helpful. I learned some new words and that's about it."

He teased, "Ain't investigations fun?"

"Thanks a lot. How'd you make out?"

"Let me look at my notes. Okay. Leslie Cahill, Arnie's secretary, had very little to do with the operations of the place. She described herself as his bookkeeper rather than his secretary. She was responsible for making sure invoices went out, the bills got paid, and the tax records were all in good order. She was mother hen to all the part-timers, you know, the trackers, or whatever they're called, when Arnie would ruffle their feathers because they weren't getting him what he wanted.

"She did confirm that he was going to retire at the end of the campaign. She also said that, to her knowledge, Vidal had only met with him a few times, but she wasn't sure exactly how many since she didn't have access to Arnie's calendar. Apparently Arnie only told her when he was going to be in and out of the office, but he didn't give her a lot of detail.

"I got the feeling she didn't like Vidal very much. She also said Carlos would come to the office every once in a while, sometimes on legal matters, sometimes just to hang out. She's very fond of Carlos."

"Anything else?"

"Not much, but I think you'll be interested in this. Two things. First, Carlos called Leslie at home today asking her for contact information from the Thurman campaign. She told him that anything she had, she had given to Vidal when they closed the office. Second, she confirmed what we heard from Vidal and Carlos – that Arnie was really on edge for a few weeks before he was killed and that was quite different for him, especially because the campaign was doing so well in the polls."

"Did she have any idea why?"

"No."

"Shit."

"Yeah. What's up with Carlos?"

"He's decided he's a top-notch investigator again and he's gone silent. I've been trying to reach him. So has his wife. Nothing. All calls go to voicemail. No responses to text messages."

"What's your guess?"

"I haven't a clue. What concerns me the most is that he has not gotten in touch with his wife."

"Is that unusual for him?"

"According to her – very."

Chapter 25: Chipo Honore

I was frustrated. Everything I was learning from my interviews was opinion, with a few facts thrown in. What did I actually know? People who knew him said Arnold Nunnely was scared. Jason McCloud was a misogynist creep and a campaign manipulator who had zero respect for truth and campaign finance laws, but so far there were absolutely no dots tying him to the murder of Arnold Nunnely. Motive? Possibly, maybe even probably. But not one provable link between McCloud, or anyone on his staff, to a drive-by murder at a bus stop in Boston. Maybe the police were partially right, but three shots center mass? No way. This was an intentional murder, and the target was Nunnely.

Henry Gore had shut down the only link I had to the other side of the campaign where there might be a motive, *might* being the key word. Carlos thought Gene Douglas was too experienced to launch a vendetta, but I felt I had to pursue the possibility that someone associated with Douglas, or Douglas himself, had something to do with the murder. I had to consider it, even if simply to eliminate the possibility so I could start looking some other place.

I called Eve and told her how frustrated I was and how incompetent I was feeling. She said, "So, let's enjoy a nice dinner tonight at Avellino's. We'll work it off tomorrow morning at Takuma's. You and Blackie have both been slackers."

"Great idea." I smiled. She knew me and exactly what I needed – not a pep talk, not empathy – I needed to feel competent at something.

Takuma's was Takuma's Endo, where I had been a long-time teacher of martial arts. I loved him and the space he'd created. He had remodeled an old Bridgeport factory into a state-of-the-art martial arts center that included a meditation room, quiet rooms for yoga, and a basketball court. Eve had been going to yoga classes there since we got together. It was a second home for me and had been for years.

When we got to Takuma's the following morning, I went straight to the locker room and changed, and then Blackie and I headed for the basketball court. It was early and I was able to enlist Takuma, himself, on the way. When we got to the court, Takuma started setting up obstacles while I got Blackie into work mode. I took him through basic obedience commands while I was right next to him and then from the other end of the court, facing him and then with my back to him. Then we ran the obstacle course a few times. It was harder on me than it was on him. We did some tracking exercises that engaged Blackie's three hundred million olfactory receptors and forty percent of his brain. In the gym we could only do air tracking. Ground tracking in winter ice and slush was not my idea of fun. That's what our weather had been for over a week – snow a little, warm a little, freeze a little, snow some more. New England winter crud.

Finally we cleared away the obstacles and Takuma got dressed in his protective gear. He walked towards me, shouting and waving his arm in a threatening manner. Blackie stood right by my side, waiting until I said, "Placken." Off he went. Takuma started running away. Blackie was on his arm and tugged him down within seconds. "Aus," Blackie let go. "Pas auf, Gib Laut." Blackie went into the guard position and barked loudly at Takuma. "Hier." Blackie stopped barking and returned to me. "So ist brav." I leaned down and scuffed his neck. He stood up on his hind legs and gave me a kiss. It was obvious he was in good shape, but what about me? It had been two weeks since I had done a rigorous workout.

Takuma took off his protective gear and walked over to us. "Come here, Blackie." Blackie went to him and got some more loving. Takuma asked, "You want to warm up and then do some sparring? Remember that kid you taught years ago, Greg Landry?"

"Vaguely." I had taught hundreds of kids over the years I had been with Takuma.

"Well, he's now in college and has gotten quite good. He'll be here in a half hour."

"Sure," I said. "Why not?"

An hour later Greg and I began sparring. He was fast and strong; at twenty he should be. But he was also predictable, and I had no trouble blocking every one of his moves. The more I blocked, the more frustrated he became. The more frustrated he became, the more mistakes he made. Then I started to go on the offensive. Five minutes later I was feeling as competent as ever. Greg laughed it off, bowed, and said, "Someday."

I responded, "Maybe next year."

"Debrief?" he asked.

"Sorry, but I need to get to my office."

Takuma had been watching. "I'll do it," he said. "He'd be too kind to you, anyway. I won't."

"Great. Thanks a lot, Frank."

"Any time."

Eve was waiting for me and Blackie in the lounge area when I finished showering and dressed for work. "How'd it go?" she asked.

"We both did quite well," I answered.

"Good. By the way, I just got an email from Henry. I think he was feeling badly being so obstinate about not wanting you to talk to Gene. He sent me contact information for Gene's campaign manager and suggested you talk to her. She's a tough cookie and may be reluctant, but Henry included her in the email so she knows what's going on."

"You talked to Henry, didn't you?"

"We may have had a little chat."

"Thank you, darling."

"You're welcome."

Chipo Honore was Haitian according to the biography I found on the internet. A graduate of Sarah Lawrence with a master's in Foreign Affairs from Georgetown, she was fluent in English, Creole, French, and Spanish. She had gotten into politics through work in Costa Rica, Ecuador, and Chile. Returning to the United States, she was recruited by one of the Democratic campaign consulting groups.

Marriage and children pulled her off the campaign trail and into the Hartford office of United States Senator Raymond Walcott, where she worked for several years. With children launched and Walcott retiring, she was wondering what was next when Douglas, at Walcott's urging, asked her to run his campaign for Walcott's seat. It was to be her first campaign as the lead. What was supposed to be a slam dunk turned out to be a disaster. It was not an auspicious beginning to her new career. I wondered if she would see me, let alone open up to me. She agreed to see me. She wanted to defend him – from me.

She invited me to meet her at her home in Simsbury, a rural suburb of Hartford. Rated the fourth-best town in which to live in Connecticut, Simsbury is small with around twenty-five thousand people and Chipo must have stood out when she shopped at the local Stop & Shop. Simsbury was ninety-five per cent white, as was her surgeon husband. They had met when she was at graduate school and he was in medical school at Georgetown. His last name was not Honore.

Driving down the long driveway past fenced in pastures, I noticed the barn first, then a cute sign warning of horses: *Whoa. Horse crossing.* I wished I had looked the property up on Zillow. I was guessing a couple million easily. Maybe more. I was sure their children, now adults, had been raised with their own horses and had competed. There were two horse trailers parked under a carport-like structure that jutted out from the barn.

Chipo Honore came to the door after the first ring. Perhaps a bell had sounded as I entered the driveway a quarter of a mile away. She led me into a large entrance hall facing an elegant staircase leading to the second floor.

I don't know what I had expected. Her hair was covered in a bright blue scarf and she wore a white loose-fitting top that set off her black skin. She wore jeans and was barefoot even though it was a cold day and there was snow on the ground. As informally as she was dressed, she was elegant.

"I have a fire going in the library. Would you like something to drink? I have some hot water on: cocoa, tea, coffee?"

"No, thank you."

"Well, I'm going to make myself a cup of cocoa. It's definitely a cocoa day. Are you sure you won't join me?"

"I'm fine, but thank you." I realized I was a bit anxious and I had no idea why.

She told me to make myself comfortable, and when she returned with a cup of cocoa in her hand, she began, "So you're investigating the death of Arnold Nunnely."

"Yes, at his daughter's request."

"Losing a parent is always very difficult. Losing one in this way must be horrible for her."

"I think it is. They were not close, which in some ways, I think, has made it more difficult."

"Hmm. I can see that. How can I help you, Dr. Kelly?"

"Please, call me Frank."

"How can I help you?"

I noted I was not invited to address her as Chipo. "I know you spoke with Henry. I'm convinced that Nunnely was the target in that shooting. He was not an accidental bystander."

"Henry did tell me of your beliefs."

So that was how she was going to play it. "Ms. Honore, it is more than beliefs. The forensic evidence is quite clear. He was shot three times. The shots were grouped in the middle of his chest. He was assassinated. None of the others were shot in the same way nor with the same weapon."

"I thought the police were calling it a drive-by shooting and that Nunnely was an innocent victim."

"They're revisiting their original theory."

"I didn't realize that."

Damn it, Henry, I thought.

I continued, "In addition, Nunnely had received a message telling him to be at that specific bus stop at that time."

"Oh."

"You can understand why I use the word assassination."

"Yes, I guess I can. Do you or the police have any suspects?"

"We're pursuing leads."

"Which is why you're here."

"Which is why I'm here."

"I can assure you Gene Douglas had nothing to do with it."

"How can you be so sure?"

"He was at a campaign rally in Winstead when Nunnely was killed. I was with him. One of our campaign workers heard the news on a Boston station and told us. We talked about it driving back from Winstead that night."

"Do you have any thoughts about who might have done it?"

"Not specifically."

"Not specifically?"

"No."

"How about un-specifically?"

She smiled, "I'm not being very helpful, am I?"

"No. A man was deliberately killed."

"He was not a nice man."

"He was a father."

"And you're working for his daughter."

"Yes, I'm working for his daughter."

She had been sitting on the couch with her legs tucked up against her body. She uncurled herself and leaned forward. "I do understand, but I'm not sure I can help."

I looked at her and wondered what her "can" meant. Did she mean she was obligated not to help, or she had no useful information? I asked, "Who associated with the campaign, or the family, was most affected by what Nunnely did? I'm not saying that would mean they had anything to do with the assassination, just who was the one most affected?"

She answered quickly, "It certainly wasn't Gene. He and Sandra had both expected that the Wilkinson situation might emerge the minute we knew that Nunnely was involved. Nunnely loved bringing up old scandalous affairs if he could find them. We had actually been more worried about the way the campaign was already going. The money Thurman was spending was staggering for a senate race, and the message that Gene was not sophisticated enough to be a player on the world stage was having an impact. They never said, 'Because he was a local black boy,' but that was the underlying message. And it was working. The Wilkinson story added to the narrative and it, too, had an underlying racist appeal, an old one: black man and white woman."

"And then…"

"The fabricated stories about sexual liaisons with non-existent women."

"That must have made people furious."

"Of course it did."

"Gene? Sandra?"

"Not because of the stories as much as the impact it had on Vivian."

"Vivian's their daughter."

"Yes. High school sophomore. The cruelty of high school students knows no bounds. She was called names. Her father was called names. She was taunted, mostly by white boys. Horrible things. They wanted to know if she was like her father and wanted some 'white meat.' The teachers and administrators were not at all helpful."

"Must have been awful for her. What did her parents do?"

"Gene and Sandra don't have a lot of money, but they pulled her out of public school and enrolled her in a private Catholic high school even though neither one of them is Catholic."

"Was that better?"

"In school, yes. Outside of school she was still a target of abuse. She wound up retreating into herself and staying home most of the time. There were some other problems and she began therapy."

"Who else was affected?"

"What do you mean?"

"Any other family members? Don't they have a son?"

"Frederick's in college. Boston University. I don't think any of his college classmates cared. It was Connecticut after all, not Massachusetts."

Her demeanor and voice had changed just a little. I decided to take a flyer. "A lot of older brothers feel very protective of their kid sisters, especially in this kind of situation."

"Have you heard something?"

I said, "Just generalities. Can you help me with the specifics?"

"There was one boy in particular who was tormenting Vivian. Frederick confronted him and started a fight with him. Frederick is not much of a fighter, though, and the other boy was much bigger. Frederick came out on the bad end of the battle which didn't last more than a couple of minutes."

"Any damage?"

"Bruises and a tooth. I think more pride than anything else."

"What did he do?"

"His parents read him the riot act and he went back to school."

"When did this happen?"

"I'm not sure. Maybe late September. Possibly early October. The fabricated stories hit at the beginning of October so it was probably October. Why?"

"Just curious."

"You're not suggesting Frederick had anything to do with Nunnely's death, are you? Frederick was not involved in the campaign. He didn't talk much about it with his parents."

"I'm not suggesting anything. I was just curious. Who else was affected by the accusations?"

"We all were. I had exquisite fantasies about what I would like to do to Nunnely, but they were fantasies. I never did anything. No one did. We just countered as best we could, but the narrative was already established and we were not able to recoup."

"I've been asking everyone this: do you have any thoughts about who might have killed Nunnely?"

"No. Given Nunnely's complete lack of ethics and cruelty, I think a lot of people would have at least thought about it. I know some people felt he had it coming to him when he was killed."

She took a sip of her cocoa before continuing, "What about Thurman and his people? Nunnely would have been looking into Thurman. Did Nunnely find out things about Thurman? Thurman is scum, smart scum, but scum, and Jason McCloud is even worse."

"So I've heard."

We spent time talking about the campaign and all of the people who were involved. I asked her about members of the family, background information, almost as though I was a reporter who was going to write a campaign puff piece. Chico described the Douglas family glowingly, lovingly. At one point she said, "Imagining them doing anything illegal, or as horrible as murder, is ridiculous."

She told me family stories. One story caught my attention. Chico told me that at the end of his junior year at Boston University, Eugene Frederick Douglas, Jr., told his parents that he had legally changed his name. He didn't ask permission or tell them ahead of time he was going to do it. He dropped his given name, Eugene, and told them that henceforth he was to be known as Frederick Douglas in honor of former slave, author, and orator Frederick Douglass. It wasn't much of a change. He had always been called "Rick" to distinguish him from his father. Furthermore, it was to be Frederick, not Fred or Freddie, and absolutely not "Rick." The newly renamed Frederick had just finished reading all three of Frederick Douglass's autobiographies as part of his minor in African American studies. Only one had been assigned.

Chapter 26: Called to Boston

O n the way back from Simsbury I got a call from Vidal. "Have you heard from Carlos?"

"No. I've been trying to get in touch with him myself. I even called his house and spoke to his wife. She seemed concerned and asked if I knew where he was."

"She just called me and left a voicemail. He didn't come home last night, and she's worried. She said he's never done anything like this before. She knew we had met for dinner and wanted to know what we had talked about. What should I tell her?"

"I'll give her a call."

I had nothing to tell Carlos's wife. I started second guessing myself. Should I have been that concerned about the differences in the stories that Vidal and Carlos had told me about her relationship with her father? Did the difference really matter that much? Should I have told Carlos about what we were finding in Arnie's files? I never expected that this would activate him. If anything, I was trying to scare them both. I wanted them to be careful.

When I reached Carlos's wife, she was frantic. She said, "He loved Arnie and would have done anything for him. Carlos also hated how old he felt and, in his head, he was still a thirty-year-old. He told me he could do a better job than you were doing and he was going to prove it. He was acting nuts he was so excited."

"Do you know what he planned on doing? Where he was going?"

"No. The only thing he said was he was going to track down some man by the name of McCloud and get information about him."

"Have you called the police and reported him missing?"

"No. I thought you had to wait twenty-four hours."

"No, you don't. That's a myth. You can report him as missing now. Carlos is over sixty-five, right?"

"Yes."

"Good. Tell the police you want to file a *silver alert*."

"What's a silver alert?"

"It's a generalized alert that goes out to the media as well as several agencies in addition to the police when a senior is missing and has dementia or Alzheimer's."

"Why? There's nothing wrong with Carlos."

"I know, but a *silver alert* gets much more attention than a missing person notification and it will be broadcast on the radio and sometimes on local television. Local hospitals will immediately check on any John Does they have. I suggest you do it right now. Have every piece of information you can think of ready for the police: car registration, driver's license number, social security number. Check any credit card expenses he has had since last night. Give the police anything they ask for. I'm also going to call my partner, Sam DeRosa, and have him call the Norwalk detective bureau. I know it sounds strange, but since he's only been missing since yesterday, it will get more attention."

"Okay. I'll do it right now."

"One last thing. Is there any place that you can think of where he might go if he wanted to get away?"

"Like what?"

"Is there any place the two of you go, or that Carlos goes on vacation, or just to escape for a couple of days."

"No. What are you thinking?"

"If he stirred up a hornet's nest, he might choose to go someplace other than home. Did he take a computer with him?"

"Let me look."

She was back on the phone in a minute. "He took his iPad."

"Does Carlos have a gun?"

"Now you're really scaring me."

"I understand. There may be nothing to worry about, but I thought I should ask. Does he?"

"Not that I know of."

"Good."

"I'm going to call the police. *Silver alert*. Are you sure?"

"Yes."

"All right. I'll do it."

She hung up. I called Sam and told him about the conversation.

"Damned fool," Sam replied. "Good thinking about the *Silver Alert*."

"He's going to be really pissed if that's how he turns up."

"Serves him right. I'll call Norwalk. I know several people there."

"So do I, but I thought it would be better coming from you."

"Probably. What are you going to do?"

"About Carlos, nothing right now. I want to find out more about the Douglas kid."

"What are you thinking?"

"He was angry enough to get into a fight, he lost, and it happened just before Nunnely was killed. Apparently, the parents were able to handle the shit thrown their way, but the kids took the brunt of it, especially the daughter. Frederick is very close to his sister and may have been much more tuned in to what was going on in the campaign than his parents, or anybody else, was aware of."

"What are your next steps?"

"First, I want to check with the detectives in Boston and then I want to learn more about the program the Douglas kid was in at B.U."

"The program?"

"Classes he's taking. Stuff like that."

"Why?"

"Because I need something to do and it may help me get into his head a bit."

"Okay, professor. I'm going to call Norwalk."

"Thanks, Sam."

Back in the office, I went on to the University website. I already knew Frederick was a sociology major with a minor in African Studies. Chico Honore had told me he had spent the summer in

Zanzibar as part of his program. I didn't know specifically what classes he had taken, but I could get a good sense of what he might have taken from the school website.

Reading the course descriptions, I became fascinated by some of them. They made me aware of my own ignorance.

- CAS AA 316 African Diaspora Arts in the Americas
- CAS AA 385 Atlantic History
- CAS AA 396 Atlantic Africa and the Slave Trade
- CAS AA 489 The African Diaspora in the Americas
- CAS AA 514 Labor, Sexuality, and Resistance in the Afro-Atlantic World
- CAS AA 588 Women, Power, and Culture in Africa

Moving around the online catalog, I paused and read the description of the Zanzibar summer program and wondered what it must have been like for Frederick to come back home and encounter the things being said about his father. Then he would have learned about the abuse being heaped upon his sister when she started school in the fall. I wanted to talk to him, but would he talk to me?

Going through the catalog I found something that caught my attention. B.U. encouraged students to participate in an outreach program before their Freshman year began: *Participants will build connections with Boston, its neighborhoods and people, community organizations, our campus, and each other.*

I wondered if Frederick had participated in that program and what he had done. I wondered what friendships he had developed.

I called Chipo back. She answered on the first ring. "I'm glad you called. I was about to call you."

"Oh. What's up?"

"After I talked to you, I called Gene and told him about our conversation. He was not happy about it, nor about the fact that you got to me via Henry. He chewed me out for not having checked with him first and even more so for having told you details about his kids."

"I'm sorry to hear that."

"You should also know that he's calling everyone connected with the campaign and asking them not to talk to you."

"Do you think I should call him?"

"I doubt that he would accept your call."

"I'm sorry if I've caused you any trouble."

"I'm sure it's nothing that will not pass. However, I'm not willing to give you any more information. I'm not sure I have anything more that you would be interested in anyway."

"I understand. Thank you for letting me know, though."

I hung up and I called Gene Douglas. He answered the phone. I introduced myself. He said, "Go to Hell and stay away from my family and friends or I will start filing harassment charges." He hung up.

I called Henry Gore. My call went to voicemail. "Henry, I just talked to Chipo Honore and to Gene Douglas. It looks like I've stirred up a hornet's nest. I'm sorry if I've put you in a difficult position. I know Gene is a friend of yours."

I called Eve and left her a message telling her what had happened. She called back about ten minutes later. "You're doing your job. I think everyone thought this was all behind them and it clearly is not. Do you think Frederick might have been involved?"

"I have no idea. But I can't discount it. He sounds like an angry young man."

"What are you going to do?"

"Try to find out more about him."

"Good luck. Can we change subjects?"

"Sure."

"The broker sent me a listing for a place that looks perfect. It's in Stratford, on the Housatonic River, and has its own marina and a boat slip that comes with the unit. Two bedrooms, two and a half baths. The price is right."

"How much?"

"Three-seventy."

"You're kidding."

"No."

"When can we see it?"

"Tonight."

I hung up and started to call Detective Colm Galvin in Boston when Claire buzzed me. "You have a call, but he wouldn't say who it is. Should I put it through?"

"Sure."

I answered my line, "Frank Kelly."

"I hear you want to talk to me?"

"Who is this?"

"Frederick Douglas."

"Gene's son?"

"No, I'm a fucking ghost."

"Sorry, how can I help you?"

"You want to talk to me?"

"Yes, I'd like to, but your father has made it clear he doesn't want me talking to you."

"That's how I knew you wanted to talk to me. I make my own decisions. He doesn't tell me what to do."

"I understand, but I don't want to cause any problems for you with your father."

"Do you want to talk to me or don't you?"

"Yes, I'd like to."

"If you want to talk to me, you're going to have to come here."

"Here being?"

"Boston."

"When would you like to meet?"

"Tonight. Seven o'clock. Just you."

"Where?

"Franklin Park. Entrance off Sigourney Street where Robeson comes into Sigourney. There's a crosswalk on Sigourney that leads into the Park. Be on the Park side of that crosswalk."

"Why are we meeting?"

"Do you want to talk to me or don't you?"

"Yes. I'd like to. We're talking now."

"Fuck you."

"Why there?" I asked.

"Because I live there, and I don't want anyone to see us talking together."

"You live in the H Block?" I asked.

"Fuck you. You want to talk to me, that's where I'll be." He hung up the phone.

I waited, wondering if he would call back. He didn't. I called Eve. "There's a chance I might have to go to Boston tonight to meet Gene Douglas's son. Could we reschedule with the real estate agent, or would you mind going alone?"

"There's no way I'm going to see any of these places alone. We really need to walk in together the first time we see a place. I'm just getting used to this together thing, and I like it."

"You're sure?"

"Absolutely."

"Okay, then we'll reschedule."

"I'll call her later. When do you think you can make it?"

"How about first thing in the morning?"

"Can't. Class."

"Afternoon?"

"Wait a sec." I knew she had switched to her calendar screen.

"I can be back by four."

"Perfect."

"Tell me about tonight. Sam going with you?"

"Kid wants to meet me in Boston at Franklin Park and wants me to be alone."

"You're not going to do it are you? It sounds like Arnie all over again."

"I'll have Blackie with me."

"Frank, don't be an idiot."

216

"Don't worry. I'll be careful."

I knew she would worry. I also knew Frederick had information. I had a hard time thinking he was stupid enough to try to repeat a Nunnely type ambush. He had to know I would tell someone I was meeting him. He probably wanted to show me something about how it had happened. What did he know? How in hell did he know anything about the murder?

When Sam arrived in the office, he thought the exact opposite. "Bullshit. He's a kid. Kids do stupid things."

Chapter 27: Franklin Park

Of course kids do stupid things. I had taught in a college for too long not to know that. Kids from so called "good" families can be idiots. Still, Chipo Honore's defense of the Douglas family was unreserved, as had been Henry Gore's. The "good family defense" was being applied to Frederick and Vivian and the parents.

I couldn't help but think about the absurdity of the New Jersey judge who didn't want an accused sixteen-year-old rapist tried as an adult. The judge's reasoning: he was from "a good family" and he was doing well at school, and he was going to get into a good college. The victim, a teenager, was intoxicated when the boy raped her. Since when did "good families" always make good kids. And what the hell was a good family anyway?

Sam made it clear, I was not going alone. Nutmeg's ex-state police weapons expert Pat Brady and Sam would both be there. So would Jackie. When I began to argue that Frederick had said to come alone, Sam shut me down. "You're my partner. I hear you about what Frederick wants, but this is non-negotiable and you're going to be wearing a vest. First, you don't know for sure that it was Frederick on the phone. Second, you don't know who this kid has been hanging out with. Third, Nunnely went to the H Block in response to a similar call."

I stopped arguing. I knew he was right. Maybe I had gotten caught up, at least a bit, in the "good family" myth. The image of Arnie Nunnely getting shot three times in the chest floated across my consciousness.

Our plan, although it was really Sam and Pat's plan, was simple. Sam would be on the street dressed in a big overcoat. He would use a walker with a bag. Inside the bag would be two Glock 22's each loaded with thirty-round magazines. He would have additional magazines in his coat pockets. He would walk and look like an old man on his way home from who knows where.

Pat would be in the Nutmeg van with an assortment of weaponry including two HK416s, each capable of firing 100 rounds in ten seconds. The van would be dirtied up and wearing signs advertising a Boston painting contractor. License plates would be swapped out to be from Massachusetts. The Connecticut plates would be kept in the van, just in case they needed to be quickly swapped back. The van would arrive at its parking place at 5:00 PM, an hour before I was supposed to meet Frederick.

Jackie would be in the van with Pat. We would all be wearing communication devices. In addition, Jackie would be scanning the surroundings with infra-red video cameras that made nighttime and darkness a non-issue. We would all be wearing vests. On this day I appreciated Sam and his love of toys even more than I usually did.

We debated talking to the detectives in Boston about the planned meeting and finally decided not to. At this point all that we could tell them was that the son of Thurman's opponent wanted to talk to me. We had nothing connecting Frederick to Nunnely's murder. That Frederick went to school in Boston would be treated as a *so what*.

An entrance to Franklin Park as a place to meet in January seemed strange but certainly nothing to get alarmed about, unless Frederick Douglas had been responsible for Nunnely's death, and we had no reason to believe that he had been. Still, the choice of place nagged at me.

I did want to find out if Detectives Dolan and Malone had uncovered anything new in the days since I'd talked to them. I also wanted to ask about the three cars that Joe Lewis had seen, the car that dropped Nunnely off, the car the shots had come from, and the third car, the one that had stopped and then driven away.

I called the investigations bureau and asked for Alice Malone. She had been far less hesitant about my involvement in the investigation than her partner, Brud Dolan. I was not interested in getting into a prolonged discussion with Dolan about how we should be working together and how we all wanted the same thing.

Alice was not as welcoming as I had expected her to be. She said, "I understand you convinced our boss that Nunnely's death was an assassination and he was not a by-stander victim."

What I wanted to say was, "Okay, Alice, so you and Dolan missed the three shots to the chest as evidence that this was anything but the murder of an innocent by-stander, I picked it up, and you two wound up looking like jerks." Instead, I tried to stay professional. I had promised their boss I would share information, so I did: "Yes, that's our belief. Sorry if it caused any trouble. I wanted to tell you about something else we've discovered that I thought would interest you."

"What's that?"

"Nunnely received a call telling him where he was to be and at what time. We think he was set up."

"Who did you get that information from?"

"His own notes."

"Seriously? His notes."

"Yes. He took notes on everything." I sounded much more collaborative than I was feeling. I continued, "Actually, a car dropped him off there. He didn't drive himself."

"Who told you that?" Alice was questioning everything I said.

"Joe Lewis. The witness."

She said, "Can you wait a minute. I'm going to put you on hold. I'll just be a minute."

"Sure." I guessed she was finding Brud or her notes or both. She found both.

It was Brud Dolan who got on the line. There were no preliminaries. "This is Dolan. Lewis didn't give us any information about Nunnely being dropped off by a car."

"Really. Hmm." My collaborative mood was fading rapidly. "How about the car that stopped right after the shooting?"

"What car?"

"Mr. Lewis told me that another car slowed down and stopped right after he heard the shots from the first car."

"He didn't say anything about a second car."

"Okay, it may be nothing. In fact, Mr. Lewis thought it might be someone who just didn't want to get involved, so they took off. Did the two victims who lived say anything about a car that stopped?"

"No. Nothing. Lewis is probably right. I can see someone stopping, looking, and taking off. No one who lives around there wants to get involved." Brud sounded anything but kindly towards the residents of the H Block neighborhood.

I had been thinking about something ever since we learned that Arnie had been given a time and place to meet the mystery caller. We knew he had not taken his own car. Maybe he had taken the train from Greenwich and had taken an Uber or Lyft to the bus stop. Uber or Lyft wouldn't talk to me, but they would to the police. I asked Dolan to work for me. "Could you check with Uber and Lyft and see if they had a drop off on that date and time and find out where the pick-up was?"

I must have been on speaker phone. Alice responded, "Yes, we can do that. What are you thinking?" Her tone had changed.

"We know it probably wasn't a cab. I'm sure Mr. Lewis would have said if it was a cab. If it wasn't Uber or Lyft, then who drove him there?" I wanted to add, *Will you please start paying attention to this case*, but didn't. Instead I asked, "What have you folks been able to find out?"

Alice responded. I couldn't tell if Brud was still near the phone or had left the room. Given her answer, I assumed he had left the room. She said, "Nothing really. Honestly, we haven't done much digging."

"Caseload too big?"

"That's putting it mildly. Thanks, though, for keeping us up to date on what you've found."

"Glad to. Let me know what you find out about the car that dropped Nunnely off."

"Will do. Frank, one more thing."

"What's that?"

"I think it might be easiest if you and I communicate from now on. Galvin really reamed Brud out about missing the wound pattern. Brud's not feeling very generous about helping you."

"Fine with me."

A few hours later, Pat drove the van into the garage under the office building where Nutmeg has its offices. All of us gathered there. Pat, Sam, and Jackie put on their vests. All of the weapons were loaded. The communication devices were tested for transmitting and receiving. Jackie checked the video cameras in different modes.

When Pat asked me what weapon I was going to carry, I replied it had to be concealed, so my Glock 23. He shook his head as though I was hopeless. "Where's your 20?"

"Glove compartment. But that thing's too big to hide."

"Get it out. I have something for you."

With its five-inch barrel, I never thought of the gun as having a concealed holster, but Pat had brought a Springfield shoulder holster with him. Covered by my winter parka, there was no way you could tell I was armed. He also had two additional clips with him that would fit in the holster.

Pat said, "I have one more thing for you. Actually, it's for Blackie." He reached into the van and pulled out a small harness type Kevlar vest with a D ring. *State Police K9* was emblazoned on the top in white letters.

He handed it to me. "For Blackie. He'll have to wear it inside out, though."

"Where the hell did you get this?" I asked.

"Friends in low places," he answered as he started adjusting the straps to fit it to Blackie.

"Thank you."

Putting on all of this equipment, I felt like we were engaging in a dramatic form of over-the-top absurdity. When I said this, Sam, the ex-detective, and Pat, the ex-state trooper, both looked at me and shook their heads. Finally, Sam reminded me, "Are you forgetting last year?

You came close to having your head blown off."

"Sam, they were terrorists. We knew they were dangerous. This is a college kid we're talking about. He's never been arrested for anything."

"That's why you were going to wear your 23. Sure."

"Okay. I admit it. I'm a bit spooked. The call did come out of the blue."

"And he wants to meet you at the entrance to the park in the same neighborhood where Nunnely was shot. He's a college kid. So why didn't he try to get a free meal off you at The Cheesecake Factory or Legal Seafood? You damned well should be spooked," Sam replied.

"I don't know, Sam. He says that's where he lives. Maybe he doesn't have a car."

Sam just looked at me. So did Pat and Jackie. None of them said a word.

When my three colleagues left New Haven in the van heading to Boston, I took off Blackie's vest, my vest, and my gun and shoulder holster and put all of the gear in the back of my car. I wouldn't be leaving for another hour and after that I'd be in the car for a couple of hours more.

I wondered what was happening at that very moment in Boston. What was Frederick doing? What was he thinking? I thought about calling his father. Maybe it would be best if I told Gene his son had called me. I started to imagine the furor that would lead to. As Frederick had pointed out, he was old enough to make his own decisions and he had made it clear he wanted to see me alone. There was no good option.

I went upstairs to my office to wait.

Chapter 28: At the Park

I had an hour to kill. Jackie had given me both a map and satellite images of the neighborhood and the park where Frederick wanted to meet me. Sam wanted all of us to have a visual orientation to the site. I wanted more and I had the time, so, as usual, I went to Google.

Between Wiki and the park website I learned that Franklin Park was the largest park in Boston, five hundred and twenty-seven acres. It had a zoo, a stadium, ballfields, playgrounds, and wooded areas. It was considered to be the final, and most glorious, park in the "Emerald Necklace" of parks designed by Frederick Law Olmstead for the city of Boston. Developed in 1837, it had, during its lifetime, gone in and out of disrepair. Today, parts of it were still in disrepair.

I would be meeting Frederick close to White Stadium. The irony of the stadium name made me smile. One of the articles I read said that back in the sixties the Black Panthers used to hold rallies at White Stadium. The Black Panthers at White Stadium. I wondered if young Frederick Douglas knew about that.

The crosswalk where I was to meet him was close to a path that led to the Overlook Ruins. I loved the description of the Ruins: *Sitting lonely and overgrown in Boston's historic Franklin Park, these puddingstone ruins were once one of the only buildings ever designed by Frederick Law Olmsted, the father of landscape architecture, whose egalitarian ideals set the standard for public parks as a place equally accessible to anyone and protected from private interests.*

I focused more on the "lonely and overgrown" than the ideals of Olmstead. I wondered if Frederick's plan was to take me on a walk to the Ruins. At seven o'clock in the middle of January, it would definitely be a lonely place. Why had he chosen the park as a place to talk? Frederick had said he didn't want anyone to see us together. Was it really so no one would see us together? Who cared if we were seen together? Sam was right: wouldn't a restaurant, a diner, a bar, or a lounge at Boston University have worked just as well? Maybe he had information about Nunnely's murder he wanted to give me. If he did live close to the H Block, meeting there would make some sense. My mind was generating and sorting through "what ifs and whys" over and over again.

If Frederick's plan had been to take me for a walk into the park and to the Ruins, he was out of luck. Sam had a different plan. I wasn't going anywhere. I was going to stay put. That way both Sam and Pat could station themselves so they could see me and Blackie at all times.

About thirty minutes into my self-imposed tutorial on Franklin Park, Detective Alice Malone called. "You were right," she said. "Nunnely took an Uber from South Station. I also looked up the train schedules. He probably took an Amtrak from Stamford. All the timing works: train arrival, Uber pick up, and drop off. I have the name of the Uber driver and have a call into him."

"Alice, thanks. That answers at least one question. I really appreciate it."

"No problem. You still think the burned-out car in Providence was the killer's car?"

"It fits Lewis's description, which was pretty detailed."

"Yeah, it was," she agreed. "By the way, I've talked to Galvin and Brud and I've got the go ahead to go back and talk to Braxton and Wilson and ask them about a third car. It may have been a trailing car to make sure the killers finished what they came to do. Lewis said it slowed down, but maybe it actually stopped and someone got out and did a quick snatch of Nunnely's briefcase. That would account for the missing computer and cellphone."

"You may be right. Thank you."

"We'll see. Braxton and Wilson were really shaken up when we first interviewed them. It's been months now. I may get nothing from them, but they may at least acknowledge there was a third car."

"Or…"

"I'm thinking they may have recognized the people in the third car and were too scared to say anything about it. We'll see."

"Thank you for doing this."

"Glad to help. I'll let you know what I find out."

I thought about telling her about my upcoming meeting with Frederick but decided not to. All we had were dots, with no lines between them. If Frederick did have any information that would prove useful, I didn't want him to run away and take it with him because I lost his trust if the police got involved. Having Sam, Pat, and Jackie there was already bothering me.

I gave myself an extra half hour for the drive. I knew I'd hit traffic leaving Hartford in the middle of rush hour. It wasn't as bad as I thought it might be though, and I made good time. I stopped at the Willington truck stop on Route 84 and pulled around back where some big eighteen-wheelers were parked. I pulled in between a couple of them where I wouldn't be seen. I got out, opened the back of the car, took off my parka, and put on my Kevlar vest, then my shoulder holster with the Glock 20. I put the two extra magazines in the holster and inserted the third magazine into the gun.

I closed the back of the car and was putting my parka back on when the driver of the eighteen-wheeler next to me came back from his break and saw me. "That's a lot of fire power," he said suspiciously.

I took out my wallet and quickly showed him my state marshal's badge.

He said, "Oh. Good luck," and climbed up into the cab and started his truck, belching diesel particulate into the cold night air as the engine turned over and finally caught. He revved up his engine, engaged his low gear, and slowly moved towards the entrance to the highway.

I finished putting my parka back on and dangled Blackie's vest in front of me, figuring out the placement of the straps since it had to be inside out. Once on, the blackness of the vest against Blackie's all black coat made the vest disappear. We were ready to go.

As I had predicted, there was almost no traffic the rest of the way to

Boston. I knew where I was going because of my previous trip to the H Block and arrived at the crosswalk to the park entrance at six forty-five.

There was no parking allowed on Sigourney Street. I saw the Nutmeg van parked at the corner of Robeson and Sigourney facing Sigourney. I drove around the block and pulled in and parked behind the van. Without acknowledging the van or anyone in it, Blackie and I got out, walked down Robeson to Sigourney, crossed over Sigourney at the crosswalk, and stood waiting for Frederick to appear. When I was in place, Jackie called for a communications check, and we all responded. Everything was working.

Five minutes went by, ten minutes, fifteen minutes. I decided to sit down on the wall at the edge of the sidewalk right next to the path leading into the park. Another five minutes went by, but there was still no Frederick. A few cars passed, slowed for the stop sign – some even stopped – and continued on their way.

Another five minutes went by. The stone wall was cold. I got up and started walking around. I was beginning to wonder if Frederick was going to be a "no show." I didn't see Sam. I asked where he was.

"I'm up on Glen Road, at the corner. I can see you. I'll move when something starts to happen."

A couple of minutes later Pat said, "The black Dodge Charger. It looks like it's circling the block. Sam, has it come down Glen Road yet?"

"No. Haven't seen it."

Pat asked, "Do you think you've been made?"

"I'm scrounging in a waste bin. Doubt if anyone's paying attention to me."

"You might want to start moving," Pat said.

"Will do. I'll cross over to the park side of Sigourney now."

I went back to the wall I had been sitting on and stood there. I gave Blackie the command to stand, "Steh." A single command in German and he immediately knew I wanted him to be in work mode. He would stand exactly where he was until I gave him another command or

227

released him by saying "gut."

The black car drove by again, only this time it pulled into Robeson Street, stopped, backed up, and reversed direction. Rather than staying in the right-hand lane though, it switched lanes, drove over against traffic, and stopped in front of me. I zipped my parka down halfway.

The driver's window was open and the driver leaned out. I had seen enough campaign family pictures to know it was Frederick. He said, "Get in." With that the back door opened. I could see another man in the back seat and he was aiming a gun at me. I could also see there was a third man in the front passenger seat.

"What's this all about?" I asked. "You said we were meeting alone. What are these two doing here?" I could imagine Sam and Pat beginning to move when they heard me say there were two other people in the car.

The man in the back seat slid across the seat and swiveled towards me, half in and half out of the car. He said, "Do you want me to do him here?"

"No. He's mine." Frederick got out of the car and aimed a gun at me. I could hear the passenger side door open on the other side of the car.

"Frederick, what the hell are you doing? Why the guns?" I asked.

"God, you're an idiot," he said. "You want to know who killed that miserable piece of shit? I did. There. Satisfied? Want to destroy my family some more? Fuck you!"

He raised his gun. "Placken," I shouted. Blackie had two potential targets. He went for the man who was in the back seat and latched on to his forearm. A fit human male has the bite pressure of about one hundred and fifty pounds. A full-grown German Shepherd has twice that force. The man screamed in agony as Blackie's canine teeth sliced through nerves and muscle and his molars crushed bones.

Frederick started to swing his gun toward Blackie. When he saw me move my hand towards my parka, he brought his aim back towards me and fired. One, two, three times.

They all hit. The ballistic panel of Kevlar dispersed the energy across my chest. It felt like I had been hit full force by a baseball bat. I fell backwards onto the pavement and hit my head and lost consciousness.

Sam told me later that he had gotten his gun out when Frederick came out of the car. When he heard the shots, he fired. Some of his shots hit Frederick, some missed. Pat had gotten out of the van when he heard me ask about the other two people in the car. He already had his HK416 trained on the car. When Frederick got out of the car, the man in the front passenger seat had opened the door and started to get out. Pat could see he was carrying an AK-47. When Frederick fired at me, the man with the AK-47 started to move toward the back of the car. Pat shot him first in one leg, then in the other. Pat then shot out the front and rear tires on the right-hand side of the car and started running toward the car.

Blackie was still fast onto the arm of the man who had been in the back seat and was now on the ground where Blackie had pulled him out of the car. He continued to scream and punch at Blackie until Sam arrived and told Blackie to "Aus." Sam kicked the man's gun away and told him to stay on the ground. Blackie limped over to me and started to lick my face. I was just regaining consciousness when I heard the sounds of sirens and knew Jackie had called 911.

Chapter 29: The Aftermath

No one died that night at Franklin Park, but no one was happy. There was a great deal of pain, blame, and misery. Violence, guns, and shooting. So stupid, so predictable, and so unnecessary. Power and greed. Politics and lies and harm. Harm to innocents leading to fury.

Arnold Nunnely and Tom-Tom Garcia had been killed at a bus stop in October. Charles Braxton and Yvonne Wilson had been wounded and watched two people die. Power and greed. Politics and lies. Gangs or government. Didn't seem to matter.

It had all happened at an entrance to a beautiful park, the crown jewel of Boston's Emerald Necklace where Frederick Douglas and his two companions came close to being killed. And, if Frederick had aimed higher, I would have been killed.

The Boston Police Department detectives were furious. A shoot out was the last thing they wanted to happen, let alone have to investigate. Media, media, media. They knew the coverage would be extensive. The mayor wouldn't be happy. The police commissioner wouldn't be happy. Their bosses wouldn't be happy.

Brud Dolan called us a bunch of over-the-hill cowboys and swore he'd get our licenses revoked. That the Boston P.D. had one less homicide case to close did not seem to mollify him, even though it had been his case. All he saw were several people with gunshot wounds, two ambulances, a lot of guns, a growing number of neighbors, and two television trucks. At one point he even called the four of us a gang. When I told him he was being absurd, he threatened to arrest me. When I pointed out to him that I had not fired a weapon, he said through clenched teeth that Blackie was my dog and I, "…was responsible for what happened to that man's arm." Fortunately, Jackie had switched the license plates from Massachusetts back to Connecticut when she heard the sirens and saw the police cars converging. Using Massachusetts plates so the van wouldn't stand out was the one thing we had done that was illegal.

Frederick and Baako Johnson, the man in the back seat whom Blackie had tangled with, were loaded into one ambulance. I was loaded into the other with Jojo Johnson, who had been in the front passenger seat.

Blackie didn't want to leave me, but Pat put a lead on him and took him to the Nutmeg van. Jackie did her best to try to soothe him.

I was able to convince the patrolman who rode with us to make a call. I called Ben, gave him a very brief rundown, and said we would probably need a lawyer. He called back a few minutes later to let me know that he and his boss Emily were on their way and not to give any statements until they arrived. Emily had also called in a favor and a Boston lawyer she worked with was going to meet us at the hospital.

If Sam hadn't been so insistent on the vest and the plan we developed, I would have been dead. On the way to the hospital that awareness kept cycling in my head like a whirlpool. My marriage to Eve, my kids, their marriages, grandchildren, moving to a new home. I had put it all at risk, and for what? To prove I could "do" what I taught? I was alive, though, and bounced back and forth from being scared to being angry to feeling stupid, but I wasn't dead. Instead I was sore. Very sore. Frederick's bullets didn't penetrate my protective vest, but their energy did.

When we got to the emergency room and they took my vest off, I had big welts where the bullets had hit. I had turned various shades of red, black, blue, and yellow. I had been lucky. The emergency department x-rays showed that none of my ribs had been fractured or chipped. I had a big egg on the back of my head and a bruise from where I had fallen, but my loss of consciousness had been momentary. I was told to watch for signs of a concussion for the next twenty-four hours, but nothing developed.

On the way to the hospital, Pat took off Blackie's vest and turned it right side out. Seeing the State Police K9 vest, the emergency department security guards let Pat bring Blackie into the emergency room. He was limping and when I went to pet him, he whined. I asked Jackie to take him over to the Angell Animal Medical Center and get him thoroughly checked out. Because they had fired shots, the police wouldn't let Pat or Sam leave.

The Angell Emergency Department was faster than the one I was in, and Jackie called back with good news. Blackie was bruised from where he had been punched and thrown against the car while holding on as Baako Johnson fought to shake him off. Blackie might limp for a day or two but a complete set of x-rays showed that nothing was broken, but we were both going to be sore and taking painkillers.

Baako's arm would be saved, but it was going to take several surgeries and rehabilitation before it would be functional. Given that Baako was going to shoot me until Blackie stopped him, I wasn't feeling terribly empathic and I didn't care how long it would take, as long as his rehabilitation took place in jail.

His cousin Jojo was not so lucky. He would live, but it would take reconstructive surgery to save one of his legs. The other leg had severe muscle damage. He was alive though, and damned lucky Pat was such a good shot. Pat thought Jojo might have been wearing a vest and, fortunately for Jojo, made the decision to shoot him in the legs rather than the head.

Of the three of them, Frederick was the luckiest. Sam was about fifty yards away and firing quickly when he shot at Frederick. Still, Sam hit him twice – once in the shoulder and once in the hip. Frederick went down from the force, but no vital organs were injured.

It was early the next morning before we finally got out of there. Dolan and Malone took our statements as soon as all of the lawyers arrived, then the detectives and the lawyers met in a conference room someplace in the hospital. Ben and Emily returned and told us we could go home just as Eve and Meg arrived.

The hell Sam and I caught from Brud Dolan was nothing compared to what we got from Eve and Meg. Sam told me over lunch the following day that Meg didn't talk to him the entire car ride home. When she did talk to him at breakfast the next morning, she had told him, "That's it. You're retired as of right now. You're not going into the office today, tomorrow, the next day, or ever again. I don't care what you do with your time. I will take care of the business until we sell it or transfer it to Frank and possibly new partners, but you no longer have an active role. You are going to be the most silent of silent partners or you had better start looking for someplace else to live. You're done being a cop, and I'm done being a cop's wife."

Sam said he tried to protest that he wasn't a cop, but Meg would have none of it. He told me she said, "Stop it. Just stop it." She slammed the door on the way out and shouted, "I'll be at Vicky's."

Eve was loving but quiet in the emergency room. So was Molly, who had arrived with Ben. She had insisted on coming when he called her. When I finally got released and our lawyers said we could go, Eve and I dropped Molly off at my car so she could pick up Blackie and then drive back to Fairfield. When it was just Eve and me in the car, she was all over the place. She was furious; she was loving. She screamed; she was compassionate. When I asked her if she wanted me to drive, she basically told me to shut up and listen. My chest hurt and I appreciated the Percocet. When we passed through Hartford, Eve mercifully stopped and let me sleep.

I slept for a few more hours when I finally got home and then, against Eve's wishes, met Sam, Pat, and Jackie for lunch at Olives and Oil in New Haven. I left Blackie at home. My chest was still very tender and was now completely black and blue. Sam had offered to come to Fairfield, but Eve was working at home and I needed a break from the silence interrupted by the repeated exasperated question, "What were you thinking?"

Ben joined us for a few minutes at the restaurant to give us the latest legal update, but he had to get back to his office for a meeting. Because we were legitimate private investigators, and because we had been collaborating with the Boston Police right along, and because we were just being cautious, and because all of the weapons we had were duly registered, and because we were in imminent danger, and because Frederick and his companions were armed and intended to do me harm, and because Frederick fired at me before Sam or Pat fired, there would be no charges. It helped that the media was being very kind to us about our role in capturing a killer.

After Ben left, Sam asked me, "Have you talked to Vidal?"

"I wanted to get to her before she heard the news, so I left her a voicemail early this morning and she called back first thing. I was asleep, so she left me a message. We're going to talk tonight. I am concerned though. She's been keeping in touch with Carlos's wife. Still nothing from Carlos."

"You don't think…"

"No. I have a hard time believing that Frederick and that crew even know who Carlos Barlotti is."

Pat asked, "You think he's alright?"

"I have no idea."

Jackie said, "I liked him. Want me to do some digging? If his wife is willing and gives me numbers, I can go pretty deep. Might help."

"Legally?" Sam asked.

"Yes. Legally, if she gives me social security, credit cards, license, and all that stuff."

"Do it," I said. I was feeling responsible.

We spent the next hour over lunch debriefing the night before. None of us were in a rush. Sam had ordered a bottle of Prosecco to have with appetizers and a bottle of Sangiovese to have with our entrees. I had sips to be sociable, but even though I was only on Motrin now, I didn't want to test the lasting effects of the Percocet. We rehashed and rehashed. Sam insisted we each have a cannoli.

When we were finished with our meal, Sam picked up the tab. I was getting up to go when he said, "Frank, would you wait a minute."

Pat and Jackie left to go to the office.

After they had walked out the door, Sam said, "Meg's serious, Frank. I've never seen her like this. I'm done. She doesn't even want me to go to the office to clean out my desk. She's going to pack everything up and bring it home."

I didn't say anything and just waited for him to talk. He continued. "It's been a good run, but it's time for me to really retire. I knew it when I heard those shots last night. When I saw your chest at the hospital, I knew I couldn't do this to her anymore. You understand?"

"Of course."

"She expects you to step up and take over. You ready for that? She's going to start crunching numbers today."

"I don't know, Sam. Eve and I are on shaky ground right now. She's really upset with me. What about this young guy?"

"Jake Barlow?"

"Yeah."

"He's not ready to lead Nutmeg. You are."

"I appreciate your confidence."

"It's both of us. Meg wants to stay for about six months, a transition period until you…"

"Learn the financial workings. Spreadsheets."

Sam smiled, "Yeah, spreadsheets."

Chapter 30: The Home Front

Eve and I had not been together that long. I knew she was very smart, strong, compassionate, fun, and a wonderful lover. I knew, at a far deeper level, that she was a good person. I trusted that she loved me. I trusted that when she decided she wanted to marry me, it was the end of a process of discernment and prayer that was profound. Still, she had been clear with me. Even before the events at the park, she had said that she wished I would go back to teaching, that my work scared her. It made sense; she had lived through violence around me. We had just gotten together when I was shot at by terrorists. It wasn't that long ago, just a year, that I was trying to, and eventually did, save a young Turkish law student who was being used as a pawn in the political turmoil that was Turkey. Last night, though, was different. I was hit three times and only alive because Sam had ordered me to wear a Kevlar vest. This may have been too much for her. It may have been too much for me, too.

At dinner that night she said, "You know what I want, but it's your decision to make. Hon, I don't want to talk about any decisions for a couple of days. I think we both need time to process what just happened and what it means for each of us and for us together."

When she said that, it scared the shit out of me. "Are you thinking of calling off our marriage?"

"Please, Frank, don't ask me what I'm thinking right now because it changes minute to minute. When I look at your chest, I want to cry one minute and hit you the next. I need some time. Please, give it to me and don't push."

"So, you are thinking of…"

"Frank, please! What I want right now is some time and space to think."

"Okay. Take it." I sounded angry, but I was really scared. I didn't want to lose her.

Then she stunned me, "I don't want you to make more of what I am about to say than it means, but I've been on the phone with Em and she knows how upset I am. I'm going to have dinner with her tonight. I need to talk to someone and get some perspective. I'll probably spend the night at her house."

My fiancée was going to go have dinner with her best friend, who also happened to be my son's boss and the person who introduced us, and she was going to spend the night. I felt betrayed, angry, and frightened. Unfortunately, it was the anger that came out, a need to control events, a need to control her and keep her close. "Sure, go ahead. Go take some space. I'll still be here if and when you come back."

She was so much clearer than I was, so much more mature in that moment. She said, "I'll be back. I'm just going overnight. Frank, this isn't about whether I love you. I do. I just need to think about the kind of life I want for us, and, yes, for me. I was petrified last night. I can't lose you."

I'd stopped listening. "I'm going for a walk with Blackie. See you in the morning." I walked out. At least I didn't slam the door.

There was a light snow, and under different circumstances I would have thought it was beautiful. Blackie and I didn't walk far. Blackie was still limping and I didn't want him to overdo it. At one point we just stood and looked at the snow coming down. I became fascinated with the way it looked against the streetlights, the halo it made. When we started back, I saw Eve's car back out of the garage onto the street and then drive away. The garage door came down. I took a deep breath and felt as empty as I had when I first discovered that Patricia had a lover, a long-time lover, a lover who was a "doer" not a teacher. I knew that Eve was not Patricia, at least my head did, even if my stomach didn't.

I had been wonderfully happy these past months since Eve had moved in and then elated when she said yes to getting married. I had been looking forward to finding a place for us to live on the water. I had imagined a sailboat, right there in front of where we lived, in front of our place – not my place or her place – our place. I remembered reading once that hope was nostalgia looking forward. I was hopeful. That was it. I had been filled with hope, and now it was gone.

As Blackie and I walked back in the falling snow, I realized that it wasn't just Eve. It was my life. Retiring from teaching and joining Nutmeg was one of the best decisions I'd ever made. These past couple of years I had been feeling alive, like I belonged, like I was doing what I was meant to do, like all of my skills and interests had come together.

I remembered something a friend of Patricia's had said. She had left a job she loved and moved to Tucson to be with a man she was dating. When I asked her about it, she had said, "It's easier to find a good job than a good man." He was a teacher at the university there. She had found an "okay" job when she got to Tucson; they got married, and two years later she caught him cheating with his graduate assistant. She was still in Tucson as far as I knew. Was it really harder to find a good mate than a good job? I had no idea.

My anger returned. I was angry at everyone. I was angry at Nunnely for being such a despicable human being that he would do anything to get his candidate elected. I was angry at the whole political system that seemed to require that opponents destroy each other. I was angry at Thurman and Jason McCloud, especially McCloud, for lying about Gene Douglas and affairs that had never happened. I was angry at Frederick for being young and stupid and self-righteous and a killer. A killer. In his twenties. "Good family" was meaningless. And now Eve was driving to Emily's house to talk and figure out whether she wanted to stay with me. I was angry at both of them too. I was angry at Emily for inviting her; I was angry at Eve for going.

When Blackie and I reached the house, I was raging inside, a kind of rage that was new to me, a rage I had never experienced before. I had to go somewhere. I had to talk to someone. I had to go to Takuma's. I had to go to Takuma.

When Blackie and I got there, he was in his office. I talked, I raged, he listened, and slowly the rage began to go. When the rage went, the tears came. He listened. I found that I wasn't talking about Eve. I was talking about Patricia and her betrayal. I was talking about her dismissal of me and my work as a teacher. I went on talking for an hour or more. I would say something, he would encourage me to say more. Once in a while he would ask me to clarify something.

I started to relax. I came back to my distress about Eve going to Emily's.

He asked, "You like Emily?"

I said I did. He asked if I thought Emily was a good person. I said that I did. Then he said words that changed everything.

Takuma said, "I like Eve. She is taking care of herself. So are you. Soon you will take care of each other."

I chuckled. Damned wise Buddhist. I thanked him.

As I left the office and was about to open the door, he called to me, "Frank." I turned. He was standing, his hands were in front of him, his right hand was in a fist and nestled in his left hand where I knew his thumb was tucked under his fingers. The traditional Wushu greeting: I honor that place in you – the strength of the right fist, the humility of the tucked thumb, the friendship of the four fingers. I returned the greeting.

Blackie and I climbed the stairs to the third floor where the meditation room was. It was an hour before we climbed back down and headed home. Vidal called. I didn't want to talk and let it go to voicemail.

It was a hard night. The house felt empty and cold. It had taken me almost a year to get over the empty feeling after Patricia was killed. Tonight, it was worse, far worse. I had gotten more connected to Eve in one year then I had to Patricia in all of the years Patricia and I had been together. The talk with Takuma had helped a great deal as had the hour in the meditation room. Still, sleep wouldn't come. I was sore but probably didn't need the Percocet for pain as much as for sleep. It was cold out, but I opened the window more than usual. Not enough to freeze pipes, but enough to make me want to stay in bed. Blackie joined me.

The bedroom was very cold when I woke up. I closed the window, got dressed, and took Blackie for a walk around the block so he could do his business. When we got back to the house, Eve's car was in the driveway. I could smell coffee the minute I opened the door and the house was warmer. I unhitched Blackie and he ran into the kitchen. I threw my parka onto the bench in the hall and, for some ungodly reason, got very silly and shouted out, "Honey, I'm home."

The answer from the kitchen was, "Get in here you creep. How do you want your eggs? And tell your dog to get off of me." I started to get teary. I knew that she was home. Her back was to me when I reached the kitchen. Even though he had been limping, Blackie was standing on his hind legs with his front legs on Eve's shoulders and he was licking her face.

"Blackie, down." He disengaged and lay at her feet. "You could have done that, you know. He obeys you."

"I know, but I liked it, and it was more fun to complain." She walked over and hugged me. "Don't worry, I'll be gentle. How is your chest this morning?"

"Better now that you're here."

"I am here, you nutcase, and I'm not going anywhere, but I do have some things to tell you while I am cooking. And how, master of the house, would you like your eggs?"

"Yeah, master. Sure. Scrambled, please."

"You got it. Do you want to pop some toast in?"

"Sure."

"Pour yourself a cup of coffee, have a seat, and be prepared for a lecture. I couldn't sleep last night and spent a few hours on the internet."

I had absolutely no idea what was coming but did as I was told. Then she started.

"Did you know that being a policeman is the fourteenth most dangerous job in the United States. Logging is number one followed by fishing. I knew how dangerous fishing was, and logging makes sense to me. Then come roofers. That makes sense. Pilots are up there which really surprised me. But garbage men, truck drivers, farmers, groundskeepers, construction workers, and supervisors in construction work are all more likely to be killed or injured than police.

"Private investigators don't even make the list of the top fifty, probably because there aren't enough of you. However, the anecdotal evidence is clear that the degree of danger is highly individualistic. As one of your kind wrote, 'If you are doing forensic work, a paper cut might be the worst thing that ever happens to you.' However, if you are going after bad guys, which you have a knack for doing, it is probably closer to being a cop.

"So, given all that, if you don't want to return to teaching, which clearly you don't and I understand that, perhaps you should consider paper cuts as a viable alternative to bullets while maintaining your current occupation."

The eggs were done, the toaster delivered perfectly browned toast, which she collected, and added to our plates. She sat down opposite me. Her coffee was already there. Blackie was still lying down where I had forgotten to release him, "Blackie, in ordnung." He gave me one of those *It's about time* looks.

Eve lowered her head and closed her eyes for a minute. When she looked up, she smiled at me and said, "You sure you want to spend the rest of your life with an academic? We can be very boring."

"I do," I said.

"Right answer, but during the ceremony I believe it's now 'I will.'"

"We're getting married I take it." It was more of a question than a statement.

"Some doubt is often a good thing and can lead to stronger commitment, my love. Remember, I am very acquainted with doubt and consider myself to be somewhat of an expert. And, for me, this was the shortest doubt spell ever."

"Okay, what happened last night?"

"I talked, Emily listened. For a lawyer I am always amazed at how good she is at that. Then she reminded me of what I went through leaving the community and how hard and necessary that decision was to me. She asked whether or not I considered that it might have been the same thing for you when you left teaching. I confessed my total and complete lack of empathy to having ever considered that anyone in the world, let alone you, might have struggled with such a decision. When I did, I felt embarrassed, ashamed, and wanted to rush home. She stopped me and reminded me that the bullets were real, both this year and last year. And that it might be possible that it would happen again, and, if it did, what would I do? In other words, sleep on it.

"So, rather than sleep, I did what any good academic would do and hitched a ride on the information highway via Google, which I did and have already bored you with it. You must promise me, though, that you will not become a logger or a fisherman. A farmer I could handle as long as it was a gentleman farmer and we didn't raise anything that smelled too bad."

"I can make that promise."

"I got scared, Frank. I was more frightened than I have ever been in my life. I do want to ask something of you."

"What is it?"

"When you went after those terrorists, you did it alone."

"Sam was coming behind me."

"Frank!"

"It was stupid. I should have waited."

"And this time it was Sam who insisted you go prepared. What if Sam wasn't there? What happens when Sam is no longer active? Emily said something I had not thought about."

"What's that?"

"You know investigation. You know what makes criminals tick. But you're a novice when it comes to safety and safety procedures. You've never worked in a law enforcement agency where that kind of thinking is drummed into you until it becomes second nature."

"I know."

"Will you please have Sam train you?"

"Meg wants him out of the business. She wants me to take over."

"Are you going to?"

"Only with your blessing."

"Only if Sam or someone trains you. I'm sure Meg would not object."

"I'll ask."

"Right answer. You're getting the hang of it." She reached across the table and took my hand. "Now, tell me about your night."

I did. When I finished, she said, "We're really lucky to have people like Em and Takuma in our lives."

"Very lucky."

On Saturday when we woke up, Eve and I didn't read the newspapers or listen to the news. We left Blackie at home and went for a walk. While I napped in the afternoon, she went out and picked up an ice pack that was filled with little beads so it would conform to my body. I think it was more so she would have something to do rather than thinking the ice cubes wrapped in a towel that I had been using were insufficient.

Eve arranged for Ben, Molly, and Stan to come for dinner. She did something that I never thought would work. She said, "We'll talk about Thursday night for an hour and then we are off to the movies, *The Ballad of Buster Scruggs*. The movie was funny and at times very poignant. It was a great choice.

Sunday morning Eve went to Mass at Fairfield University. For some reason I picked up an old copy of *Huckleberry Finn* that I must have had since high school. I spent the day on the Mississippi or napping. I couldn't seem to get enough sleep.

243

Chapter 31: A Good Family

When Monday morning came, my chest felt better and Blackie's limp was imperceptible. I called Vidal after Eve left for school. I told Vidal about everything that had happened at the park. She listened, asked a few questions, and said something that surprised me. "That poor family. I can't imagine what they must be going through, and it was all my father's fault."

I told her, "I have to admit my own feelings and judgments are all over the place. The kid shot me. He wanted me dead. I hadn't hurt his family."

"I'm sorry, Frank. I understand, but you were investigating, and he knew that. His father had told him. He had to have felt threatened. I'm not trying to excuse him. He killed my father. I was talking about his family, not him. To me, they're the real innocent bystanders. My father was culpable in destroying Gene Douglas's political career. His methods hurt that entire family and also cost them a son."

I said, "It's a filthy business. Don't forget, though, your father didn't distribute the misinformation about Douglas having current affairs."

"No, but he didn't stop them or resign from the campaign either. I'm not kidding myself about who my father was. His moral compass pointed in whatever direction he thought would benefit his candidate, and him. I'm afraid my father's primary interest was in his reputation and his pocketbook. I hate saying that, but I am not going to delude myself."

There was no anger in her tone, just acceptance and clarity.

I said, "I agree with you. There are a lot of victims. Frederick's parents and sister must be going through hell. The kid's going to be charged with first-degree murder. Your father's memo about the set up for his meeting with Frederick, and then Frederick's confession about shooting your father, which we have a recording of, is probably enough to convict him. If the gun he used on me turns out to be the gun he used to kill your father, I have no idea what on earth his defense could be."

"What kind of sentence do you think he'll receive?" she asked.

"In Massachusetts? If he's convicted, it will probably be life imprisonment with no chance of parole. He'll spend the rest of his life in jail."

She said, "He's a twenty-year-old kid."

I was struck by her empathy. She sounded more sympathetic to Frederick than to her own father. I could tell that she blamed her father for all of this – his own death, Tom-Tom's, and now she saw Frederick's future as still another death. Maybe she was right. It was done, though. Tragically, it was all over except for the courts.

She said, "I can't help thinking in terms of, 'What if.'"

"What do you mean?" I asked.

"What if Dad had gone to another university and not gotten caught up in the whole Vietnam thing at NYU? What if he had worked hard and gotten into a good law school? What if he had been made a partner at Goldman and Bunch, or had gotten the promotion at the prosecutor's office? Would he have been so bitter? What if I had not gotten so mad at him and been more understanding when I was younger? None of this might have happened. He might still be alive."

I answered with pablum because it was all I had. "We'll never know."

She was silent for a moment before she asked, "Do you believe in atonement?"

"What do you mean?"

She said, "I'm not an observant Jew. I go to Bubbe's for Passover and that's about it. There is one exception, and that's Yom Kippur. I don't go to temple. I stay home. Believe it or not, I fast. I don't watch television or visit with people. Sometimes I do some writing or I read something; this year it was *The Wisdom of Hypatia*.

"I'm not familiar with that name."

"Fourth-century philosopher; extraordinary woman; incredible teacher. On Yom Kippur I do the best I can to reflect on my past year.

I'm afraid it's the repentance part I'm not so good at."

"What do you mean?"

"Making things right." Again she was quiet and then asked, "Frank, do you think you can atone or repent for another person's sins?"

Again I asked, "What do you mean?"

"Correct me if I'm wrong, but don't victims and family members of victims get to speak at sentencing hearings?"

"I believe they do in Massachusetts, but I don't know for sure."

"I'm wondering about approaching the Douglas family and offering to tell my father's story and not mince words about the harm that he has done in his life and to their family and that I hold no desire for revenge or retribution."

She was feeling far more generous than I was. "I'm sure they would welcome that."

"Do you think it would make a difference?"

"I have no idea."

"I'll have to figure out how to get in touch with them so they don't think I'm an enemy."

Henry Gore immediately came to my mind. "I think I can help you with that."

"Oh, that would be wonderful, and Frank, I'm still worried about Carlos. Have you considered that Frederick might have something to do with his disappearance?"

"I've thought about it, sure. In fact, I'm going to ask the Boston detectives to consider it as well. Honestly, though, I seriously doubt that any of them have any idea about what happened to Carlos. I'm going to ask the detective you liked, Alice Malone, to check on alibis for all three of them at the time we know Carlos went missing. My best guess, though, they don't know anything about it."

Vidal said, "I talked with Carlos's wife just before you called. Nothing yet. Frank, Carlos and Dad were close, and I hope to hell that he doesn't turn out to be still another victim. I know our original agreement was confined to finding out who killed my father, but would you consider staying on this until we find out what happened to Carlos?"

I was about to say, *I would like to, but I'll have to check with Sam*, but I stopped myself and said, "I'd like to do that." I'd check with Meg later.

She said, "I'll pay you your usual fees plus expenses. I want to see all of this right to the end, whatever it may be. I need to. Carlos, Frederick, all of it."

"I understand." Atonement and repentance. The daughter was taking on the sins of the father.

I called Meg and told her about my conversation with Vidal and my unilateral decision. Her answer was straightforward. "I agree. Just don't involve Sam."

"I won't. I may ask Pat and Jackie for help."

"You can ask Pat, but remember, Jackie's only part-time. She still has to finish this semester."

I said, "She's been so helpful that I forget that sometimes."

"By the way, I've ordered new business cards for you and have drafted a letter to our clients informing them about the transition. I'm going to have Claire help me pack up Sam's office, and I would like you to move in there as soon as you're ready. Speaking of unilateral decisions, I called Jake Barlow and invited him to come up for an interview with you. I hope you don't object."

"No, not at all."

This was really happening. Meg was moving quickly so there could be absolutely no doubt in anyone's mind that this transition was real. My appreciation for her grew even greater than it had already been.

I was still a bit shaken and needed to be with Eve. I didn't want to wait until dinner, so I called and asked if it would be okay if I drove up and could we have lunch together. She said yes, but she only had an hour, so I was tasked with picking up a salad for her and whatever I wanted for myself. In other words, please pick me up a Greek farro salad from the Crown Market on Albany and you can have whatever your heart desires, which was not a Greek Farro salad. We had done this before, and I had the Crown Market in my cellphone. I called on the way, ordered Eve's salad and a turkey on rye with coleslaw and Russian dressing for me. It was a Jewish deli after all, and since it was the Crown, a Dr. Brown's diet cream soda. I knew that Eve would be drinking tea.

When I got to her office, I was surprised to see Henry Gore sitting with her at her conference table. Well, maybe I wasn't all that surprised. They seemed to be engaged in a very serious conversation, so I knocked even though the door was open. Eve looked up, saw me, came over to the door, kissed me and said, "Henry needs to talk and he wanted to talk to you in person, so I told him to join us. Hope you don't mind."

"No, in fact I was going to get in touch with Henry." I turned to face him. "I'm glad you're here."

Henry got up and we shook hands. "Sorry for barging in on your lunch like this," he said, "but Eve assured me you wouldn't mind."

"Not at all. I was going to call you about something."

"Really. Well, this is fortuitous, then."

We sat down. I spread our lunch fare out and said, "Sorry I didn't pick up something for you, Henry, but I'm sure that we have more than enough to feed the three of us."

"No thanks, I've already eaten." He launched right into what was on his mind. "Frank, I owe you an apology. I knew that there was no way that Gene could have been responsible for something like Nunnely's death. To be honest, it never even occurred to me that Frederick might be involved. I'm still having a hard time believing this. I've known that boy for years. But I haven't really seen or talked to him since he went away to school."

"No apology needed."

"Yes, there is. I tried to convince you that no one in the family was capable of something like this, and it could have cost you your life."

"Okay. Apology given and accepted. How is the family holding up?"

"They're devastated. Frederick is being held in the hospital and will

248

be released tomorrow. I doubt a judge will even consider bail. He confessed to killing Nunnely, then the attempt on you, and the lawyer they've hired had more bad news. The ballistics on the gun Frederick used to shoot you indicate that it was the one of the two guns used to kill Nunnely.

"Their son is a murderer. I don't know how any parent can cope with that. I went over there last night. We sat and talked, cried, tried to explain it…"

"How are they explaining it to themselves?" I asked.

"Differently at different times. Sometimes they are together. Sometimes blaming one another."

"What do you think?"

"I have no clue. What Sandra is saying makes the most sense to me. Gene just seems overwhelmed by everything."

"How does she explain it?" Eve asked.

"She doesn't quite blame the school, but sometimes I think Gene does. Anyway, apparently Frederick participated in a program the school offers the summer before freshman year. The idea is to learn about Boston and maybe do some community service as part of it."

"I read about that in the school catalog," I said.

"Sounds great on paper, doesn't it? Well, Frederick wanted to participate, and he worked that summer with some kind of kids and art project in Roxbury. In the process, he met some guys his own age who he made friends with. They lived in the area. Unfortunately, they also happened to be members of a gang, not one of the more violent ones Sandra said, but one that wanted to be better known, have more street cred, so to speak. In that area, that meant be more violent.

"This was all new territory for Frederick – socially, psychologically, in every which way. Even though he had been brought up in Waterbury, he was very much a middle-class kid and, apparently, he found all of his new friends to be very exciting. His parents are liberal politically, but when it came to raising their kids, they were pretty strict and protective. Sandra thinks that was part of what happened."

249

Eve said, "He was rebelling and just chose the wrong group to rebel with."

"And gangs can have a cult-like aspect to them where you're either in or out, and you don't dare choose out," I added.

"Something like that," Henry said. "And then, according to Sandra, he started taking classes that taught him the history of the Middle Passage, the slave trade, the years of Jim Crow, and the entire ugly history of white supremacy in the United States. He started to get in fights at home with his parents. Gene said Frederick, his own son, started calling him a white wannabe and a Tom. Sandra said they were fighting all the time when Frederick was home, and then he stopped coming home.

"She said the only people he associated with were his new friends from the gang and the other black students in the program at BU. Then he went to Zanzibar at the end of his sophomore year, as part of his BU program. While he was away, they Skyped once a week. Frederick never asked about the campaign. Instead, he gave his parents mini lectures about the history of Zanzibar. He used his newly learned Swahili words whenever he could and talked about staying there. He was told that under no circumstances was he going to stay in Zanzibar, that they were in the middle of a political campaign, it was getting dirty, and voters needed to see the family together. Apparently this pissed Frederick off and he stopped Skyping.

"When he got home…"

"All hell had broken loose," I said.

"Yep. Sandra thinks that what pushed him over the edge was when Vivian got bullied at school. It was very, very bad. When he found out she had been cutting herself, he lost it."

"Chipo told me some things about it," I said.

"Sandra said that the he descended into a very dark and angry place that she had never witnessed before. He blamed Gene for not doing more to protect Vivian. He told Vivian he would take care of the bullies."

I said, "And thus, the fight that he lost."

"More, which I didn't know, until now. He stopped communicating with Gene and Sandra. He also moved out of his dorm and started living someplace in the H Block. Still went to school. Stayed in touch with Vivian. Nunnely became the evil one who was responsible for everything that had happened to Vivian. Sandra said every time they talked, he was fixated on Nunnely."

I asked, "How did he even know about Nunnely?"

"Early in the campaign Gene had mentioned Nunnely and the Thurman campaign bullshit that Gene was not sophisticated enough to be a senator."

"How is Frederick now?" Eve asked.

"I have no idea. Neither do Gene and Sandra really. He talks to his lawyer. When his parents visit him, he is distant and totally inside himself."

"He belongs to a gang," I said. "He's trying to live up to a code."

"That's what Sandra thinks. Gene rejects it. He says he refuses to believe it."

After we ate Eve said, "You two can stay here as long as you want, but I have to get to class."

After she left, I told Henry about my discussion with Vidal and her offer. He said, "That's very generous of her. She must be an extraordinary person."

"I'm beginning to see a lot about her I hadn't seen before," I answered.

"I'll definitely pass this on to Gene and Sandra."

We chatted a while longer and then Henry had to leave for Storrs. I walked him out to his car. When we got to his vehicle he turned and said, "Frank I can't believe this is all happening. Every time I think about what might have happened to you, I…"

"But it didn't, Henry. It didn't. From what you've said, Gene and Sandra are going to need your friendship more than ever. I'm fine; they're not."

251

Chapter 32: Boss

I had promised Vidal that I would look into the disappearance of Carlos Barlotti, but all I wanted to do was sleep and relax for a few days. Even though no bones were broken and Blackie and I were doing better, we were both sore, and, if I wanted to be grandiose, might be classified as *the walking wounded*. I think it was much more psychological than physical for both of us, although when I moved, I knew just how physical it was. Blackie stayed close to me and followed me from room to room when I got home. Even at Eve's office, he had stayed at my feet rather than in his bed.

I took a nap – a delicious, middle of the afternoon nap. Blackie hopped up on the bed with me, usually a no-no, and I let him be. At first, he came up and snuggled next to me. Then he moved down to the corner of the bed, between me and the door to the hall. Sore or not, if anyone was to try to get to me, they would have to go through him.

When I finally got up, I wanted a drink. It was the middle of the afternoon, and I wanted a drink. I remembered Jackie's recipe for a "Frank Sinatra" and decided to try one. Why the hell not? If I went back to sleep, I went back to sleep. I settled in front of the television set and thought about watching an old episode of *Will and Grace* on Netflix. I needed to laugh.

I never turned the television set on. Instead I just sat, sipped my drink, and thought about the conversations with Vidal and with Henry. I thought about Arnie and Frederick and the histories which had led these two human beings to a bus stop in Boston. I thought back over all of the "what ifs" that Vidal had been pondering. I thought about Henry's description of the radicalization of a young man and the history of black people in the United States. The surprise is not that Frederick experienced a kind of radicalization. The mystery is that more young black and brown people don't.

252

Every time I moved, though, and my chest hurt, my empathy diminished. These men, Arnold Nunnely and Frederick Douglas, had made choices. Choices that had led them to that moment last October. It had been a beautiful fall day. A bus stop. A God-damned, lousy bus stop. Frederick Douglas, a kid, would be held accountable for murder and attempted murder. Arnold Nunnely was dead. I had been shot.

I was halfway through the second "Frank Sinatra" when my cellphone rang. It was Jackie. She was excited. "Carlos had a second credit card, for expenses back when he worked with Arnie. It was in his name only. His wife only checked on the card that was in both their names. She said she knew he had a second card, but he hadn't used it since he'd retired."

"How'd you find out about it?"

"When I called to talk to her, I asked if she would mind if I came over to their house and looked around. You know, if he had a desk or something, or maybe the garage. I found an old statement with only one name on it in his desk. I asked her if he used the same password for everything the way most people do. She said yes. Sure enough. It worked and I was able to get into his account online. Frank, he's been using it, and I know exactly where he is."

"Great work, Jackie. Where is he?"

"Wait a minute. There's more. Wait until I tell you this. Remember his wife had said that he wanted to talk to Jason McCloud?"

"Yes."

"So, I called McCloud's office in Washington to find out where McCloud was. His secretary told me that he was on vacation. She was not about to tell me where. Remember Sheila Neverdowski?"

"Of course."

"Well, I called her. She knew where he was and guess who had called her and asked the same question?"

"Carlos?"

"Yep. Apparently he talked to her right after you did. He told her he was working with you. Well, she hates McCloud and wanted to help

253

you and thus Carlos. She called McCloud's secretary. Apparently, the two of them were BFFs when they were working for McCloud, and they both thought he was a son-of-a-bitch. McCloud's secretary told Sheila, and Sheila told Carlos and now me."

"So, where are they?"

"Wait, there's even more. From the credit card I was able to find out where Carlos was staying. I called Sheila back and asked her where McCloud was staying.

"Same place?"

"Nope. Apparently, McCloud always stays at the Marriott. I can't believe what they charge a night. Carlos was staying someplace else. Costs half as much."

"Great work, Jackie. Where are they?"

"Wait, there's more."

"More?"

"Yep, I called the hotel where Carlos is staying and asked for Mr. Barlotti. The hotel said he was no longer there. I asked for check in and check out dates. The reservations clerk wouldn't give them to me. I tried to act official and told her that he was missing. I told her everything we were doing to find him and that he was the subject of a police investigation in the United States. That got her attention. She referred me to the manager who was on duty. He was much more cooperative. It turns out Carlos checked in, but never checked out."

"I thought you said he wasn't there?"

"He isn't. The hotel thought he skipped without paying his bill. He hasn't been in his room, and nothing was left in his room. Believe it or not, they're still charging his credit card."

"Shit. Okay, where the hell are they?"

"Tax haven of tax havens, the Cayman Islands."

"Jackie, this is fantastic. Great work."

"Thanks, boss."

Boss. No one had ever called me boss before, not in a real way. Everything in me wanted to call Sam and let him know, but I couldn't.

I had promised Meg and had sort of promised Sam. Damn it. Sam would want closure on this. I called Meg and told her what I had just learned from Jackie and then said, "Meg, this thing about Sam. Not talking about cases with him is…"

"Bothering all of us. I know. Sam and I talked for hours last night. I still want him to fully retire and not be active, but if you want to consult with him and keep him up to date, go ahead. I may have gone a bit too far in setting up a stone wall around him."

"Thank you. I also have another question. And this is a partner decision. I want to go to the Feds and tell them what we know about the campaign finance problems. There are a lot of issues here, and I want to sort them out with the people at Lawton, Chase, and Harrison first. What do you think?"

"Sam and I also talked about that last night. Do it. Go get 'em."

"It will mean a lot of investigation of us and our involvement, and perhaps of our delay. They're going to want the complete Nunnely files, all of them. Years and years. That's going to create an incredible firestorm. We only looked at the dirt he was collecting on Thurman and Douglas. Can you imagine what might happen if all of his material became public?"

"We know. We both think it's worth it, and it's our duty. The decision, though, is Vidal's. Legally, she owns those files. I think our only obligation are the files related to the Thurman campaign. You haven't looked at any of the others, have you?"

"No. We had no need to."

"Talk to Ben first. Let's get a read on this from his firm, and then we have to talk to Vidal."

"I agree. I'll call them both today."

She asked, "The Caymans?"

"I'm going."

"With?"

"Pat. If he'll go."

"Don't worry. He'll go. When?"

"A couple of days. I need to talk to Eve tonight."

"Good luck."

"Thanks, but I think we're okay."

"I know."

"You do?"

"We've talked."

"Oh."

"I called her," Meg said. "I thought she might need the perspective of the wife of a former police officer."

"Thank you."

"Wedding still on?"

"Yes."

"I have a suggestion, if you would like it."

"Sure."

"Go see the condo you told me about before you leave for the Caymans, even if it means you delay a day or two longer. The case will always be there. You need to take care of your life, first. Don't make the mistake of forgetting that, Frank."

"I'm learning."

"I know. Sam and I love you both."

"Thank you."

I never finished the second "Frank Sinatra." I had too many calls to make. First, I needed to call Vidal, tell her what we had learned about Carlos, and I had to talk to her about the FBI and the likely scenario of what they would do and what they would want from her. I had to tell her that we were consulting counsel before we did anything, and she might want to do the same.

Then I had to call Mrs. Barlotti and tell her what we had found out and that we were following up. I had to ask Pat to join me on a trip to the Caymans; Claire would get us tickets and reservations. I had to call Alice Malone and ask her to check alibis for Frederick and his buddies at the time when Carlos went missing. I also wanted to know if the AK-47 Jojo Johnson had at the park was the same gun that had shot

Nunnely, Tom-Tom, and the other two at the bus stop. Henry had told us about the ballistics match for Frederick's gun, but what about the other gun? If it matched, Jojo would also be charged with first-degree murder.

Before all of that though, I had to call Eve and get the number for the real estate broker. Eve and I had a place to see in Stratford, on the Housatonic River, with a dock. I wondered how big the boat slip was that would go with our unit.

Acknowledgements

My partner in life, Melody Barlow, read, suggested, and did the initial copy editing of the manuscript. I am lucky in many, many ways to have her in my life. This is just one of them. I am grateful to be a member of a writing group with people who are wonderful writers, great companions, and whose feedback I value immensely. Sometimes I disagree at first, but then... The Reverend Doctor Judith Campbell, author of the Olympia Brown and Viridian Green mystery series; Pamela Claughton (Pamela Kelly) author of best-selling mysteries, romances, and cookbooks; Bob Knox, author of *Susso's Lane* and numerous short stories and poems; Florence Noonan, author of *In Blood and Stone* and *A Season for Evil*; and Kalina Vendetti, who is working on a historical novel about a fascinating madam in the Old West.

The daily news gives us more than enough information about the current state of oppositional research in the United States, but two books helped me get an insider's view: *We're With Nobody* by Alan Huffman and Michael Rejebian and *How To Rig and Election* by Allen Raymond.

Many years ago I had the privilege of working as a consultant to the Sawyer Miller Group. Although my task was focused on organization development issues, I was in a position to observe this super smart group of campaign consultants at work. I have managed some local political campaigns, but these folks operated in a different orbit, and it was exciting to watch them strategize and execute.

As with any book of this nature, the final product is my responsibility.

www.ingramcontent.com/pod-product-compliance
Lightning Source LLC
Chambersburg PA
CBHW070906180626
46817CB00003B/939